WILD ENCOUNTER

EMMANUELLE

USA TODAY BESTSELLING AUTHOR

SNOW

Smart Lily
Publishing

SAVE THE DATE
LOVE
NASHVILLE
HOCKEY
WEDDING
Green Mountain, Tennessee
A & NICK

Wild Encounter
Emmanuelle Snow

First edition - November 2022 (V_1) (2025 update)

ISBN eBook: 978-1-990429-63-7

ISBN paperback: 978-1-990429-64-4

This book is part one of the Breathless duet.

Editors: Shalini G. and SLE

Cover: SMART Lily publishing inc.

Published by SMART Lily Publishing inc.

———

Emmanuelle Snow
emmanuellesnow.com

CARTER HILLS BAND UNIVERSE
(SUGGESTED READING ORDER)

Carter Hills Band series
False Promises

<u>HEART SONG DUET</u>
Blindsided
Forevermore

Whiskey Melody series
Sweet Agony

<u>SECOND TEAR DUET</u>
Cruel Destiny
Beautiful Salvation

<u>BREATHLESS DUET</u>
Wild Encounter
Brittle Scars

Upon A Star series
Last Hope

Midnight Sparks

Love Song For Two series
Lonesome Heart Duet
Fallen Legend
Rising Star

Two of Us Duet
Snowbound

Wicked Love

All titles available at
emmanuellesnow.com

For the best experience, read in the order as shown above

WHAT THE REVIEWS SAY

- "I've been a HUGE fan of Emmanuelle Snow since I got my hands on her first book, so it should come as no surprise that I absolutely loved this book. This is without a doubt Emmanuelle's best work yet!" **(Tanja, OMGreads)**

- "There are a lot of subgenres in romance, but Ms. Snow is a genre of her own. Because she writes about life and what we all live through. Love is not just words for her, but the actions her characters show, the way they are committed to each other. Every single day. That is what makes this book so special." **(Book Reviews by Shalini)**

- "I wasn't prepared for their story. It was beautiful and heartbreaking. Full of hope and love too. Now I can't decide which one of Emmanuelle Snow's books is my favorite. They're all special in their own way. " **(Goodreads)**

- "I couldn't put this book down as it was a real page turner and had you on the edge of your seat while turning the pages wondering what would happen next and it was so addictive with great characters and a storyline that pulled you in and just wouldn't let you go and kept your attention throughout the whole book." (**Goodreads**)

- "Emmanuelle Snow always delivers a fun, spicy and heartwarming read." (**Goodreads**)

TRIGGER WARNINGS

Disclaimer

My books are realistic and emotional love stories.

I'm an advocate for mental health, and some topics could be sensitive for certain readers since they are portrayed as close to real life as possible.

I've listed the potential trigger warnings for each title on my website.

Be advised that those trigger warnings could potentially be spoiler alerts for the storylines.

Those sensitive topics have been written with the utmost care and respect. Please reach out if you have questions or comments.

All books contain sexuality, mature content, and language not intended for people under 18 years of age.
For other readers' sake, please avoid spoilers in your reviews.

Thank you and have a wonderful day!

Emmanuelle

emmanuellesnow.com

Lou, I believe in you. I'll always believe in you.
It's you and me against the world, remember?
Fight for what you want.
You'll do great things because you're a special kind of someone and
there's only one like you.
You may be small today,
but you'll be the bigger man one day.

I love you
Mommy xx

BECOME A VIP
TO NEVER MISS A THING

Snow's VIP

Join **Emmanuelle Snow's VIP newsletter**

Be the first to know about new releases, giveaways, sales, and special events. And step into a space where big emotions are celebrated, love is messy and beautiful, and stories linger long after the last page.

emmanuellesnow.com

Snow's Soulmates

Join Emmanuelle Snow's Facebook VIP group, **Snow's Soulmates**, to chat with her and other readers, get updates, and more bonus content.

facebook.com/groups/snowvip

A GIRL LIKE YOU
THE SONG

Girl, I noticed you for the first time
    last night
Looking pretty with your hair down
    and flushed cheeks
My heart sizzled when you
    walked in
But drowned as you stood too
    far away
Because all I wanted was to call
    your name
All I wanted was to claim you
    as mine

[CHORUS]

Girl, I wish you could see yourself
    the way I do
'Cause your smile is bright enough
    to light up my days

The sadness in your eyes should be
    stolen away
And replaced by a million dancing
    sparks
Girl, I wanna be the man who adds
    colors to your life
'Cause I would cherish your heart
    and never let you go

A girl like you can change the world
    with only a smile
A girl like you can jolt my heart
    back to life with only a glance
You looked my way, and my pulse
    ran wild
My body buzzed to life, and your
    pink lips I wished I could kiss
The sea of your eyes drew me in,
    sapphires beckoning me into the
    night

[CHORUS]
A girl like you should stay wild in
    her dreams
A girl like you should take the world
    by storm
Let me be the guy who anchors your
    life and holds your hand
And when you need a rest, I'll lend
    you my shoulder
And when you need a hug, my arms
    will hold you tight

[CHORUS]

A girl like you belongs with a guy
    like me
And a guy like me loves a girl
    like you

Music and lyrics by Carter Hills

Chapter 1
Addison

I slumped down on the couch of the posh hotel we were staying at all weekend and huffed, a wine bottle hanging from my fingers by its neck. Glasses were overrated, anyway. "That's it. I'm over men. I'm done."

My childhood best friend snickered.

"I'm serious, Dah. This time I mean it. You know I do."

I scanned the space around me. Large windows with a direct view of Nashville's busy streets below, high wooden beam ceilings, dark flooring, and handcrafted wood furniture. Chic and tasteful, with an unmistakable country vibe.

"Yeah, right. I'm sure you won't last a week. Two at the most," Dahlia teased.

My friend, and the bride-to-be, inched closer, and I zipped her up. Her cut-out mermaid gown was a gray-lavender hue and looked both sexy and demure, showing just enough skin without being indecent. Perfectly Dahlia Ellis.

Before I could sink back into my lazy position on the couch, she beckoned me to follow her with a finger. Sitting on the edge of the bathtub, I glugged the wine straight from the bottle while I watched her apply mascara.

"Addi, there are good men out there who would appreciate your light. Don't punish all of them because you dated a few who were total dickheads." She grinned at her reflection, but it was meant for me. It warmed my heart as she continued, "I'm confident you won't last in your quest to ignore them all when they turn on the charm."

"Laugh all you want, girlfriend. You'll see. Be prepared to be shocked. This time, I'm not backing down. Anyway, remember Felicia from college? She messaged me last week. It's destiny."

"The one you 'experimented' with?" my friend asked, curving her fingers into elaborate air quotes, her gaze fixed on her eyelashes in the mirror, not sparing me a look.

Another sip. "The same. We could have been in love and lived happily ever after. The timing was just not right back then."

"Huh, you said the same thing about Carter once. Besides, I thought women weren't your thing," Dahlia added with a quirked brow.

"It's not the same. And perhaps I changed my mind. Who knows? I might be into women more than men after all. Think about it, we should have been a couple, you and I. Everything would have been much simpler."

"You think?"

I shrugged. "We get along fine. And we're friends, so our relationship would have had a solid foundation. Look at you and Nick. Friends, then lovers. I believe that's the secret to long-lasting love. Back to business..." I sighed.

"Felicia and I experienced some pretty memorable moments together. It's just Shawn happened to cross my path, and I couldn't resist him. Stupid me. Stupid men. I'm telling you their species is old news. You're lucky you found two awesome ones in your lifetime. What are the odds? God knows I've tried. I usually don't back down easily, but hey, maybe it's time I try something else. That I understand once and for all what life has been trying to tell me all these years…"

Dahlia shook her head, focusing her attention on me for the first time since I started the conversation about my disastrous love life. "Addi, you know how much I love it when you're not being overdramatic, right?"

I poked my tongue out, and we both burst out laughing. A sense of peace washed over me. Dahlia Ellis had that effect on me. Her presence was always enough to ease all my doubts and bring a curve to my lips, even when I didn't feel like expressing joy. "That's why you love me. I'm entertaining…despite myself. Anyway, where are the bridal shower festivities taking place? I can't wait to party all weekend. The distraction will do me good."

My best friend reached over and landed a kiss on my cheek, her eyes searching mine. Worry shimmered in them. "You okay?"

I nodded.

"You'd tell me if it wasn't the case, right?" I sensed the apprehension in her question.

"Always. You're the only one I willingly confide in."

With a warm smile that promised everything would turn out just fine, she went back to applying her makeup. "All over town. Tonight, we're having dinner with only the people closest to us. Tomorrow, we'll have a get-together with some friends and the guys on a yacht before splitting up and maybe meeting again later."

"Rewind for a sec. We're having your bridal shower with your future husband and his friends?"

"Yep. His best friend. Guys from work. That's the idea."

"Yeah, I should've been the one organizing the whole thing." Dahlia raised a hand, ready to argue, but I kept going. "For what it's worth, I'm sorry I let you down. I was really looking forward to throwing you the bachelorette party of the century."

A new weight grew heavy on my shoulders. In the fog of my latest relationship blowing up, I had lost focus on what really mattered. This time, my tears had knocked me out more than ever. But I was back now, and no way was I failing the girl I considered a sister again.

Dahlia pulled me into a hug. "It's okay. Don't chastise yourself. It'll still be fun. And you did plan most of the wedding already. You deserve a night off…to enjoy yourself… You, me, booze, music. And the man I love and his friends."

I leaned back, studying her for a moment. Dahlia had no ounce of evilness in her. She really meant everything she'd just said.

"What is it?" she asked, a frown marring her forehead.

"Real sweet, Dah. After I told you I was done with men, you're going to make me spend hours with a bunch of Nick's buddies. And alcohol. If I didn't know your heart, I'd think this was a test. To check my newfound determination." One more sip of wine. *Be strong, Addi*, I repeated in my head. I flicked my hand and pasted a smile on my lips. "Know what? It doesn't matter. I won't back down. I'm done with men, and I'll prove it to you. Tonight. I won't flirt, and I won't kiss. Nope. Nada. D.O.N.E. Just watch and learn, girlfriend."

I held out my hand, and we shook on it.

Chapter 2
Tucker

"I was really hoping we'd go to a strip club or fly to Vegas or do something crazy and fun. When you said bachelor party, I never thought in a million years it would happen in Nashville." I sighed because it was a real bummer. "I should've known better, man. You're a stupid fool when you're in love, a sucker for all things romantic. Remind me to buy you a pair of brand-new shiny steel balls as a wedding present. You might need those sooner than you think."

Nick rolled his eyes, handing me a beer.

"Tuck, you're just jealous. Always have been. If I remember correctly, you're the one who stated, and I quote: 'Settling down isn't for me. I love diversity. And to be able to sample everything on the buffet.' I can still hear and see you when you announced it."

With a frown, I threw my beer cap at him.

"Yeah. When you say it like that, I sound like a fucking ass."

"Man, it sounded the same when you said the words as a teen. Lucky for you, Nashville is full of hot women. One rule, though." My best friend, and the future groom, lifted a finger. "Stay away from Dahlia's best friend, Addi. She's been through a rough break-up, and she doesn't need you to complicate things even more. Okay? She's family, and her heart is hurting. Women get attached to you easily... even if you're not interested in a relationship. No games this time. She's off-limits."

"Is this a warning?"

He breathed out. "It should be."

Nick waited for me to say something, his bottle hovering in midair just in front of his lips.

"Is she hot?"

Something bitter twisted in my stomach, but I spoke the words he expected—the ones everyone assumed I was heartless enough to say.

"Tuck. Come on. You think all women are hot. You never look at their faces, only their tits and their asses. Stay. Away. I'm not kidding this time. We're getting married in six weeks. Don't do anything to make things awkward. Don't get on Dahlia's bad side before the wedding."

I threw my hands up in the air between us. "Impossible. Your future wife is a fan of mine."

"Yeah, she is. But don't give her a reason to change her mind."

"Fine. The maid of honor is off-limits. What about the bridesmaids? Are they also forbidden?"

Nick shook his head with a crooked smile. "Did you even hear a word I said when we spoke about the wedding before? It will be small. No bridesmaids. Just us four at the altar, which means you better behave."

I jumped up to stand and adjusted the cufflinks of my crisp white shirt, a sharp contrast to my dark skin, and continued, "Change of plans then. I need a date for tonight. Where can I find some pretty creature in a short amount of time?"

Nick rose to his feet and clapped my shoulder. "No date needed. It's only dinner with friends and family. You, me, Dahlia, Addison, and Carter. A few other people. And Dahlia's parents. Fuck, you really registered nothing."

"I did. Me, groomsman. You, groom. Women in dresses. Booze. Music. Everything that's important. Anyway…wait. Your sister isn't coming?"

"No, Jessica is attending some surfing competition in Hawaii. It's fine. Good news, though. Your bestie Jack will make an appearance, but he'll be with a babysitter so we can enjoy some grown-up time. He's spending a few days at Dahlia's parents' afterward."

"Just pause for a sec, will you?" My brain had just processed what Nick had said a minute ago. "Carter Hills will be there?"

"He's Dahlia's best friend. What did you expect?"

"How's your relationship with him? Still strained?"

Nick huffed. "Better… I guess. We're not quite friends, but I still have high hopes one day we will be."

"All good for me then. Do you think he'll sign something for me?" I teased with a big smile spread across my face. "Autograph my chest or my shirt? Do you think he keeps posters in his trunk?"

"Okay, you gotta see a doctor, man." He shook his head, reeling in his smirk. "Since when did you become a groupie? Last fall, you faked having too much work to avoid coming to his show with me. Tickets you bought, remember? And now you want him to sign your man boobs?" He sent me a knowing gaze, with barely contained amusement and despair at my idiocy. Yeah, Nick Peterson could call my bullshit from miles away. My lips parted, but he kept talking. "Never mind. You do you."

I shrugged, bearing an all-teeth smile. "Do you think black ink would look good on my skin tone? Or should I get one of those golden markers?"

"If I were you, I'd opt to transform the autograph into a permanent thing. I know a guy who can ink you for cheap."

I tapped my chin with a finger, pondering it over for his sake. "Would you add a guitar or a heart next to it? Or maybe a music note?"

"Tuck, you're incorrigible. Geez, it's been too long since we hung out."

"Hey, I said nothing."

"No need." He shook his head. "Just in case a part of you is serious in some ways, we must set some ground rules until the wedding. Tell me. Why didn't I pick Jace as my best man?"

My smirk widened, and I winked. "Because he's married to your ex-fuck girl, who owns his balls and who happens to think you're a pathetic loser because you refused to date her when she decided your little arrangement didn't suit her anymore. And let's be honest. I'm the best choice." I scanned the suite. "Why isn't he here this weekend, though? I thought he said he was flying in this afternoon."

Hurt flashed in Nick's eyes.

Jace was our other best friend. We all grew up together.

If I had known Jace would be a no-show this weekend, I would've carried him here myself, regardless of the excuses his wicked wife came up with. She had a record of perfectly timed excuses to keep our friend away from us.

The devil, or Pamela White according to her driving

license, had organized a fishing expedition, something she knew Jace would never miss—somewhere in the Atlantic Ocean—the same weekend Nick was getting married. Such a low blow.

The guy chose to marry a mean control-freak. Nobody forced him. But he had promised he wouldn't miss this weekend. He swore he'd be here.

Nick was like a brother to me, always there, and Jace, the pesky cousin who was flitting around. The three of us had been inseparable growing up in Chicago, and we got into trouble more than once. Jace distanced himself after he eloped with the devil.

"What's the reason this time?" I asked. "Let's not kid ourselves. We both know Pam is behind Jace's whereabouts."

"Her birthday. Her sister is in town one week before-hand to celebrate with her. He said he felt bad about leaving her behind in Chicago, even though she was the one who refused to come along," Nick said as he took a sip and shrugged. "It sucks. We've been friends forever, the three of us. I still don't get why she hates me so much. I don't think I ever will… She's the one who slept with one of my two best friends—"

His stare moved to a spot on the carpet as he peeled the label from the bottle, lost in his thoughts.

Feeling a bit like a jerk for bringing that bitch up, I asked, "What are the rules? You're never not organized, so you already must have a list ready for me… Just in case I was planning on going rogue."

"Tuck, don't be a jerk."

"It's me, man. You can trust me. I promise to follow them the best I can. But only for the weekend."

"Six weeks, Tuck. Not just this weekend." He exhaled, and flecks of annoyance tinted his words.

In our relationship, I was the unpredictable one, the wild friend always in pursuit of good times and short-term fun. Nick was more thoughtful, aiming for long-term commitments and a conservative way of living.

"But—"

"No buts," my friend cut in. "You sure you wanna do this?"

"Yep. Give it to me."

"Okay. First. No getting too close to Addison. Second. No fangirling over Carter. For whatever reason. If that's really the angle you wanna play. The guy is now able to tolerate me for more than a couple of hours. Don't give him a new excuse to hate me."

I chugged the rest of my beer. "Man, the guy can't hate you. You're the kindest and the most harmless person I know. You're almost boring with your lovey-dovey ways. Don't forget you were nicknamed *Chicago Lamb* back in the day."

"No. I wasn't."

I shook my head. "You should have been," I muttered. "No kidding. You're too soft. Give Carter Hills a run for his money. I can help you. I don't care if he's mega-rich or the president of Nunavut."

"Focus, Tuck. For once. It's important to me. And to my future wife." Nick pinched the bridge of his nose. "And by the way, Nunavut isn't a country. No president there."

I smirked. The guy was so predictable—at least, he was to me, most of the time—and bantering with him prevented me from thinking about all that was bothering me these days.

"Smart ass, I know where Nunavut is. I was just testing your geography skills." *And doing my best to make you forget the fact that Jace isn't here.* "About Carter Hills hating you, I'm sorry. But you can't blame him. You're the guy in the middle. And that woman of yours is quite a catch. I'd be possessive too if I were him. Just sayin'."

Nick exhaled a noisy breath. "Let's just say he's over-protective of Dahlia and Jack and sees me as a threat… Or he used to. Now we're surfing a calm wave. We're getting along fine, and I wanna keep it that way."

"The guy is a douche."

"I wish. But he's not. I swear. You should have come to that concert. You would've seen for yourself instead of taking my word for it. What he did for Derek… I'm still speechless when I think about it. Truth be told, he's amazing to Dahlia and Jack. Their friendship is truly special. Getting into their close-knit circle—or rather duo—can be challenging. After everything they've been through, it's understandable. One last thing. Don't tease me in front of him for entertainment purposes. Please. That would be shitty. Even coming from you."

"Never. After all, I'm the reason you and Dahlia found each other. If I hadn't sent you to Green Mountain in the first place, you'd still be alone and miserable. I'm glad my cupid ways worked. You still owe me for that one. I'll cash in on my dues soon. Once I figure out what to demand in exchange."

Nick tilted his head back and let out a heartfelt laugh. "Keep sending yourself flowers, man. You know you're delusional, right? Nobody owes anybody anything. If we'd kept tabs down all those years, you'd be the one in debt. For every single time I saved your ass." My friend pointed to the scar across his eyebrow. The one he got after he jumped into a fight because I kissed a football player's girl-friend and the entire team decided to get revenge. "Tuck, about those rules…are we good?"

"Yup. I'll stick to those two. For the rest, I intend to make this weekend one to remember." I uncapped two more beers, and after I handed one to Nick, I raised mine to clink with his. "To you, man."

———

"Are you ready, pussy-whipped man? Your woman can't wait to see your sorry ass. I bet the girls are curling each other's hair in the room next door. Or maybe they're rubbing each other's bodies with oil. Geez, I'm getting hard just thinking about it." I shook my legs to remove the tension tightening my crotch. "While I'm here, do you want me to gel your hair or shave your butt? That's as far as I'm willing to go for your bachelor party weekend. Just say the word and I'll give you a beauty makeover."

"She said that?"

Did my best friend hear a word of what I'd just said or only process the part where I told him Dahlia was getting ready next door? "Her friend arrived one hour ago. They'll meet us in about thirty minutes at the venue. Your fiancée dumped all this info plus sent a dirty text while you were in the shower."

"Tuck, don't read my stuff. Already told you that. Like ten thousand times in the last twenty years. Gimme my phone."

Nick rolled his eyes, and I laughed, unable to take my friend seriously when he was acting like a baby over a text message. It wasn't even *that* dirty, anyway.

Dahlia and Nick had rented half the top floor of City Garden, Nashville's finest hotel, for the weekend. It helped that the future bride had founded the Carter Hills Band with her best friend when they were kids. A few years ago, before Dahlia retired from the music scene, the band was the biggest country music sensation in the world.

Dahlia and Nick were two of the most incredible and

generous human beings I had ever met. Their hearts were in the right place, and they never did anything half-assed. Both successful small-business owners, I bet they spared no expenses for this weekend. From what I'd seen so far, renting half a hotel floor for a couple of days to celebrate their upcoming nuptials didn't seem like a big deal.

"We're ready to leave, I think," Nick said as he exited the bathroom. "I can't believe this is happening."

"Man, are you getting cold feet?"

"Never. I love her, Tuck. She's the one. I knew it the first time I laid eyes on her."

I clapped him between the shoulder blades. "I know, man. Seeing you with Dahlia is almost enough to make me believe in love. Almost." I winced, but his honest smile shattered my train of thought. "You guys just fit. I don't know how to explain it, but she's the one for you. No questions asked. I'm happy you two found each other and that I put you on her radar, if we're being honest."

His grin widened. "Thanks, man. It means a lot. Not the radar thing, though. Whatever."

I took a step forward and adjusted his shirt's collar and the lapel of his jacket. "There. Better. You missed the Tucker touch."

I winked, and he pulled me into a hug. "Thank you, Tuck. For always having my back. And for being here this weekend and everything."

I tsk-tsked. "Don't go all emotional on me, man."

He straightened his back and regained his composure. "Not a chance."

Three inches shorter and less muscular than me, Nick and I looked like complete opposites. With his blond hair and amber-colored irises, he had the serenity of a guy who'd experienced the ups and downs of life reflecting in his eyes. More comfortable wearing a pair of jeans and a

T-shirt than a suit, he preferred nights in with his family to the loud music of any bar or nightclub.

I, on the other end, was built like a pro football player —dark-skinned, broad-shouldered, crew cut, always dressed to impress. I had expensive and diversified tastes. Amazing food, grandiose apartment, designer clothes. And women.

And yet, our friendship had lasted over two decades. Even in our differences, we were similar. And always had each other's backs. No matter what.

"Now let's go. I can't wait to meet the two people I'm not allowed to get too close to," I teased with a wink.

We made it to the top of the building, two doors down the street. For the entire night, we had the rooftop to ourselves. A green, faux-grass rug lined the concrete floor. A bar in a little shack made of reclaimed barn wood was on our right, next to a makeshift dance floor with fairy lights hanging from beams above. A long white table decorated with golden plates and green foliage was set in the middle. Tall vases filled with pink dahlias and baby's breath gave a country-chic vibe to the decor. From here, we had a perfect view of the Nashville skyline from every angle. No doubt that was the main reason why my friend and his fiancée chose this place for tonight. It was magical.

Even my untenable heart felt giddy as a server passed pink champagne in crystal flutes around.

"Let me introduce you to everybody," Nick said, tugging at my elbow.

Before we could move, Dahlia came to us, with a tall girl in tow. Blonde hair and the most vibrant blue eyes I'd ever seen overpowered my senses.

"Hey, Tucker. So glad you could make it." Dahlia leaned forward and kissed both my cheeks before stepping back. "This is my best friend, Addison." She motioned to the girl, now deep in a conversation with Nick, before moving closer. "I hope Nick has already warned you not to mess with my friend. The two of you together are sure to create wildfires and leave chaos in your wake. She's been through enough already. If you tango with her, I'll break your neck myself."

"Are you joking?"

"Try me and find out," she said in a deadpan tone, a mixture of humor and something fierce like protectiveness dancing in her moss-green irises.

"Jesus, Dah. You and Nick have become a pair of cutthroats."

She tipped one eyebrow as if to say, *Did I make myself clear?*

I lifted both hands between us. "No maid of honor for me. Understood."

Who knew Dahlia Ellis, the girl with the voice of an angel and the sweetest person I'd ever met, could serve threats the Chicago way? Guess the Southern ways weren't too different from ours after all. She leaned back and offered me a warm smile, all traces of her harsh words gone, her voice smooth as honey. "I'm so happy to see you. You don't visit us often enough. Enjoy yourself tonight, and let's catch up later."

Nick wrapped an arm around her waist and drew her to him, kissing her temple and whispering something in her ear that made her giggle.

"Addi, this is Tucker, Nick's best friend," she said, introducing us in record time, making sure we couldn't exchange more than a "hi" or a "hey." She tugged at her friend's hand. "Come on, Carter is here. Let's have a drink, the three of us. It will be like high school all over again."

Addison stared at me, giving me a slow once-over, a gleam in her eyes. The girl was *trouble*. I could already tell. I hoped the future bride and groom had served her the same warning they gave me.

Just a thought.

She parted her lips and mouthed something I didn't quite catch, her eyes still trained on me.

I offered her my most dirty look, zooming in on her rack and making sure she noticed it.

Dahlia led her friend away, offering one last silent "hands-off" warning when her eyes met mine over her shoulder.

"Whoa, what did you do to piss off my future wife, man? I thought you two were best friends. Your words, not mine. You usually have a blast together." Nick scratched the side of his head, his gaze following the girls traipsing away.

I sipped my champagne, offering him my most unaffected expression. "Oh, we're good, man. More than good, actually." A smug grin stretched my lips. "She just threatened to break my neck, but hey, we're all right. Don't worry."

"Damn, she's hot. Every time she stands her ground with you, I love her even more." They grinned at each other from a distance. Love was like newborns or puppies; it turned people into weirdos. "Don't meddle with a Southern woman. Whatever you do, don't ever say I didn't warn you."

Carter Hills came to introduce himself next.

"How is it going, man? Heard a lot about you," I told him as we shook hands.

"Great things, I hope." His eyes darted to Nick for half a second.

"Always."

Something—or someone—caught Carter's attention behind us. A wide smile curled up his lips, and he excused himself. I turned around to see a middle-aged couple, whom I assumed to be Dahlia's parents, holding their grandson Jack's hand as they exited the elevator.

Carter hurried across, and after he greeted them—now I was sure they were Mr. and Mrs. Ellis—he swept the boy off his feet, his broodiness now forgotten. Carter's face lit up as if he'd just won something priceless. From his well-over-six-foot height, he resembled a giant next to the little boy.

"Okay... From up-close, the resemblance is even more striking. Fuck. Right now, I'd bet my savings they're father and son."

"Yeah." Nick downed the rest of his champagne. "I'm pretty sure his brother and he could pass for twins."

Dahlia neared them, and Carter enveloped her in his arms and pressed a kiss to her forehead. They exchanged smiles and seemed to understand each other without speaking a word.

"Now a lot of things you said before make sense. Don't you feel like kicking his ass or something? I know I wouldn't like my girl being all cuddled up in another man's arms if she were mine."

Nick blew out a long breath. "Well, I've learned to accept it. That's the way they are. Dahlia could've dated Carter during all these years, but she never did, so why should I be jealous? That would just make me miserable. They are family, as they say. Nothing more. I trust her. I really do. Now I am just happy to be a part of her life. And Jack's."

"Carter too?"

"He will have to be the acquired taste."

A burst of laughter escaped my lips at his drawl. "For sure. Anyway, she's head over heels in love with you. That much is evident." I studied them for a few more seconds.

"You're right, man. She doesn't look at him the same way she looks at you." I raised my hands in surrender. "I won't meddle in your relationship. You guys can have three-somes, if you desire, none of my business. Unless you want me to join in... But I'm telling you, I'm not doing you, man. Tried it once. A man, I mean. Not my thing. Never doing it again."

"Shut up," Nick said. "Too much info, Tuck. Your sex life is your thing. No need to gimme the 4-1-1. I already know more than I should. Way too much. Stop putting these images in my head. They never fade away afterward."

I let out a loud laugh and ordered two whiskeys from the server as he neared us.

An hour later, we all sat around the table. Riley, Dahlia's former manager, rose to his feet to make a toast. "Let's see. I've known Dahlia for a long time. We used to travel the world together. Without a doubt, she's one of the most amazing and caring women I know. Dah, I've seen you at your highest highs and your lowest lows, and I can honestly say that today, you shine. No, you sparkle. It was about time you got your groove back. I've met Nick a few times already, and I can predict you two will go the distance. You're made for each other. And come on, when was I ever wrong?" Carter tossed a balled napkin at him. "See? Carter agrees. He knows I'm speaking the truth. He's the living proof." Everybody laughed. "Anyway, I wish you guys many years of happiness. You're what we should all aim for. Unconditional love. To Dahlia and Nick. And to soul mates."

We all cheered.

"Nick, welcome to the family. You're now officially one of us," he said, lifting his glass one last time before sitting back down.

A few more people said words before we dug into our five-course meal.

The blue of the sky transformed into multiple shades of pink, and someone turned on the fairy lights over the dance floor, giving the rooftop a warm glow.

We ate like royalties. The food was insanely delicious, with our wine glasses and tumblers always full.

Addison stared at me from across the table, the blue of her eyes hypnotic. I'd felt the heat of her gaze from the moment we sat down. For the past hour, I'd been averting my eyes, doing everything I could to avoid meeting hers, no matter how tempted I was. Somewhere between the third and fourth course, she rubbed my shin with her foot under the table. I pulled my leg back. No, I wouldn't go there. Not a chance. I was strong. I gave my word to my best friend. Addison was off-limits, and I loved my life way too much to risk Dahlia putting me in an early grave, way before my time.

With one mission in mind, veering as far as possible from the troublesome maid of honor, I went to the restrooms, needing time to cool down—and give my overzealous teammate a stern talking-to. I usually never backed down from a challenge. Even less, a lady challenge. I loved women. Always had. A little too much, according to my friends. And I could never stay away when they shot me *come-hither* glances. But I didn't do relationships, though. Never. And I never saw more than one woman at a time. Those were my rules. And to wear a rubber. All the fucking time.

I was freakish about catching some disease or shit. Heard they made your junk red and itchy. *No thanks, I'll pass.*

In front of the mirror, I adjusted the collar and rolled the sleeves of my Esteban Fu button-up shirt, my everyday go-to clothes and my designer of choice, my jacket already discarded. Yeah, I looked elegant—and fucking hot. I smirked at the image the glass reflected.

Too bad I couldn't use my charm on anybody tonight. I would enjoy a good chase…get my blood boiling and more. But no, not tonight.

When I exited the men's room, the blonde temptress cornered me, drawing a hand over my chest, her long pink fingernails toying with the buttons of my dress shirt. I held my breath, curious about this encounter. Wearing a steel-blue gown that tied at her nape and ended mid-thigh along with strappy high heels, she looked gorgeous. Even with those extra inches, I towered over her as I watched the goddess in front of me. A star amongst a sea of dark dresses, her blonde hair fell over her shoulders like a radiant aura around her. She sported an intoxicating smile, and her heavy-coated lashes made her irises appear bluer than before. More alluring.

"Tucker, right?"

"Yep," I said. A server walked by and offered me my drink of choice. I accepted and brought the tumbler to my lips, studying her features and the fire in her eyes. "At least it was the last time I checked."

"Oh, a sense of humor. I like that." She laughed and lost her balance on her four-inch heels. I clamped my fingers around her waist to steady her. Something coiled inside me, warming my core where our bodies connected.

"*Ooooopsy*. So *sorrry*," she slurred, revealing how drunk she was. Addison pushed her hair over her shoulder, her smile devilish and enticing. "Stop looking at *meee* like this, *Tuuuck*. I can call you *Tuuuck*, right?"

"Guess so." I shrugged, keeping my back straight and doing my best to look unaffected by her antics. I had made a promise to my best friend, and if nothing else, my words counted for something. But Jesus, this woman.

"Anyway, *Tuuuck*," she said, her voice sultry and sinful, putting emphasis on my name, "just so you know, I'm *ovvver* men."

Every molecule in me woke up, reacting to the intimacy of her touch. To her tone. And the luring energy emanating from her.

The heat circulating within me surged to a searing point.

My grip tightened around the glass in my hand. "You are?" I asked, my voice a loud growl, my interest in her growing with every passing second.

"*Yesss*," she said with a firm slant of her head. "Men break hearts. No matter how *muuuch* you love them or how many times you *suckkk* their dicks in a week, they always end up breaking *youur* heart." She waved her fingers at me. "This means *youuu* too break hearts. I can tell. *Youuu* have this thing that makes women *cravvve* you." She leaned closer and sniffed me. *Yes, she fucking sniffed me.* I blinked, wondering if Addison was for real or if she was playing a game. "Oh, and *youuu* smell too," she added, her voice a whisper against my skin.

With a step back, I lifted my arm blatantly and took a whiff of my armpit, scared I really did smell, then dropped it back down. "You're crazy, sweetheart. I don't smell."

She scrunched up her nose and sighed, then waggled a finger at my face. "*Nooo*...not like that. *Youuu* smell like sex. You probably have a *biggg* dick and are very capable with *youuur* tongue. Am I right?"

Who was this girl, and where had she come from? No wonder Nick warned me off her. I was wrong when I thought she was trouble. She wasn't. She was pure evil. Sent on this Earth to be the end of me. I realized I had to be careful. All this time, I thought I was a player. But here she was—pure dynamite—and could play the game too. Damn it.

Speechless for one of the first times in my life, I stared at her. Amusement danced in her eyes, and I was pretty sure it did in mine too.

My body pulsed to her symphony. I rolled my lips over my teeth to avoid saying something I wouldn't be able to take back or doing something I'd regret. Like getting the explosive tension out of the way by locking us in the restroom and ramming into her until I fucked the *sassiness* out of her. Addison was drunk. I'd promised to keep my distance. Two major turn-offs.

I breathed out, barely in control, countless scenarios running through my mind. All of them involved us getting naked and panting.

She lowered her small hand down my abdomen.

My stomach muscles clenched.

"Are those *abbbs* you are hiding underneath that shirt? Six-packs are a *reaaal* turn-on, by the way. Do *youuu* agree?" Her sensual voice twined around my control, cracking the tough shield I had erected around myself.

"You tell me, sweetheart. I'm not usually patting a man's stomach the first time we meet."

She fought a roll of her eyes, never breaking the contact. "Women possess *themmm* too. Don't discriminate. Like I said, I'm *ovvver* your species. God should've named *youuu* T-R-O-U-B-L-E. I should re-baptize all of *youuu*. It's a good thing I *lovvve* women now. Not being picky."

I chuckled. "And yet, you're the one feeling me up right now. Are you enjoying it? Wouldn't have guessed you're into women."

She let her fingers drift lower, and a shiver coursed through me. Addison's eyes turned to slits, and she cocked her head to the side. "Nobody ever told you not to make assumptions?" she asked.

"Nobody ever told you not to send mixed signals?" I countered.

She ate me up with her gaze, and I could almost touch the electric charge sparking in the air between us.

The fire that had been simmering low inside me for a while now rekindled. My senses heightened. My heart did what I'd call a complete revolution. Whatever this woman did, it worked. I felt alive facing her. Like I hadn't in quite some time.

We fixated our gazes on each other. Her throat rippled, and her breathing accelerated.

My cock pushed against the zipper of my trousers, bewitched by the blonde tornado ripping through my control.

I downed the rest of my drink, wishing it was cold water and that it would kill my arousal.

Addison gave me a doe-eyed look, not backing down from inspecting me as if I were her next meal.

Two words: excruciating torture. A test of my willpower. All I could imagine now was that sinful mouth around me.

Back down, I ordered my dick. *Don't expect anything from this woman. Not happening.* I whizzed a quick breath out, urging my common sense to make an appearance.

As if she could hear my train of thoughts, Addison blinked away whatever spell had taken her hostage, shutting down the desire that had been simmering between us. "*Backkk* to business. The thing is, I know *I'mmm* right. I know my men. *Youuu* are all the same. Except for Nick. Nick is *finnne.* He passed the test. Anyway, he doesn't have that alpha-vibe pouring out of him like *youuu* do. You're dangerous, *Tuuuck.* Very dangerous." She got lost in her own head for a moment. "Now that *I'mmm* choosing to only *lovvve* anyone but hot-blooded men for the rest of *myyy* life, guys like you can't hurt me anymore. I'm done being *playyyed*. Women don't have *dickkks*, so they're safe. And they aren't heartless. *Mennn* are. Women are more compassionate. I had a… I had a girl lover once, and she used her *tonnngue* much better than all of *youuu* Neanderthal specimens combined. She could *givvve* you lessons. Do *youuu* want lessons, *Tuuuck*?"

"Oh, believe me. I need no lessons, sweetheart."

She tsk-tsked. "Don't get cocky on me, *Tuuuck*. Every man requires a woman's help. Adam, Eve. Barrack, Michelle. Harry, Meghan. Anyway, *youuu* get the point." She swept her bottom lip with the tip of her tongue, and it was one of the most erotic displays I'd ever seen.

I blinked and perused the space around us for another drink, desperate to cool off the arousal sprouting in my dick and slowly climbing its way up my being.

Something was going on, right? Was I being pranked?

Where were the cameras? And the crew? Was Nick on it? Was the entire flirty encounter a setup? A test? Not that it was his style, but still, a guy had to ask.

I made a split-second decision to keep playing along. "My tongue is made of gold, sweetheart. Don't judge a product you've never sampled before." I sucked a deep breath in, trying to keep my composure intact.

"Too bad my vagina isn't interested. Guess we'll *nevvver* know." She offered me a one-shoulder shrug. "See *youuu* around, *Tuuuck*."

As if she couldn't convince herself to walk away, Addison studied me a moment longer, tracing the curve of her mouth with a finger, devouring me with her eyes, completely unaware of the battle consuming me. The one I could lose any second now.

She opened her mouth to speak, and like an idiot, all I could focus on were those juicy lips, just sitting there, begging for trouble.

A heat wave crashed over me, flooding my body with sensations I'd never experienced before. Well, I had…to some extent. But never close to the intensity searing inside me right now. I memorized the line of her neck and the freckle below her left earlobe.

The womanizer in me had been poked, and all he yearned for was a little fun of his own and to have his way with her. Rip her clothes off and make her come until she passed out from too many *pleasure induced by me* orgasms. The kind of things she'd remember forever, stamping my name on her for eternity.

We watched each other, my pulse throbbing in my temples. Addison closed her teeth around her forefinger. Was she even aware of how sexy and diabolical she acted, or was it all rehearsed? My blood boiled hotter at the thought that it came to her naturally.

With a wink, she traipsed away, and I fought the desire to call her back, to settle this thing between us. To get the upper hand and lead my team to victory.

Armed with a loaded weapon in my trousers, I watched her retreat instead, once more urging my on-alert cock to stand down. Recede. Play dead.

A couple of deep breaths later, it finally listened, going from a strained, full-on superstar to a half-mast, second-string team player.

I scanned the rooftop. From the dance floor, Dahlia and Nick looked in my direction. My friend offered me a subtle shake of his head, pinching his lips like he was about to burst out laughing.

Dahlia made a cut-throat gesture with her finger and mouthed, *Don't even think about it. Off-limits.*

They were in on it. All along, they knew Addison was a risk to my sanity—and to my dick.

From afar, Addison looked all sweet and harmless, but she was a vixen wearing colorful clothes and hypnotizing smiles. One I was now dying to taste. I could read every strategy in her playbook. Because we shared a similar one.

I stood there, bothered and mesmerized.

Fuck.

Why did I promise to keep my distance?

Chapter 3
Addison

I pushed Tucker away with one hand, ignoring the slackened jaw and *what the fuck just happened* expression in his eyes, and resumed my walk toward the pre-wedding party now filling the dance floor. When I had touched him, his shallow breaths and pounding heartbeat had vibrated under my open palm. I had chosen to disregard it because the zing traveling through me and the warmth pooling down my belly meant nothing. Instead, I focused on my steps. The ones taking me away from the temptation dressed like some Adonis. The more space I put between us, the more the thoughts of my encounter with him faded, making me relish the boozy bliss my head was swimming in. Even if my life depended on it right now, I wouldn't have been able to walk a straight line. But hey, who cared, right? I felt happy. And relaxed.

Alone in a chair, sipping a clear cocktail that I knew to be water—because Carter Hills didn't drink anything else since his brother died—my favorite country singer was watching our friends dancing and laughing, a somber look etched on his face. Back then, when his brother passed away, he had chosen to clean up his act and be there for Dahlia and Jack.

"You're not joining them?" he asked, pointing to the dance floor with his chin.

"I'm a *litttle* bit"—I squinted and pressed my thumb and forefinger together—"drunk. That wine was *deliciooous*."

Carter straightened his back and leaned forward, resting his elbows on his knees. He fixed me with an intense, scrutinizing gaze. "Why are you so sad, Addi?"

I flicked my wrist as if it was nothing. Inside, an earthquake shook my foundations. Up to now, I'd been doing a great job, or so I believed, at keeping my feelings bottled up. But something in the way Carter looked at me threatened to fracture my fragile facade.

"C'mon, girl. We've known each other for a long time. I can read you, you know? And right now, you're hurting."

"It's nothing," I said, averting my gaze. I used my fingertips to wipe the moisture building in the corners of my eyes.

"If you say so, but that sadness in your eyes is kind of a giveaway. All night, you've been acting like everything is good, but I know better." He shrugged. "If you want to talk, I'm here. How's Phen? I haven't heard from him in ages."

Phoenix was my twin brother and one of Carter's closest friends growing up. He moved to England to attend college, got married, and never came back home. "Still on the other side of the Atlantic Ocean. Has twins of his own now."

Carter's eyes flared. "Wow, he didn't lose time to settle down. I'm glad he's doing okay."

"I miss him, you know. We used to do everything together. Now I'm lost without the only guy who never played me." Hot tears prickled the back of my eyes, and I blinked them away. The conversation had somehow sobered me up. "How are you holding up? I know it must be hard for you to be here tonight. This whole month and a half will be…"

Carter scratched his forehead. "I love her so damn much, Addi, but I'm learning to let go of her. Getting better at it," he said, staring in Dahlia's direction as Nick spun her around on the dance floor, both so fucking blissfully happy it was sickening. "She always chooses the other guy. It's fucked up. I can't do this anymore. My love is always one-sided. Nick is fine. I'm not upset with him. He makes her happy… Jack loves him too. I'm mad at myself for not being enough. For not being what she wants…or needs. And for not being able to get over her sooner, like she had asked. I hope she doesn't get married a third time. I'm not sure I'd survive watching the girl I've forever been in love with get hitched once again. Twice is more than enough for this lifetime."

I pulled my chair forward and hugged Carter.

The guy had the biggest heart on Earth. Both times Dahlia fell in love, I'd witnessed his heart getting crushed.

"It would have been easier if you'd agreed to date me in high school. We'd have had each other to be miserable with," I added in a teasing tone. "Or maybe we'd have been happily married by now. Who knew what would have happened if you hadn't pushed me away when I kissed you…" I wiggled my brows, and Carter snickered.

"I'm sorry, Addi. I never apologized, but I acted like a jerk that time. You took me by surprise, and I panicked. I should've been flattered you liked me like that instead of running away and giving you the silent treatment afterward, like I did."

I rested my head against his muscular shoulder. "It's okay. We weren't meant to be. We'll be fine… Both of us. We just need time to heal. Or find whatever we're looking for."

"You think so?"

"I know so. One day."

"What's eating you up? Right now, what are you thinking about?" he asked.

I shrugged, doing my best to come up with words that would make some sense. "In a way, I guess it feels like my life isn't the way I'd imagined it'd be." Carter said nothing. Perhaps what I said resonated with him too, so I continued. "I have dreams and expectations. For myself. But I have no idea how to make them happen. When I try too hard, when I push ahead, it always backfires instead of going the way I expect it to."

Carter spoke in a low voice, "Then don't. Don't push it. Be yourself. Let them come to you, Addi. You've always been the happy-bubbly person we all aspire to be. Things will work out. When, huh, when they are meant to… You just gotta be patient."

I snorted. "Can I serve you the same advice?"

He shook his head, his protracted silence speaking volumes.

Feeling a tad better, I rose to my feet and held out my hand. "Wanna dance? For old times' sake. And for what could have been."

"Addison Wilde, you know I don't dance."

"I'm sure you can make an exception for me, Country Boy. The last time, when Dahlia got married, you were a drunken mess. For the rest of the night, let's stick together to survive the next few hours."

He nodded and knitted his fingers through mine. "One dance. I can't believe you're making me do this," he said, shaking his head. "Only you, girl."

"Oh, Cart. I'm full of surprises. Never underestimate me. You should be aware of it by now."

"That sounds more like the Addison Wilde I know. Welcome back."

He wrapped his strong arms around me, and I felt so delicate in his embrace, Carter towering over me by almost a foot.

"Thank you for being my friend," I said as I sank into his chest and forgot about the things I had no control over.

———

"I'm calling it a night," Dahlia said as she hugged me hours later.

"Already?" I asked. "Is it even midnight yet? The night is still young."

"Almost. If I stay out too late two nights in a row, my face will be all puffy. I'm not used to partying this much. You should get some sleep soon. We're having a full day tomorrow. I've planned some great stuff for us."

I shrugged. "Don't worry about me. I'll head to that bar we like for an hour or two. Blow off some steam. You've always been too level-headed, girlfriend."

"By yourself? You sure?"

I nodded. "Yeah. I still have friends in town. I might give them a call. Or I'll make new ones. Don't worry about me. Now go and make love to your man while you're still a free woman."

I winked as Dahlia's smile stretched. "Addi, you'll find

your man too. He's somewhere out there. Don't be a pessimist. You'll get your happy ending. I promise."

I brushed a strand of her hair back with my fingers. "I love how you have faith in me, Dah, but did you forget I'm not into men anymore?"

She let out a loud chuckle. "My bad. For a second, I forgot."

"You'll see. I'll impress you. My next lover will be worthy of my love. I won't offer my heart to anyone not reaching the highest standards anymore. The next one will be marriage material. No, correct that. The next ones, with an *S*, will be rebounds. Hot and sexy. Tempting and forbidden. Then I'll find *the one*."

Dahlia hugged me again. "You deserve the best. I'm glad you got your smile back. Even if it's just for tonight. Even if it's slightly pretend. I love you. Don't get into trouble. And if you do, call me. Night."

She kissed my cheek and joined Nick, who was standing near the elevator, his palm outstretched, waiting for her to slide hers in it. That. The simple gesture. This defined true love.

Not ready to let the thought bother me, I yelled at everybody and nobody, "*I'mmm* hitting the bars. Those who want to extend the fun, follow *meee*." I downed the glass of wine in my hand. And another one, just because I felt like it, and headed for the exit.

Before the elevator doors closed, a large hand glided between them. When they opened again, Tucker entered the car, looking fierce. The flutters in my stomach returned. Fast. And invasive. No one said I couldn't enjoy a great sight when presented with one.

Taking his place beside me, he stole all the vital air from the car, and I sucked in a jagged breath in response.

His proximity made me feel lightheaded. Or was it the huge amount of alcohol I had drunk all night?

"Where are we going? I don't know the city, and I need a guide. I think you might be up for the job. Anyway, I'm pretty sure it's in my best man's job description to look out for the maid of honor."

Oh, he wanted me to play tour guide. Nothing else.

I could deal with that. This would keep me and my weak heart safe.

The low baritone of his voice as he let out a deep chuckle shook my core.

Girl, get a grip on yourself. Yes, in my intoxicated state, my willpower had no solid ground.

If I couldn't find a sure way to stay away, this night would end badly. I could already tell.

All my radars were attuned to the man standing feet away from me. About six feet two, built like an athlete, with broad shoulders and a lean waist. His dark skin gave the impression he'd been molded from the most exquisite chocolate, with even darker, enigmatic irises and a smile showing perfectly aligned white teeth.

Tucker was everything I had a weakness for.

Smart. With a touch of sarcasm.

Even if I denied it, no way would I ever be indifferent to how he made me feel. Not me. Scratch that. My body. To how he made my body feel.

I got drunk on his cologne, the scent of sea breeze enveloping me.

I clenched my thighs, refusing to let my imagination run wild.

I was over men. Over. Men. T-R-O-U-B-L-E.

I had to come up with an exit plan. An excuse to remove myself from his gravitational pull. My drunken brain made it almost impossible for me to map out an evacuation plan.

"You're not chaperoning *meee* all night," I warned, pointing a finger at him. "*I'mmm* on a mission. To get laid."

Tucker rolled his jaw back and forth and arched one eyebrow. Its sharpness alone could tear my new resolution to shreds. "And I can't help you with that because? Other than the fact I promised your best friend I wouldn't seduce you."

"Wait. What? *Youuu* did what?"

He shook his head, shoving his hands into his pockets. "It's no big deal. Dahlia might have threatened my life if I fucked with you."

"Ohmygod. She's the best." I snickered. "I love her so much right now. Anyway, she's not *myyy* mother, and I'm free to do whatever I-I want. But to... *Sorry*, my head is all over the place right now. Too much wine… Huh, what was I saying?"

"That I wasn't on the list of potential fucks tonight, and I was asking you why."

"Ahh, yeah. That. I…huh…I remember now. Well, first, *youuu're* Nick's friend. That would be weird, right? Second, you're…*youuu*." I drew circles in the air inches from his face.

"Me? What's wrong with me? What does that even mean? The last time I checked, it wasn't such a bad thing."

"God, do *youuu* need me to spell it out for you? 'Cause I will. *Youuu're* a man, *Tuuuck*. T-R-O-U-B-L-E. You lose all your points right there. *I'mmm* over your species. I already told you. Not that I…I don't appreciate your gender. In fact, I do. A little too much. Like a pricey wine. In both cases, *theyyy* come with promises of a great night but with the risk of a major hangover the next day. Tonight, *I'mmm* looking for a woman. Someone sweet who can think with her brain and not her *dickkk*, for a change. Someone who knows how to use her tongue expert…*expertisely*…nah…oh yes, expertly. And her fingers. Don't forget the fingers. *Youuu* can't compete with that."

"Oh, sure. Right. Got it. You think women make better lovers." He rubbed the skin of his nape. "See? I agree."

"*Youuur* mother taught you right," I said.

He flinched at that, and his face hardened. "Keep my mother out of it."

"Don't get *alll* worked up, big guy. I was just complimenting how she raised *youuu*." I paused because the grimace on his face unsettled me. What did I say that put him on edge? With a hand, I stroked his forearm.

Tucker relaxed under my touch. The hard lines around his eyes receded.

He blinked, and a devious grin spread across his face, his harsh reaction to my compliment forgotten—or pushed aside for now. "If I understood you right, tonight, we're both playing the same field?"

I nodded, pride filling me.

"I'm willing to prove to you I'm much more qualified than you to entertain the ladies."

"In…huh, in that case, let's make things interesting," I said. "Let's see who *brinnngs* someone to their hotel room first. What do *youuu* say? Deal?"

Tucker seemed to ponder the idea in his head. "Oh, so you're not only a tease, but also a player."

I mustered the widest smirk my lips could stretch into. "Tell me, *Tuuuck*. What will I get once I win this challenge? The stakes *havvve* to be high. Like super high. To keep them entertaining."

He stared at me, his gaze so dark that my feet melted into the floor as he pinned me to the spot. "A weekend in Vegas, all expenses paid. If I win, you pay. If you win, which I'm pretty sure will never happen, then the bill is on me."

I extended my hand. Finally, I'd found someone to play with. "Deal. A three-day stay with a view of the Strip. Not some *shittty* motel in a clandestine corner of the city. The real *thiiing*. Classy and unforgettable."

"Good luck," he said with a wink. But under his confidence swam something I couldn't define. It must've been my imagination. Or the alcohol I'd drunk. Everything about Tucker screamed cocksureness and nights of limitless pleasure.

In Dahlia's and my favorite bar, we parked our asses for the night. It was one of my preferred nightlife spots in the city. I'd been living in Atlanta for the last few years, but every time I was around to visit my parents, I ended up here. Dahlia knew the owner; they'd toured together. So, he usually set us up with VIP rooms and the best champagne. Not tonight, though. Tonight, I was on the prowl. To forget all about my last relationship—and men in general. No special treatment needed.

Tucker ordered shots, and we each chugged three as we hung by the bar.

"If we fraternize, we'll look like a couple. No one will make a move on us," I said, dabbing at my lips with the back of my hand, careful not to smudge my lipstick.

"Sweetheart, I can melt panties from yards away. See how it's done and pick up a trick or two. That's why I'll win this little beginner's challenge tonight. Hands down."

"Tuck, I can play dirty. You've never seen me in action. Get ready to have your mind blown."

I tsk-tsked and walked away, swaying my hips, knowing the effect it would have on him. And just because I could. "I'll win," I whispered to myself as I watched him over my shoulder, his jaw slack and his eyes glued to my backside.

In a corner, I spotted a group of women, all wearing short dresses, showing off their bare legs and too much cleavage, looking drunk and ready to party.

"Hey, ladies," I greeted, sliding between them. "I'll come straight to the point. I'm looking for a girl to rock my night. You see that guy over there? The one with the dress shirt?" They all eyed Tucker, giggling like schoolgirls. "Well, we've made a bet, and he thinks I won't go through with it. If he nears you tonight, please ignore him. He's cocky as hell. If one of you wants to make out, just say the word. I'm your woman. He thinks I'm bluffing, but he's wrong."

A girl with long jet-black hair, ruby lips, and a sleeve tattoo inched closer. She looked like a model in her tiny leather skirt and high heels, her infinite legs tanned and skinny. "Honey, you wanna give him something to talk about?"

I nodded. Nervous excitement coursed through me as she gave me a slow once-over, observing me through her thick, curled lashes. She cupped my cheeks, and without breaking eye contact, dipped her tongue into my mouth, moaning as she did. After a few seconds, I relaxed and lost myself in one of the most sensual kisses I'd had in a long time.

Everything inside me soared.

I was breathless and longed for more.

The girl, whose name I ignored, kneaded one of my breasts, and I dissolved into her touch.

When we broke apart, I was panting, lacking viable oxygen to my brain.

Yeah, I had forgotten how amazing being kissed by a woman was.

My cheeks warmed up. I cocked my head and noticed

Tucker watching us, his mouth agape. My gaze traveled down to the bulge in his pants.

Our little bet got even more interesting.

Now he didn't stand a chance. At this rate, I'd get him so hot and bothered that he'd forfeit, and I'd win.

"Shots?" I asked my new group of friends. They all cheered, and I waved the bartender over to take our order.

———

The pounding on the door brought me out of my slumber. I tried to open my eyes but couldn't. My head hurt. No, my brain hurt. The pain was anchored deep inside my pulsing skull. I darted my tongue out to moisten my lips, but it was so pasty it made my stomach churn. My body felt heavy as if someone had wedged me in fresh concrete. Where was I? I patted the bed around me, but it was hard. Was I sleeping on the floor? Acid filled my mouth. This was bad. I had no memory of the previous night. The last thing I remembered was yelling at Tucker because he flirted with the girl I had been working hard to bring back to the hotel. She said we were bantering like children and we should get our shit together and left us.

Tucker?

Where was he?

Did we even make it back to the hotel? Every part of me ached, and whatever was beneath me was far too hard for comfort. My face felt as if it had been scraped with sandpaper. A buzzing sound reverberated against the walls of my skull.

The banging on the door resumed. Someone—a man —was angry. My brain was too numb to understand a word, or to make out whose voice it was, but by his tone, I could tell he was pissed.

Sensations returned to my hands, my arms. Slowly, it made its way down to my toes.

Something happened last night. The flesh of my inner thighs was tender. I wriggled a hand down my front. No panties. Okay, I was butt naked. I could deal with that. I moved my hand back up and slid it between my breasts and the hard surface. I had no clothes on.

What did I get myself into this time? I begged my brain to give me a clue. Nothing. Zip. Blank slate.

With a push of my hand, I lifted my upper body and opened my eyes. The room was trashed with junk food wrappers and sample alcohol bottles scattered everywhere. I was sleeping on my front on the carpet of the hotel room. Not my best moment. How could my amazing night have turned into this? Right now, I missed the comfort of a fluffy mattress.

The banging on the door intensified. Oh yeah, that guy was upset.

"Come on, open up. We'll be late. You were supposed to meet me an hour ago."

Oh God, did I make some woman cheat on her husband? This was a nightmare. How would I get out of this one? Of all the people I chose to fuck last night, I had to pick a married one.

The irony wasn't lost on me.

I let out a shaky breath and closed my eyes, trying to stop my head from spinning and my stomach from churning.

A warm hand slapped my ass cheek, and I gasped.

"Hey, sweetheart. You awake?"

The blood froze in my veins.

This was bad. So bad. Kill me now.

What did I do last night?

Chapter 4

Tucker

I stretched my arms and pried my eyes open, the thumping on the door about to crack my skull open. I didn't remember the last time I got so wasted. The little challenge between Addison and me last night had turned into a full-blown competition. The girl could play. She deserved a medal just for her efforts.

Minutes after we had arrived, she kissed a woman, full tongue, right in my face, offering me the most perfect jerk-off vision I'd ever seen.

The girl was a devil dressed like an angel.

She was bad…so bad, and had almost killed me with every flick of her tongue.

And truth be told, I had a weakness for bad women. All of them. No exception. Even the ones I'd promised to stay away from.

My dick had been hard for hours, watching Addison

make out with strangers, caressing their tits, gripping their asses. Staring at them with intense lust.

Just thinking about it got my dick stiff. Again.

The soft breathing of the woman next to me brought a smirk to my lips. At least I got laid last night. *Yeah, congrats, Dick. I knew you still had it in you.*

If only I could high-five my wingman...

Guess I won after all.

The more I'd drunk, the hazier last night's events became in my mind. I remembered my conversation with Addison up on the roof, then she'd danced with Carter Hills. The sight of them had sent a wave of misplaced jealousy through me. They laughed together, looking intimate. How well did they know each other? He clearly didn't get the same warning that I did. To avoid making a scene because I somehow felt as if looking after her was my dutiful job, I had asked Mrs. Ellis, Dahlia's mom, if she would like to dance. She ended up being quite a dancer, and I'd spent hours twirling her around.

Then I had followed the maid of honor to the bar. Because I had no idea how to escape her magnetism. And because my dick was a selfish prick and enjoyed her attention.

We had drunk shots.

She had gotten me hard by kissing a woman.

A surge of envy had stirred inside me. One that I could barely contain.

Desperate to be the one her lips were molded to, I had downed more shots to forget about her.

My memory faded from that point onward.

From then on, my mind was flooded with flashbacks of our night.

I flipped to my side and looked around. Why was I lying here?

With my fingertips, I rubbed my throbbing temples. Nothing two painkillers couldn't fix.

A foot away, my hand found the curve of a bare ass. The porcelain flesh was a great contrast to my darker skin.

My dick twitched. Perhaps we could have one last round before we go our separate ways. Just to get all the lust out and secure it away for the rest of my stay.

"Hey, sweetheart. You awake?"

The woman turned her head, and my words died in my throat.

"Wilde? What the fuck." I stretched my arm to grab a piece of fabric and used the discarded shirt to hide my junk. "Why are you here?" She blinked, watching me as if I'd grown horns. "Fuck, did we—? Nick is gonna kill me." I ran a hand over my face. "No. Dahlia will strangle me. And then she'll throw the pieces of me to sharks, so there won't be anything left."

Would I burn in hell for this?

I closed my eyes, praying my hangover brain had conjured the entire scene, and shook my head.

When I peeled my lids open, everything looked the same. "I *will* burn in hell for this," I mumbled, mostly to myself.

The door of my hotel room burst open, startling me. Nick stood in the doorway, along with a concierge, his arms folded across his chest, an annoyed expression replacing the fleeting relief in his eyes. I grimaced. *Addison.* I raised my arm to fake scratch my nape, looking sideways to where she lay seconds ago, but she had disappeared. Did I dream of her in my room? I shut my eyes, trying to make sense of the scene unfolding before me. My best friend tipped the guy after assuring him of my well-being.

The door shut behind him, and Nick stalked forward, stopping a foot away from my sprawled self.

"What the hell, man. I've been knocking for over twenty minutes. I thought you were dead or had passed out in your puke. I really got scared for a moment." His eyes took me in. "Why are you sleeping on the floor? You're aware your room has a king-sized bed, right? Geez, Tuck. Are you all right? Should I worry?"

I stood up, dropping the shirt and forgetting all about my naked state. "Everything is fine, man. Just overslept. Somehow, it got wild last night." *Or Wilde.* Yeah, perfect choice of word.

A whistle parted his lips. "C'mon, Tuck. Cover up. Your dick doesn't have any effect on me. Anyway, you were supposed to meet me for breakfast. I got worried. Addison is missing too. Have you seen her when you went out last night?"

I shook my head. "No. Addison who?"

His eyes surveyed the suite. "Never mind. What did you do to your room? It's trashed. Did you have a party in here?"

"Yeah, got a few people over." *Did I?* I snorted. I'd bet my best man title the chaos was Addison's and mine only. We drank, we partied, we fucked. Seemed about right. Didn't I say already we shared the same playbook? "They stayed late. I'll sort it out. Don't worry, okay? It's your weekend. I'm a big boy. I won't get in any more trouble."

Bemusement flashed in Nick's eyes. "You do remember you are my best man and my only immediate family this weekend, right?"

Yeah, Jace would miss his wedding. And his bachelor party. He only had me to count on. How could I forget? Right now, I looked like an egotistical jerk.

I cast my eyes down. "I'm sorry, man. I mean it."

"Whatever. I'll be in my room when you're ready. You have fifteen minutes. It's almost noon. If you're not there, we're leaving without you. I'm really looking forward to spending time together. I've missed you since I moved to Green Mountain. And if you hear from Addison, please ask her to call Dah. She's worried sick."

I nodded, my head hanging low. Because what else could I do?

I locked the door behind my friend, and after putting last night's pants on, I reached for the bedroom. Addison was there, all dressed up, sitting on the bed, her hands locked between her thighs.

"Listen, Tuck, about last night, I-I don't know what to say because I don't…huh… I don't recall a thing…"

I stood in the doorway, raking a hand through my hair. "Huh, I don't either. Are you sure we—?"

"I'm sore. No doubt we did it. But I'm not sure we used protection, though."

"How can you…well, how can you tell? Sorry, stupid question." I paused to regroup my thoughts. "Huh, okay. I want you to know I'm clean. Got tested last month, and I've been on a dry spell since."

"Well, I'll take the morning-after pill when I get home. No big deal. I can't take birth control pills because they give me migraines. Also, I'm clean too." She breathed out. "Now at least."

My eyes flared as I stalked closer. "What do you mean, you're clean *now*?"

Fury scorched deep down in me. This was no joke. I didn't mind sleeping around, but catching some fucking disease? Not happening.

She dropped her head low, and her shoulders slouched forward. "You know my vow about staying away from men. Well, my ex...he-he cheated on me. Rather, he led me on. They all did at some point… Anyway, the guy I'd been dating for two months...it turned out he had multiple girlfriends." Her eyes dimmed with hurt. "One in many states. I only learned about it because he caught something and thought he gave it to me. Felt it was his duty to come clean about his dick's whereabouts. Like he was the savior in the story. Asshole. Anyway, I'm fine. Don't stare at me like this. I didn't screw around. He did."

Tears clouded her blue eyes.

Now I felt like an idiot for assuming the worst about her.

I sat on the bed next to Addison and held her hand in mine. It seemed like the most sensible thing to do after I fucked her without a condom and had no memory of any of it—or of doing it. Her touch quieted my racing thoughts. I breathed easier as we shared a moment. We both stayed silent, the reality of what happened hitting us.

After a long minute that seemed like an hour, I tried to ease the tension in the room. "Guess we both won the challenge then."

"Or we both lost," Addison deadpanned, avoiding my gaze. "I should get going. I'm supposed to go shopping with Dahlia, and I'm like almost two hours late. She must be running crazy."

"Huh, do you want to talk about it? Later. We could—"

She jumped to her feet. Her somber voice, lacking last night's confidence, pinched my heart. "Nah, it's okay. We shouldn't. What's done is done. Let's just forget about it. Bye, Tuck." She hurried out of the room without another glance in my direction.

Twenty minutes later, showered and dressed in a clean Jaxon Arison button-up shirt and black trousers, I looked refreshed and felt better than I did earlier. With my headache almost gone and my hangover forgotten, I sauntered toward Nick's suite with a swagger in my step.

"Any news of Addison?" I asked, acting as casual as possible, after he let me in.

"Yes, she's fine. She overslept too. Said she turned off her phone because she had a headache. Anyway, she's coming over soon. We just made a reservation for lunch at that restaurant Addi and I adore in East Nashville for the four of us," Dahlia said with a twinkle in her eyes, meeting my best friend's enamored stare.

Their love really was nauseating.

"I thought you girls had plans?" I asked. The idea of spending more time with Addison turned my spine into an ice pick. Nothing good could come out of this after what we did last night.

"Change of plans. I know my bestie. What she needs is a meal with friends, nothing too fancy, and an afternoon nap to be in top shape for tonight. Shopping can wait."

A knock on the door sent my pulse into overdrive, and pearls of sweat gathered at the back of my neck.

"Hey, Addi. Are you feeling better?" Nick asked as he greeted her and dropped a kiss on both her cheeks. She muttered something I didn't catch, my blood rushing so loudly in my head that it drowned out all other sounds around me.

"Hi, Tuck," she said as our eyes met when she walked past me toward Dahlia.

"Hey," I echoed, my voice rough, running out of words.

Dahlia clasped her hands before her. "Ready? I'm so excited we're doing this. I haven't spent this much time with grown-ups in years. And somehow, sharing this day with you guys is really important to me."

She beamed, and I felt stupid for racking my brain to find a dumb excuse to bail out on all of them.

In the small eatery, with black leather booths and dark

wrought-iron chandeliers hanging from the ceiling, Dahlia and Nick sat next to each other, and I took a seat beside Addison. The narrow booth was a tad small for my stature, so our limbs brushed against each other the entire time, and her heat shot through me where our bodies connected.

The scent of her shampoo made me dizzy. It was too intoxicating. Too fruity. Too Addison Wilde. I loosened the collar of my shirt and rubbed my throat, trying to open my airways. I was suffocating. At this rate, I'd be dead from asphyxiation before lunch hour was even over.

"You two ready for your maid of honor and best man's pre-wedding speech tonight?" Dahlia asked, the sparks in her eyes still shining. She could light up the entire town with those.

"Yeah," I said.

Beside me, Addison coughed. "Sure. Super ready. Yay," she said, pumping her fist.

I studied her from the corner of my eye. Gaze down. Dropped shoulders. Curved back. Flushed cheeks. The girl was the worst liar I'd ever met. Was her best friend blind or so overwhelmed by the wedding that she missed all the signs?

Under the table, I patted her hand, but she yanked it away as if my touch burned her. Before Dahlia could push the topic some more, I changed the subject. "When is the honeymoon?"

Nick intertwined his fingers with his fiancée's. They exchanged a ridiculous grin that only people in love flaunted. "Carter has a month off later this summer. We'll leave then. Jack will stay with him, so we'll have a full four weeks to ourselves. Two in Fiji and two at home."

They kissed, and I averted my eyes.

"You okay?" I asked Addison under my breath.

"Sure. Never better," she answered, not meeting my gaze.

Back in my hotel room two hours later, I debated between lying down for a much-needed power nap or doing the thing that the voices in my head were nagging me not to do.

After deciding a nap could wait, I gathered my phone, a sheaf of papers, and some stuff I filled my pockets with, and bolted through the door. Not knowing which room to go to, I gave Nick a call. "Hey, man. Looking for Addison's room. I grabbed her key by mistake. Can you gimme the room number so I can take it back to her?"

"Sure. Thirty-five-eleven."

"Thanks," I said, cutting the line before he struck up a conversation.

Seconds later, I knocked on the door, stuffing my free hand into my pocket and trying to look relaxed. Addison answered after a minute. Fuck, did I wake her up? She had changed into dark gray sweat shorts and a see-through white tank top.

She folded her arms over her chest, guarding her room, wearing a disapproving frown. "What do you want, Tucker?"

The sight of her brought a smile to my lips, and without waiting for an invitation, I ruffled her hair and pushed inside, not intimidated by her little act. Yeah, Addison Wilde was as scary as a kitten while trying to look disgruntled.

With a loud thud, she closed the door behind me, breathing heavily through her nose. The wrinkle across her forehead hadn't receded as she swiveled to watch me while I sat in a chair next to the bed. This little mask of fury looked adorable on her.

I took a second and perused the room. Open-floor suite

—same as mine—set up as a loft. It had panoramic windows with a stunning view of Nashville, high-beam ceilings, and a southern touch in its wooden accents.

"I'm here to help you out, sweetheart. You haven't written your speech for tonight."

"I have," she lied.

Still not convincing.

I waggled a finger. "Didn't you learn lying is bad? Stop already. I could tell earlier, and I'm here because I wanna help you save face tonight. We should get to work. I'm sure Dahlia expects great things from you. You wouldn't want to deceive your best friend, no?"

Addison neared me and huffed, the most irritated look I'd ever seen on someone now painting her face, her fists resting on her hips.

My gaze swept over her figure. I couldn't believe not remembering her naked and under me last night. The crests of her hips. The curve of her ass. The fullness of her breasts or the taste of her pussy. I shook my head, annoyed at myself. It had never happened before—having sex and retaining no memory of it the next day.

"Why? Why would you want to help me? It makes no sense. You wrote yours? Congrats, you're the perfect best man. Now leave. I can do this on my own."

"Nope, you're stuck with me until it's done."

She glared at me. I hated that last night's misadventure had created tension between us and that she would have to deal with the repercussions on her own to avoid any unplanned surprise taking over our lives nine months from now. Even though I was as responsible for our crazy night as she was, I could do nothing but hold her hand and support her through it all. Whatever happened, I refused to be just another man who failed her, one who would just abandon her in such a situation. I guessed if I were her, I'd be annoyed and pissed at myself too.

With a groan directed at me, she continued with her accusation, unaware of my thoughts. "You could shine as the perfect best man tonight, making me look unprepared. Why don't you, Tucker? Tell me. Unless you have an ulterior motive. So, what is it? I'm all ears."

This woman. Even her anger couldn't deter me from my goal of helping her.

I let out a warm laugh. "Call it team spirit, sweetheart. We fucked up last night…and fucked. If I had to guess, we went at it a lot. Anyway, I consider us friends now, and I wanna help you out. Don't overthink it. I don't usually offer my help that easily. And freely."

"Still not believing you. What do you want in return? Men always want something. They all do."

I sprang to my feet. "Whoa. I'm not that kind of guy, Wilde. I'm not being nice to get my dick sucked, if that's what you're referring to."

A dark blush spread across her cheeks. "Fine. What do you have in mind?"

I emptied my pockets on the nightstand. Her *ocean on a sunny day* blue eyes rounded.

"Sweetheart, the best way to get over a hangover is by having another drink. It's drinking 1-0-1. Make yourself comfortable. We'll be here for a long time, you and I."

Six mini liquor bottles and around thirty balls of paper strewn all over the room later—we tried our luck at basketball using the trash can but failed—we came up with a draft that pleased us both.

"See? It wasn't hard," I said once I finished reading it out loud. "I kinda like it."

"Again, why are you helping me, Tucker?" Addison

asked, her voice throaty. "You never answered the question."

I shrugged. "No idea. It seemed like you had a bad week. Or a bad month. Or whatever. I thought you could use a friend and some ass-kicking to get your speech over with. Have you written your speech for the wedding yet?"

"Yeah. I wrote it months ago. I'd forgotten about the one for tonight, though. Let's just say I've got a lot on my mind these days."

We clinked our bottles and knocked back the vodka in one gulp.

"Do you have any idea what went down last night?" Addison asked, her glazed eyes full of hope.

I shook my head. "If I had to guess, I'm sure I went down…on you."

She offered me a death stare.

"The truth? No idea. It's a shame I can't even remember the taste of you. Or how good we were together… I'll let the mystery fuel my fantasies for a while." She threw a pillow at me. "Don't think too much of it, sweetheart. You should be the one crying because you can't remember how being fucked by a real man felt like." Sitting side by side on the bed with our backs resting against the headboard, we stayed silent for a while.

"Thanks for helping me today, Tuck."

Okay, so we were back to *Tuck* instead of my full name. Progress.

"All my pleasure," I said as she rested her head on my shoulder. "I think we make a great team."

"Yeah. We do."

Soon Addison's breathing evened, and I beseeched my own eyelids to stay open. We both dozed off before either of us could make out what was happening.

The sound of sirens reverberated inside my head. They bounced against the walls of my skull. Were they real or a figment of my imagination? Right now, I couldn't tell. My eyelids weighed so heavy that it'd take an entire crew to force them open. The sirens turned into a deafening alarm. My head spun, heavy and confused. Still sleep-deprived, I couldn't remember where I had landed my ass last.

Something fastened around my waist shifted, and as if I'd been tased, I woke up. I scanned the room. Images of the last few hours flashed through my mind.

I patted the bed, looking for my discarded phone. Instead, I found Addison's. At least now I knew where the alarm was coming from. I turned the annoying sound off and stared at the screen, my brain taking longer than usual to make out the time.

I shut my eyes.

Re-opened them.

Blinked a few times.

Better. It brought the focus back.

"Wilde," I said, shaking her. "Wake up. We have to get ready." She mumbled something and sank her face deeper into my chest. "Earth calling Addison. *Wakey wakey.* Show me those blue irises. Get up right now, Wilde." I pushed her hair away from her face. Having her nestled against my body felt oddly domestic. Even if I didn't do love, this time somehow, having a woman in my arms just for the pleasure of it didn't freak me out as much as I thought it would.

She pushed my hands away as I dug my fingers into her ribcage and tickled her. "Stop. Leave me alone. I'm exhausted. I need sleep. Let's just stay here and skip the festivities. No one will realize we're missing."

I chuckled. "You're right. Neither the best man nor the

maid of honor shows up, and nobody will notice. Very clever." I squirmed from underneath her, disappeared into the bathroom, turned on the shower's cold water, then returned to the bed to lift her slumped body over my shoulder.

"Tuck, put me down," she pleaded. "Gimme another ten minutes."

"Remember, I'm doing this for you, sweetheart. Don't hate me, okay? It's for your own good."

I lowered her to her feet under the stream. A high-pitched cry escaped her as cold water ran over her. With my shoulders, I blocked her exit, my feet rooted to the tiled floor by the shower opening. Addison reached for me, pulling at my shirt, and scratching me like an angry kitten, trying to escape the glass box.

I held her in place with one hand. "Here," I said, adjusting the shower to warmer water while fumbling with the knob in my free hand. "See? Better?"

The minute I let go of her, she charged at me, jumping into my arms and twining her legs around my waist.

I risked a step back, but she didn't let go. "Come on, Wilde. This is how you repay me for caring for you?"

Her upper body molded to mine, drenching my shirt. "All my clothes are wet because of you. It's only fair yours are too."

I shook my head as she jumped to her feet, satisfaction brightening her face.

"You know this isn't actually my room and that I gotta return to mine in order to change, right? Real nice, Wilde. Well played." I unbuttoned my shirt and twisted it, trying to squeeze out as much water as possible.

Addison stood there, speechless, staring at my naked torso, her lips parted.

I flexed my biceps and my abdominal muscles to give

her something to fawn over. "When you're done drooling, you may want to undress and shower. We gotta be ready in less than an hour. I'll pick you up in fifty minutes. And by the way, I can see everything through that shirt of yours."

She yelped.

I winked and turned on my heel, leaving a mute Addison behind. My feet landed on the hallway carpet at the same moment Nick was about to knock on the door.

He scanned me from head to toe, his throat working, question marks dancing in his eyes. "Is everything all right? What are you doing here? Why are you shirtless? Two rules, man. Two."

I raised my hands in surrender, not hiding the trademark smirk I usually wore. "Easy, tiger. It's not what you think. Addison had a shower problem, and I helped her fix it. I just got soaked in the process. What are you doing here, anyway?"

My friend studied me for a few seconds longer, then shook his head, not impressed by my excuses after over twenty years of friendship. "Just…just don't do anything stupid, okay? Addi asked Dahlia to check on her in case she slept through her alarm."

"No need. She's getting ready. Give her some slack. She's a grown woman, not a toddler you two need to watch over."

"It's not like that. Told you she had a bad breakup. She's been off lately. Dahlia is protective of her right now. Anyway, once you're all ready and decent, meet up with us. We're having drinks in our suite."

"Yeah, see you in a bit." I walked away before my best friend could read through me and figure out I'd been lying to his face. Sorta. Did it count as a lie if I had no memory of breaking the rule?

Forty minutes later, I was about to go get the maid of honor when she appeared at the threshold of my room. Dressed in a floral tube dress and high heels, with her blonde hair tied into a sleek ponytail, she looked beautiful and dangerous. For all *man*kind. Men of our kind. Me included.

I fixed my gaze on hers after giving her a slow, appreciative once-over. "Wow, you clean up nice, Wilde. I knew that a cold shower would do you good. You can thank me now."

Addison didn't return my smirk. Instead, I noticed panic flashing in her eyes.

"What's wrong?" I stepped closer, trailing my fingers down her forearm. As if touching her had become my obsession—something I had to do.

"Okay, listen, here's the thing… I ordered something for tonight. A present for Dahlia and Nick. It was supposed to be here by now, but it's not. And I totally forgot to check the delivery time earlier today. I called the store, and they told me the package was on its way. If I wait for its arrival, I'll never make it to the boat on time." She sighed and rushed with the explanations, almost tripping over her words. "Do you think you could stay back with me for another hour? I'd wait on my own, but I came here by train. I don't have a car, and I don't like cabs and stuff. They gross me out. You got a rental, right?"

I nodded. "Cabs disgust you? Everybody takes them all the time, sweetheart. God, you're weird. You know what? Somehow, it suits you. Lucky you're not a New Yorker, or you'd go nuts." I checked the time on my phone. "Fine. I'll wait with you. I'll text Nick so he doesn't go ballistic on us for being late. Again."

In the lobby, Addison sat on a plush sofa while I rested

in a sable-brown oiled leather armchair, both of us sipping cocktails I got from the hotel bar. Dark wallpaper with a silver pattern adorned the walls. A stone fireplace with a wooden beam used as a mantle stood in the middle of the room. Wrought-iron chandeliers hung from the ceiling. The space looked like the foyer of a chalet-type resort in a decor magazine.

Addison kept checking the time, her leg nervously bouncing in her three-inch nude pumps. From behind my tumbler, I studied her. The girl looked amazing in her strapless dress, giving a hint of the swell of her breasts. I still couldn't believe I had those luscious globes all to myself last night and couldn't remember any second of it. Such a waste. Her blonde ponytail bounced over her shoulders every time she turned her head, and she had put on enough makeup to hide the dark circles under her eyes and make the blue of her irises pop. Addison Wilde was a gorgeous woman. The jerks who had hurt her in the past were just that, jerks. No way would I ever be able to make a woman like her cry. Or hate me.

"Enlighten me, sweetheart. Is the Cumberland River big enough for a fancy boat?" I asked, trying to dissipate her anxiety.

"Yep. You should see the big-ass ships you can spot when you're in Riverfront park. There's even a showboat offering tours, dinner cruises, and live shows. Tourists love it. It's nothing compared to the yacht Dahlia and Nick chartered, though. Wait until you see it. I saw pictures. It's huge." She whistled. "I wonder why the owner would keep it here, in a river in Tennessee, instead of at a marina along the oceanfront where most yachts are anchored."

"That impressive, huh?"

She bobbed her head.

A man dressed in a delivery company uniform passed

through the door, and she jumped to her feet to greet him, forgetting all about our conversation. They exchanged a few words, and she signed something before sauntering in my direction, a bright smile now lighting up her face, oblivious to the man's lingering gaze over every enticing inch of her. She waved the package at me, triumph in her eyes.

"Got it. We can go now."

"Follow me then," I said, pushing her forward, my hand molded to her lower back as if it had been made to rest there.

Two blocks away from the hotel, the lane merging onto the highway was blocked, a truck lying on its side. "Damn it," I said, hitting the steering wheel with an open palm. "We'll never make it on time. Wilde, get the GPS on your phone to find another route. Else, the yacht will leave without us."

"No need, big guy. I grew up around here and know just the perfect shortcut."

I sighed, made a U-turn, and followed her directions.

"Next traffic lights, on your right, then turn left at the stop sign."

I maneuvered through the narrow streets.

My gaze darted to the time on the dashboard, and I drummed my fingers on the steering wheel. We only had nineteen minutes left to get to our destination, and I loathed being late.

"Right here," she blurted without any notice, her finger pointing to our left.

I hit the brakes, the sudden motion propelling our bodies forward before we collapsed into our seats, the car behind us almost rear-ending us. Instinctively, I stretched my right arm in front of her, the gesture meant to protect her. Or prevent her from any impact.

"Jesus, Wilde. A little advance notice next time would

be appreciated." I flicked the flasher, and once my pulse settled, I followed her directions.

Addison pointed to a supermarket and said, "Turn here."

Agitation simmered inside me. The tapping of my fingers skipped to a faster beat, frustration tightening my muscles. My eyes took in the time. Beads of fury danced in my stomach. "Are you kidding me right now? The time is ticking and you wanna make a pit stop?" I dragged a hand over my face and rubbed my freshly shaved jaw.

She puffed and cocked her head toward me. "What? No. There's an alley just behind. It's a shortcut. We'll get there faster."

"Faster? I feel like we've been driving in circles for the last ten minutes." I grabbed my phone from the center console, turning the GPS app on.

Addison stole the device from my hand and held it as far away as possible from my reach.

"Gimme that," I begged, humor absent from my tone.

She shook her head. "Not a chance. I'm the one giving directions. We already agreed. I'll take you to the boat, big guy. Trust me."

I put the SUV in park. "Not now. We'll be late, and I'm not playing this game with you anymore. Gimme my phone back."

"Nope. I'm telling you. There's an alley behind the supermarket, and it will lead us to where we're going faster," she argued.

Jesus, Addison Wilde had a way of getting on my last nerve.

"Thirteen minutes left," she said with a large grin that drove me nuts.

Deciding to give her the benefit of the doubt and not waste any more time, I followed her instructions.

Once we exited the alley, we drove through a residential neighborhood, then turned right on another alley behind some sort of tattoo parlor, only to land on a deserted road parallel to the railway. Somewhere that appeared far from civilization but was actually two streets away from another residential neighborhood.

"Wilde, for the last time, you sure you know your way?"

She folded her arms over her chest, pushing those luscious tits of hers up, and I glanced at her sideways, entranced.

Eyes on her face, man, I told myself.

"No shame in admitting you're lost. Or asking for directions," I said, my aggravation dropping a notch.

"Are you serious?"

Oh-oh, now she sounded half-offended and half-amused as if about to scold me.

Not willing to participate in a battle of wills, I gave her a stiff nod and spoke before she could add anything else. "Dead serious. Now gimme my phone."

Addison angled her body until her back rested against the passenger door. She studied me for a beat, shook her head, annoyance tracing her features. "Tuck, Tuck, Tuck. Listen, you gotta learn to trust women. This is a bad habit of yours."

My insides clenched at her words, and I forced an innocent expression onto my face. "Who said…? What are you even talking about?"

"Sorry to ask, but do you have trust issues? With women? Because from what I've seen, it is evident." She wiggled her eyebrows. "Don't you agree?"

"Enlighten me, sweetheart."

She cleared her throat and raised one finger, challenge burning in her eyes. "First, I mentioned your mother and wanted to compliment you, but you flinched." She raised another finger. "Second, when I said we had sex this morning, you asked if I was sure. Come on. How could I have put your cum there myself?" She lifted a third finger. "Then you insinuated I hadn't written my speech." She sighed and shook her head. "That time, though, I'm giving it to you. You were right." With a smug expression pasted on her face, she raised a fourth digit. "And now you thought I gave you bullshit directions to the yacht. The devil is in the details. Your behavior, taken individually, seems insignificant, but when put together, it's incriminating. You also gave yourself away just now, stiffening your upper back when I asked if you have trust issues with women."

I blinked. Something resembling fury mixed with uneasiness seared inside me. I cracked my neck to the side and rolled my shoulders back, trying to dissipate the thorny vice around my muscles before it lodged there longer than necessary. "No, I don't. Since when are you a shrink?" I tried to hide the wrath lacing my words, but failed. My clipped words sounded harsher than I intended.

Addison studied me, not impressed by my weak comeback, her gaze drilling holes into my skull as if she could read what was going on in my mind. "Hey, no need to get defensive with me. It's okay. I recognize the signs. Because I don't trust men, remember? Well, most of them anyway."

She shrugged, furrowed her brows, then changed the subject as if she just hadn't uncovered my innermost fears and laid them bare for everyone to see. The ones I thought I had done a good job of burying deep when I was a twelve-year-old boy.

"Dahlia picked this part of the Cumberland River because we used to come here a lot when we were teenagers."

The knots around my stomach released their deadly grip, and I forced a deep breath in. "Fine. I'll do whatever you say. And for your information, none of this has anything to do with trust. In women, I mean. You are wrong." I stole a quick glance at her, but her face stayed neutral.

Without a word, she motioned to the deserted road with her chin.

"Show me the way," I said.

I relaxed my stance, happy the conversation had been forgotten—or put aside for now.

"There." She pointed at an old warehouse on our right that had been turned into a gym. "Turn here. We'll save a lot of time. The parking lots are all interconnected."

We raced from one empty lot to another, the SUV bumping on the uneven pavement. In the distance, I saw the yacht. It was huge and immaculate.

Tingles lined my spine. The excitement set in, replacing every tendril of tension in my back. Tonight would be fun. I could already tell.

"*Nooo*," Addison screamed, pulling me back from my admiration. "The gate. Look. It's locked." She slouched in her seat and brought her hands to her face.

We were at the end of the lot, where vegetation grew through the cracks of the pavement, the building on our right clearly abandoned.

I parked the car and angled my upper body to face her. "Wilde, what the fuck. I thought you knew the place. You said so. Now we're screwed."

"Yeah, it will take forever by road to get there unless—" An idea flashed through her mind because her eyes flared, and a smirk twisted her gorgeous pink-painted lips. "How do you feel about a challenge?"

I snickered. "Sweetheart, I never say no to some fun.

And I love a little risk. You should be aware of it by now. What do you have in mind?"

"Trespassing. Climb over the fence, jump to the other side, reach the boat. I know it's all rusty and shit, but who cares, right?"

My eyes traveled the length of her, appreciating every curve of her body. "You're telling me you'll climb a rusty fence in that dress?" I arched a brow and waited for her answer.

"I'm a lot tougher than you think, Mister *I Refuse To Get My Hands Dirty*. I'm a Southern girl, Tuck. Nothing scares me. Stop doubting everything I say and follow me." She grabbed her purse and package from the backseat and exited the car with her chin high and back firmed. "Turn around. I'll go first," she said, throwing her stuff over the fence before waggling a finger. "And don't sneak a peek up my dress."

"For your information, I saw more than your panties last night. And you're barely hiding anything with that piece of fabric."

Addison let out a long breath while removing her heels, then throwing them to the other side, one after the other. "It doesn't count if you don't remember. And my dress is perfectly fine, so stop complaining."

A wolf-whistle slipped through my lips. "Not complaining, Wilde. Never. The view is enjoyable from here. You're free to parade in front of me anytime. Clothes optional."

"Shut up. And turn around."

I faced the SUV for a few seconds but glanced over my shoulder once she started climbing. "Need a hand?"

"I'm all good on my own, big guy."

I pressed my lips together as my eyes admired the woman. I could stare at her toned legs all night if given the choice. She could really climb. I had to give her that. She swung her long leg over the fence with the ease of someone who'd done it a million times before, even in that tiny outfit, and I got a peek of her red lace panties. *I want to get fucked* panties. No women wore red underwear unless they expected some action later. My throat went dry at the thought, and I swallowed hard, turning my head back around to focus on the hood of my rental. The last thing I needed was to get caught and be on the receiving end of her ire. Even though I doubted Addison Wilde would get mad if she caught me staring. After all, she had to know how attractive she was.

Still, my brain formed images of her. Of *us*. Naked, entangled. Taking her from behind. Hearing her moan my name. Pleasuring her, my face between her thighs.

Heat slammed into me like a wave.

I blew out a breath, my mind drifting to Pamela White to kill the excitement bulging down there. Yep, Jace's wicked wife had that effect on me. Erection murderer.

"Your turn," Addison announced, quashing my racy thoughts.

Her feet hit the ground, and I rolled my sleeves, ready to join her. Something about her made me want to be close to her. For a moment, I swore under my breath, wondering how I found myself trespassing on an abandoned lot instead of already sipping drinks with my friends. I was way too old for this game. Why did I agree to go with this plan of hers? I knew it was stupid, and yet, I rolled with it like a champ. Damn it. I swept one leg over the fence, careful not to tear my pants. Grinning with satisfaction, I planted my hands on the rail, ready to swing my other leg over when I lost my footing. Instead of climbing down as I had planned to, my shirt caught on the rusty grid, and it tore open at the front on the left side. From my nipple to my waist.

Addison gasped.

I froze.

Was I topless?

Chapter 5
Tucker

"Fucking stupid idea," I grumbled, jumping down and rubbing my hands together to brush off the dirt from the fence. With a grimace, I pinched the ripped fabric as irritation boiled my veins. "Look at me now. I'll spend the rest of the night half-naked. Great. What a wonderful idea you had there, Wilde. Come on, if you'd wanted another glimpse of me, all you had to do was ask. I would've even given you a run for your money."

Addison ate the distance between us and burst out laughing, her laughter so warm and contagious that some of my anger dissolved, and I joined in. Yeah, I appeared ridiculous, no doubt.

"Tuck, I gotta say, you *do* look stupid. Not sure your pricey shirt can carry off this new design. Lucky you, you have pretty nipples. You could pretend you got hurdled by a flock of needy women on your way here, and they ripped your clothes off with their long fingernails. Or their teeth.

People would get engrossed in such a story. Super believable. They'd all talk about it, and you'd be a hero."

I blinked. And I blinked again.

She nodded, seeming convinced by her retelling of events that had never happened. Addison Wilde was... *Jesus*... For once, I had no idea how to describe her. Some of her last words replayed in my head.

"Pretty nipples?" I had fucked my share of women and never had any of them tell me my nipples were pretty.

Addison grinned. What was wrong with her? Couldn't she share my anger instead of complimenting my freaking tits? Pecs. Geez, she was toying with my mind now. Every parcel of it.

"Wilde, keep your compliments to yourself because none of it changes the fact that I'm about to board a multi-million-dollar yacht looking like a cheap stripper." I flexed my hands at my sides. "In case you haven't noticed, I'm particular about my clothes. I love expensive designer shit. This," I gestured to my chest, "doesn't cut it. Not at all. I'm freaking mad right now. And it's all *your* fault."

She moved closer, pushing her blonde ponytail over her shoulder, and grabbed my upper arms. "How is it my fault that you misjudged your step? Stop blaming me for your incompetence."

I took a step toward her. "Care to repeat that?"

My chest brushed against hers, her stiffened nipples rattling the chains of my self-control. Her breaths mingled with mine. The air between us heated up. Her lips pursed. Fuck. That mouth, it did nothing to tame my hunger. My dick sprang to life. Her soft breasts pressed against my torso. The contact drove me insane. Our heartbeats synced. The glare she sent my way turned me on instead of appeasing the throbbing in my lower body. All I wished for was to claim her as mine.

Here and now. Finish what we had started last night. Relive the episode I couldn't recall. The one urging me in such a compulsive way I had a hard time containing it in that instant.

My heart mistook my annoyance for excitement. Yearning. Lust.

No, it wasn't desire kindling inside me. Just a primal need to get her out of my system. To kill the ache.

I pursed my lips and drew a calming breath in to unknot the tension rising in my core. Her presence invaded my senses, inverting the North and South of my internal compass.

Addison, looking all feisty and alluring, sighed and rolled her eyes. I forced my desire down, clenching my fists. I had no right to feel whatever was sizzling inside me. I stepped back, desperate to evade her gravitational field. To avoid touching her. To prevent myself from kissing those pouty lips.

Her exasperated tone cooled my ardor. "Don't be a baby, big guy. It was an accident. And it wasn't *my* fault. Now, if you'd listen to me for more than ten seconds, I have a solution. Not sure you'll like it, but it's worth trying."

I frowned. So far, all her bright ideas had turned out badly. For me. Okay, for her too. Maybe. It didn't matter that she looked all adorable and innocent. Addison Wilde possessed a devilish side I wasn't sure I liked that much, but couldn't seem to escape. Did I really want to, though? My hesitation spoke volumes. I was so screwed.

She was having another one of her light bulb moments. Yeah, right. What would it be this time? She opened her sinful mouth, and I braced myself for the volley of her words. Instead of speaking, she seemed to think better of it because, without saying anything, she lifted her mysterious package from the ground and tore the plastic wrap open.

I stared at her. Waiting. My chest rose and fell quickly, my anger barely contained now, mixed with anticipation.

The sight of her, a grin on her lips and sparkles in her eyes, acted like a balm, easing my temper.

Until she unfolded the piece of fabric she fished out of the bag.

My heart stopped beating. Yes, I was pretty sure I died right there. If that was her brilliant idea, what did her shitty ones look like? Oh yeah, I already had a taste of them. My throat worked for a few seconds, air barely flowing through because I had no clue whether to burst out laughing, start crying, or just run for my life. I opened my mouth to say something—anything—when the most cock-sure and adorable smile spread across her face as she watched my reaction. My gag reflex engaged. It fucking did. This was a joke. I was being pranked. Again. This scrap of fabric shouldn't be allowed to be called a T-shirt. It was an insult to all the T-shirts in the world. I blinked. Once. Twice. No, it wasn't a dream. This nightmare was real.

I was right last night. Addison Wilde was a minx. She would ruin me.

Dear God. Please help me, I prayed, casting a quick glance at the sky.

I owned pink dress shirts, but that thing bore the ugliest shade of...of... I lacked the pertinent adjectives to characterize its uniqueness. Addison flicked a switch hidden in its seam, and a battery-powered sign at the back spelling "GROOM" lit up.

Fuck my life. She. Was. Messing. With. Me.

No way could this be real.

Dirty salmon-pink, size extra-small—sure looked like it —and blinking lights.

Jesus, I'd be the butt of all jokes throughout the night.

I closed my eyes and took a long, steadying breath, feeling the anger inside me grow by the second. My blood turned to lava. Could she see the steam coming out of my ears and nostrils? Two more seconds and I'd turn into a dragon. Goddamn it.

My molars would fuse together if I didn't relax my jaw.

Taking another deep breath in, I unclenched my fists, reining in my anger. Deep inside me. Far, far away from here. No, I wouldn't explode. Now wasn't the time to unleash every swear word in my vocabulary.

"That's the package we couldn't leave without? Are you fucking with me on purpose? It's terrible. Promise me you'll never throw a bachelor party for me. Not that I'll ever get married, but still. A man can't be too prepared for something that awful. I'm crossing your name off the guest list right now. See? All done. You're uninvited to an event that won't ever occur. Ugh, that's how bad this looks."

"Tuck, Tuck, Tuck. Why are you being a brat about it? You need a shirt. I happen to hold a brand new one in my hands. Try it," she argued, not affected by the words I just spoke.

"No. There's no way I'll ever wear...this. Whatever *this* is," I barked, pointing to the piece of pink fluff I refused to call clothing. "I hope bare chests are allowed on the boat, sweetheart. Fuck, I'll really look like a stripper."

I bowed my head, inhaling and exhaling, as a new wave of ire singed my insides.

Addison folded her arms over her chest and sighed. A mix of amusement and—was that annoyance?—danced in her deep blue eyes. She shook her head and pushed the awful atrocity against my chest with more strength than necessary. My gaze lingered on her pushed-up tits for a fraction of a second before returning to her face.

The corners of her lips were pinched together, and she had a *don't bullshit your way out of this* look plastered on her gorgeous face. Damn, even her upset face did something to me. My dick stirred in my pants. *Stay put, man. We're not playing that field, remember?* Knowing Addison was off-limits made her even more attractive. A forbidden fruit. A banned temptation. Go figure.

Her irritation brought my focus back to her, and I snapped out of my perusal. Oh yeah, the stupid "groom" T-shirt.

Her voice, as mellow as honey, dissolved more of my anger. How could she master this trick? "Tuck, don't be prissy about it. Just wear the damn shirt already."

I folded my arms across my chest, mirroring her previous stance. "Not a chance. And did you pick a toddler's size? It's so tiny. No way will I ever fit in this. My head is bigger than this dishrag."

A grin transformed Addison's face, chasing away her aggravation. "What choice do you have?" She grabbed the phone from her purse and watched the screen. "The yacht is leaving in five minutes. Either you wear this fantastic T-shirt I designed myself for our friends' special night or you spend the night in torn clothes. Not that I'll complain. Told you, your nipples look nice. Your choice. Hurry up, the clock is ticking. *Tick-tock. Tick-tock. Tick-tock.*"

Oh, this girl. If only I had the time to fight with her right now. Get that smug grin off her face.

My dick twitched again at the thought.

I don't have time for you, I told him in my head. *Stay out of it. Last warning. The girl isn't ours to play with. Boundaries, man.*

Addison knew she had me. I was weak around her.

My body firmed.

The tension between us soared.

We faced each other, neither of us breaking our stance.

Her tempting lips parted, and right now, damn the consequences. I would have kissed the shit out of her, bent her over the hood of my rental, and fucked her till morning. Until I could fulfill and then erase all the naughty images swimming in my head.

Addison Wilde had a way of getting under my skin.

To make me want to pull my own hair—if only I could get a grip on it.

Those ridiculously blue eyes were trained on my semi-bared chest. If they swept down, they'd be aware of how bad I had it for her right now. And how the challenge she brought into my life excited me.

I lowered my gaze to my wrecked shirt. Nothing I could do would fix it. "Let me tell you something. You owe me big time, sweetheart. You better open a tab because, at this pace, you'll be broke by the end of the night. And I mean it. You're responsible." I waved a hand around. "For all of this."

Addison tipped her chin up, never breaking eye-contact.

"Oh, already told you, big guy. I don't scare easily. Southern girl here. Born and raised. Your big-city threat doesn't impress me much. Sorry. You'll need to do better than that to unnerve me." She glanced at her phone. "*Tick. Tock. Tick-tock.* What will it be, *Tuuucker*?"

The way she said my name. Slow and with a hint of arrogance. Even that made me want to bend her over. Damn Nick's rules. The guy knew what he was doing when he made me swear to keep my distance. He knew I would have a hard time resisting the temptress. That I would sell my soul for just a taste of her.

"*Tick. Tock. Tick-tock.*"

A loud growl crossed my lips as I said, "Fine. Gimme the thing you're bold enough to call a T-shirt." I snatched it from her hands, held the sides of my torn shirt, and ripped it off me just to gauge her reaction, then slid the pink monstrosity over my head, gritting my teeth. Her cheeks flushed as she nibbled on her lower lip while pretending to be unaffected. She blinked and took a harsh breath. Once. Twice. Was she as unsettled as I was at this instant?

I, myself, couldn't breathe, blame the attraction, or maybe the tasteless T-shirt clinging to me. It was so tight the seams stretched as I tugged it lower. "Happy now?"

Addison hid her victorious smirk behind her hand. "Oh, Tuck. You look amazing. It was made for you. I should have got one for you in the first place. Maybe you'll let me throw you a bachelor party after all. See? I can read your mind, and my name has been put back on your guest list. Thank you for trusting me with the task of dressing you for your special day." I glowered at her for her presumptuous tone, but she ignored me and cupped her heart with both hands. "It will be my honor. I promise to make you proud. Can't wait." She paused. "Would you mind playing model for a few hours? I'd like official shots of you sporting one of my creations. I helped you, you help me out in return. Only fair."

She took her phone out and pointed it at me, her finger pressing the shutter button. "Oh yes. Show me that scowl. The ladies love a handsome grump. You're hired."

A groan tumbled out of my mouth. Guttural and animalistic. Addison was playing with fire and enjoying every second of it. The more she teased, the more I enjoyed her presence. It was a sickness. Something that poured fire into my blood. Killing my brain cells. Fucking with my existence. Addison Wilde had annihilated me, and she was having a blast doing so.

"If you wanted to make sure I wouldn't get laid tonight, well, you succeeded. Congrats, sweetheart. You could've just said so. I know I'm a pretty memorable fuck. The best you'll ever get. No need to go all possessive on me now that you've had your way with me. It's sad you can't remember it, I agree. Somehow, you'll always wonder what it felt like. My dick inside you. Your screams as I pounded into you. The sound of flesh on flesh. Your rapid breathing. Toes curling. The best lay you ever had."

She gasped and did nothing to hide the sparkle of mischief dancing in her eyes. She blinked, flustered, her eyes big and her breasts swollen. *Yeah, enjoy the self-denial, woman.*

I whirled around and stalked forward. "Let's go before our friends kill us for being late. Again."

We walked in silence through the high weeds.

Addison's stare burned into my skin. I could feel it on my back the entire time.

I cocked my head to watch her, and she offered me a lopsided smile. Pride. Recognition. Longing. Emotions danced across her face. I'd never be able to stay indifferent to her charms. Agitated, I locked my ache for her. If only the pre-wedding festivities were over by now and I could book the next flight home.

For a second, I felt bad for Addison. She'd miss giving Dahlia and Nick the gift she had made for them to help me out. Selflessness filled her heart. What else could explain her actions? I mirrored the tilt of her lips, unable to cast her out.

So far, this weekend was nothing like I'd imagined. I regretted not fighting to be in charge. After all, planning a bachelor party was supposed to be the best man's job.

Dahlia and Nick had insisted on organizing everything themselves. Deep down, I bet a part of them knew I would've gone overboard with it. Yeah, I couldn't blame them for opting to keep some control.

I refocused my attention before me, the yacht now in full view.

Addison's glee bounced on my back, and I halted, waiting for her to get in step with me, and reached for her hand. Her fingers intertwined with mine as if we had rehearsed the small gesture many times before. Her hand fit perfectly in mine. In silence, we moved forward. Together.

"Thank you. For trusting me," she said after a beat.

How could I stay mad at her? Addison possessed a strong yet vulnerable persona. I saw the two sides of her, and the mix of both was a deadly combination. I could imagine people turning their entire world upside down to catch a glint of happiness in her features. To follow her anywhere. To bask in her contagious energy. Because a part of me felt that way too.

What was her ex thinking when he slept around and broke her heart? This woman, no matter how bad I tried to portray her, was kindness personified. Sure, she was crazy, and her ideas were atrocious—she really believed they were awesome even when they made absolutely no sense—but still, she had an endearing personality and a challenging spirit. That I could tell. Because, despite myself and my best friend's warning, she had sucked me into the vibrant vortex that defined her.

"Tell me, you really designed this?" I asked, still flabbergasted that I agreed to wear the T-shirt, but trying to go back to the friendly relationship we'd shared earlier.

She shrugged. "Yeah. I design T-shirts I sell online. For fun. I'm a graphic designer. I usually do dealership banners and ads, but designing fun logos and stuff has always been a passion of mine. I've been doing Carter's merch for years now. Anyway, I lied to you. I should have ordered the T-shirts weeks ago, but with everything going on, I kinda forgot and ordered them yesterday as a rush shipment. Sorry it's boring."

I stopped in my tracks. "Are you fucking with me again?"

She released my hand and kept walking.

I circled her wrist with my fingers to force her to stop.

She spun to face me. "No. Why would I?" Even her irises were shitty liars. A flashback of the vulnerability I saw on her face this morning came back to me. When she confided about her ex and how he screwed with her heart.

It was my turn to shrug. "It's cool. The T-shirt isn't that bad. The color is enough to give me acne, and the size hasn't been thought through to fit an adult male, but other than that, I think it's pretty original. You're talented. I can tell. I had no idea you were behind Carter Hills's logo and merch. That's incredible."

Addison tipped her head forward. Was that a flush on her cheeks? "Thanks," she muttered. Was I making her shy? I thought shyness wasn't in her vocabulary.

The easy conversation and confidences we shared warmed a layer of my icy heart.

Hand in hand and feeling somehow closer to her, we resumed our walk.

She offered me a squeeze of her hand and a tight-lipped smile, her gaze filled with a hint of empathy. Or tenderness. A sign she was there with me and would have my back. Those details were not lost on me.

She put her heels back on just when we approached the yacht.

A fresh burst of energy jolted her, and she hurried forward, tugging my hand.

From up close, the motor yacht was magnificent. About sixty feet long, it had an open deck above the hull and single-level living quarters below, providing a panoramic view of the river from every side. We stepped inside the salon, and I was taken aback by the luxury it projected, with white walls and wooden trims and flooring and ornate decor. A table big enough to seat over twenty people had been set up in the middle of the salon, which led to the galley on the left and a navigation station on the right.

After a crew member welcomed us aboard, he motioned us toward the staircase leading to the upper deck. My hand rested on Addison's lower back the entire time as I climbed after her. Open-air, the deck was lined with dark plank wooden floors and white leather seats. The warm breeze swept across our faces as we reached the last step. People mingled, holding their glasses, dressed to the nines.

All conversations stopped the moment our feet landed on the deck.

Eyeballs rolled in our direction.

Laughter replaced the chatter.

"Oohs" and "Ahhs" blasted into my ears.

I dragged a hand over my face. Great. I'd been right earlier. Now I'd be the topic of stupid jokes all night.

The temporary peace that had settled between Addison and me vanished when I caught the twinkle in her eyes. Now we were back to each man—or woman—to themselves. Our banter would resume. Gone was the compassion from her features. She looked highly amused by the commotion our entrance created.

I breathed in, trying to keep the new batch of irritation swirling inside me under wraps.

Yearning and frustration blended together. With my eyes throwing daggers at the woman who had dressed me like a blind toddler, I steeled my back and upped my chin. "Showtime, I guess," I muttered under my breath.

"Ohmygod, Tucker. What happened to you? You know Nick is the groom, right? Are you trying to tell us something?" Dahlia teased, her eyes glinting and mouth twisting with repressed mirth. "In case you didn't get the memo, I'm not marrying you. Sorry. Anyway, you look... Well, you look charming."

Dahlia was as much a bad liar as her best friend. I resisted the urge to poke my tongue out at her and strangle Addison at the same time. Perhaps that sounded a bit excessive.

Inside, I cringed. *Charming.* What the actual fuck. Nothing about the way I dressed was charming. I looked stupid. More than stupid. Ludicrous.

I forced a smile to my lips and met Dahlia's entertained demeanor. "Great. I'm glad you think it's a good look on me because guess what? You get to wear one too. We'll match tonight, you and I." The humor vanished from her eyes. "That's right. Wilde got them for you and Nick, but since I ripped my shirt and didn't have time to change, I was the lucky SOB who got to wear the groom's. You're the bride-to-be, so do the math in your head, sunshine. We'll rock the town together later."

Nick joined us, sparks in his eyes, barely able to contain his chuckle. *Fucker.* He clapped my shoulder, and I groaned, jerking away from his touch. "Sorry, man. No way you're playing bride and groom with my future wife. She isn't wearing hers." He focused his attention on the maid of honor, still standing tall beside me. "Did you make those?"

She nodded, a large smile showing her pearly whites, pride undulating from her.

"I knew you'd make something. They look amazing. I'm super impressed. Sorry it ended up on this loser."

Addison sighed and waved her hand. "Yeah. The worst part is that he can't even appreciate the art and creativity behind it."

"I agreed they were originals," I protested, none of them paying an ounce of attention to me.

Nick continued as if I'd said nothing, "That's a shame. I'd wear mine with pride, girl." Why did he have to be so non-embarrassed about everything? My best friend had become the biggest no-spine doormat since he'd fallen in love. His expression almost had me convinced he regretted not being the one wearing the stupid shirt.

Now I had the certitude he wouldn't help me save face or find a solution to my wardrobe malfunction. The only person who could have had my back tonight had turned on me. Unapologetic.

I rubbed the back of my neck, trying to come up with a smart idea to fix my dressing problem on my own. Surrounded by people who acted as if I couldn't hear them mocking my look shamelessly, I massaged my temples and pondered my options. "Come on, guys, be serious. I can't be the only one wearing this," I said, motioning to my chest with a hand, a sad expression taking over my face. Would they fall for it? I tried to pinch the cotton, but it was so tight I couldn't even get a grip. "I look ridiculous. This is supposed to be a couple outfit, not a lonely-groom kinda thing."

Carter sauntered our way, laughing so loud that he had to use his fist to wipe the teary corners of his eyes. Great. Another witness to my humiliation.

Amongst all the people present, he was the only one I could trade clothes with. He had about an inch over me, but my shoulders were broader.

"I must say, Addi, you surpassed yourself this time. When you told me you had a little special something for tonight, never would I have imagined it to be so damn spectacular." They high-fived, and smoke came out of my nose. Again. "And I'm pretty sure it looks even better on Tucker here." He faced me. "Man, you look like you borrowed a ten-year-old's T-shirt. Kudos to you for agreeing to wear it." He extended his fist to bump mine, but I ignored it.

"At least on the real groom-to-be, it wouldn't have been so stretched. You wouldn't have a spare shirt in your truck by accident? One I could borrow for the night?"

"Sorry. All I have are smelly gym clothes." He offered me a rueful smile and brought his glass to his lips.

Fucking great. This night was anything but fine. And it had just begun.

Dahlia and Addison moved to either side of me. "Babe, can you take a picture?" the bride-to-be asked my best friend. "I want to immortalize this moment forever. C'mon, Addi, get closer. It will go in our wedding album. Tuck, if hedge-fund banking doesn't work for you anymore one day, modeling should be at the top of your list when applying for a new job."

I fake-grinned as Nick snapped a picture, his lips still stretched to his ears.

Anger seethed stronger in my bloodstream. "Okay, stop. All of you. I need a bride. ASAP. Anyone. Find me a woman. Someone single. No way am I going to a bar later dressed like this on my own. It's supposed to be a bachelor party. Not a *make fun of Tucker* night. I can embrace this T-shirt while we're here and give you something to talk about, but later I want an out. Think, people. Fast. Find me a fake bride, so I don't look like a stood-up groom who lost a bet."

Addison scrunched up her face and said, "Fine. I'll wear the other one. Are you happy now, Tucker baby? Geez. Where's your sense of humor?" She pushed the top of her dress down, not a care in the world that people could see her in a strapless, lacy red bra. The lace offered me a perfect view of her pink nipples, while she bunched her outfit around her waist. Fuck me already. My body reacted, recalling events I couldn't. My skin overheated. My dick swelled. Eye-fucking me, she slid her arms into the matching T-shirt and adjusted it over her mesmerizing tits. Now that I got a glance, I'd never be able to unsee them. My mouth watered at the image of her round breasts. Jesus, even that shirt looked bewitching on her. Her little act achieved what she wanted. She'd baited and hooked me, acting all innocent.

Nick elbowed me in the ribs, offering me a drink, and it broke the spell I was under. The alcohol lined my throat and returned some moisture to my dry throat. My reaction to Addison undressing here was nothing short of fierce. The sting of jealousy surprised me. All these people had a front-row seat to the show and had peeked at what wasn't theirs to admire. Not that I had more right. Still. Somehow, it felt like I did.

"Stop ogling her like she's a piece of meat. Care to tell me what happened to your shirt?" Nick teased.

I sighed, downed the rest of my drink, and explained everything. Leaving out the parts where I'd daydreamed about ravaging her pussy while bending her over the hood of my rental.

From across the room, Addison watched me, sipping on a martini, eating olives from a pick, another vision hardening my dick. Was she playing with my sanity on purpose? Was she toying with me, knowing she was off-limits? Why did I fuck the devil last night? Now I was attuned to everything about her. Her smile. Her lips. Her rack. Her hips. Her legs. Fuck Nick. Why did I agree to stay away? I needed to bang that girl out of my system—and remember it. Once and for all.

Rule number one sucked. Big time. I couldn't wait for this wedding to be over to get my hands on the maid of honor. Then the rules would be outdated. Just a little over one month to go. I could live with that. At the pace she was infuriating me, sex with Addison Wilde wouldn't be soft. It would be animalistic. Yeah, I'd make up for all the times she got me tangled up. I would ascertain the memory of my tongue between her legs haunted her forever. In the most excruciating flashbacks.

I'd bury myself so deep she'd never be able to forget how good inside her.

Staking my claim, I stared back, my irises swallowing her whole. A chill ran through her. Even from the distance separating us, I saw it ripple the length of her. Her pulse ricocheted at the base of her throat. The games had just become more challenging, and the reward would be so well-deserved and satisfying. I trembled at the thought. My lower-self hardened at the picture I painted in my mind.

By week six, you'll beg me to end you, sweetheart, I mouthed behind my hand as I brought the tumbler to my lips.

And for the first time in months, I felt like my old self again. Alive and ready for the chase.

Chapter 6

Addison

No matter what I did, I couldn't detach my eyes from Tucker's perfect torso. The shirt left nothing to the imagination. My mouth watered at all the things I wished I could do to him with only my tongue. *Stop, Addi. Get some control back. No men. You don't love them anymore. You. Are. Over. Them.*

Ignoring the heat in his stare, I resumed my conversation with a group of women. We talked about the plans for tonight once the yacht brought us back to shore. No matter how much I refused to give him any attention, I couldn't help the way my body reacted to him. It was always aware of his presence. It felt him everywhere, even from a distance. That had never happened before. With a palm splayed across my breastbone, I urged my pulse to hush and stay indifferent and in control.

Mid-dinner, I cornered Tucker as he went to the restroom. It seemed like it had become a new thing between us. Me following him to the men's room. Right now, I was a bit tipsy on wine and cocktails, ready for the party to start later. Dinner was great, but I couldn't wait to hit the town.

"How is it going, *Groom*?" I asked, giving him my most flirty smile, batting my lashes as fast as I could. Booze helped me forget about my new no-men resolution.

"Wilde, you gotta stay away from me. Every time you're around, I get into trouble."

I dragged a fingernail down his chest and felt the shivers running through him. His nipples hardened. And so did his dick. His clothes did nothing to hide the effect I had on him, and I relished every second of it.

"Go, find yourself a woman, and I'll do the same. Not playing with you tonight. I promised I wouldn't, and I'm a man of my word. Bait someone else."

"Tsk-tsk. Don't be so boring, Tuck. We're bride and groom tonight, remember? And I'm sure Nick and Dahlia's rules don't apply in this case. We're gonna pretend we're madly in love. Isn't this what it's all about? You asked for a fiancée. Don't make me regret playing the part. A little fun never hurt anyone. Did you already forget what we did last night?"

His throat worked. I had him exactly where I wanted. Men were the weak species. All of them. Nothing equaled the thrill coursing through my veins when they surrendered their power to the simple promise of a good time between the sheets. Tucker stepped back, putting some distance between us, his eyes luring me in even though his words told me otherwise.

"Anyway, I'm just here to tell you it's speech time and after that, we're splitting up. I'll miss my groom. Will you miss your bride?" I asked, unleashing the full power of my puppy dog eyes.

He flinched but recovered quickly.

Shaking his head, he adjusted the crotch of his pants, not even being subtle about it. "You're playing with fire, sweetheart. Soon you'll get burned. Never say I didn't warn you." He released his junk and pushed past me, going back to where our friends were, still seated at the table.

I breathed out. No idea why I did that. Something about Tucker made me want to be bad or brave. To test his limits. And see if I could break him. Now that all my doubts had vanished, I knew I had as much effect on him as he had on me. This pre-wedding weekend was pure torture. Men were my addiction. Always had been. I had to learn to live without one around. To be on my own. To break the heartbreak circle once and for all. Tucker was a no-go, the forbidden fruit. And lethal. My best friend was right when she had served him a warning. He owned enough power to hurt me if he got too close. The zing we shared couldn't be faked. If we yielded to the temptation of our sizzling attraction, reality would haunt me once the sheets turned cold. One-nighters weren't my thing, but Tucker made me want to get out of my comfort zone and seize new opportunities.

Two hours later, some of us were packed into a limousine. Half the party had left to go to an underground bar owned by a friend of Carter, while the other half—ours— cruised around town, bubbly pink drinks in hand, leaning half out of the panoramic sunroof as the wind whipped past us.

Dahlia snaked her arm through mine, her head resting on my shoulder. "Because I…because I was pregnant and everything went *downnn* so fast, I didn't have all this the first time," she said, gesturing around her. "Thanks for doing this with *meee*. It means the world. I *lovvve* you, girlfriend."

I caressed her hair and caught the lone tear tracing her cheek. "I *lovvve* you too. Are *youuu* okay?"

She slurred a little, but her level of intoxication was far less than mine. She huffed and smiled, the glossiness in her eyes quickly switching to happier memories. "I *ammm*. For a while, I never thought I'd be smiling again. Nick makes me happy, and my knees weaken whenever he's around. He's mine. I love him *sooo* much. We're two halves of the same heart. Even rain is exhilarating when he's there. He's *my* person. My soul mate. I want that for *youuu* too. You deserve this. *Lovvve*. Butterflies. The whole package."

I pressed my head against hers. "Dah, I want it too. But I-I just never meet the right one. *I'mmm* tired of being used by *myyy* lovers. Starting to feel like *I'mmm* replaceable, like I don't mean as *muuuch* to them as they mean to *meee*. To trust them with my whole heart when *theyyy* couldn't care less about protecting or cherishing it. *Theyyy* always deceive *meee* in the end."

"Were *youuu* serious when you told me *youuu* were done with them, though?" Dahlia cocked her head to look at me.

I shrugged. "Yes. *Nooo*. I-I…huh, I don't know. *I'mmm* just scared to put like…to put *myyy* heart out there again. I guess we'll see."

"What did *youuu* do last night?"

I could read the worry in her gaze. My best friend really cared, and I loved her so much for always having my back and never judging my actions.

I avoided her eyes for a second, then shook my head. "Do *youuu* think I…I could've inherited *myyy* father's gene… *Youuu* know…the one?"

"Do *youuu* see any similarities?" she asked.

"*Nooo*. Not really. Every time I'm down, it crosses *myyy* mind. My last relationship wasn't marriage material. I-I know it now. But it really, huh, shattered *meee* when it ended. Made me doubt myself. And that propelled *meee* into this spiral of anger…this spiral of anger and sadness. The idea of *lovvve*…never mind, it's…it's stupid…"

"Addi, it's *nottt*. It's normal to wonder. I…I would too. Wanna talk about it?" she asked.

"*Nahhh*. Tonight is *youuur* night." I breathed in, ready to change the subject. "What *abouttt* that karaoke bar we used to go to? I haven't been there in ages. Do *youuu* feel like owning the stage for a few hours?"

Dahlia's contagious energy returned as if I'd just shot her with a dose of adrenaline. Drunk Dahlia was easy to convince and was always ready for some fun. Any other time, I would have helped to plan tonight's events, or I would've even organized the entire thing myself. I always reveled in coordinating events for my friends. But she was right when she said my latest breakup had affected me. For the last three weeks, I hadn't been feeling like myself. Sure, I was bummed about being single once again, but more than that, I was hurt. Hurt that someone I believed I loved not only cheated on me, but also gambled with my trust. Now I knew our relationship was not meant to survive the test of time, but still, I had respected him once. We were friends. Or I thought we were. Until it all blew up in my face.

"Addi, I *loooooove* that bar," Dahlia singsonged the words, breaking my train of depressing thoughts, and squeezed my arm tighter. "I…I wanna sing something with *youuu*. Like we used to. Let's ask the rest of the party to meet us there. It'll be *funnn*."

I dropped down and reached for the phone in my purse and messaged Tucker. He was the groomsman, so I figured he had to be the one making the calls. Sorta.

ME

Hey, groom of mine.

He answered almost instantly.

TUCKER

Wilde. What's up? Miss me already?

ME

Karaoke. You. Us. Ask Cart, he knows where. Thirty minutes. You in?

TUCKER

With you? Not sure. It sounds dangerous.
For me.

ME

Always. But you love how much more fun your life gets when I'm in it.

He didn't answer for a whole minute. I was about to message him again when his reply came through. One simple word.

TUCKER

Okay.

ME

Don't be late

"*Alll* set," I said to my best friend, returning to my position next to her. "They'll…huh…they'll meet us in half an hour. Let's go."

———

The song ended, and the two women who had taken the stage climbed down and disappeared into the crowd. The dive bar was just how I remembered it. Dark, not so clean, and filled with people only here to have the best time. No one took themselves too seriously, and I liked that about our little local hangout spot.

"Listen, all y'all. We have a bride and groom here with us tonight," some guy announced through a microphone. People cheered and applauded. "Let's give a warm welcome to the future newlyweds. Please come on up to the stage. We have something for you." Damn it. The last thing we needed was to grab people's attention.

As if her thoughts mirrored mine, Dahlia's fingernails dug into my forearm as her voice became strained with tension. "Addi, I'm not getting up on that stage. How did they even know we were here? There's a difference between singing something with you while people are busy chatting and drinking and being up there for everyone to stare at. What if people recognize me? Not that it matters, but I don't want them to recognize Cart, or he'll feel obligated to sing and might leave so that we can enjoy the night without being bothered. You gotta go, Addi. You and Tuck. Pretend you're us. Please. You're wearing the bride and groom T-shirts. No one will suspect you're faking it."

Next to her, Nick nodded. "She's right. I know people in Nashville usually let famous people be and stuff, but are we willing to take the risk and have them come here just because Carter is hanging out with us tonight? And hassle him for autographs and pictures?"

Dahlia and I both shook our heads.

"We all agree, then." He nodded. "What's the plan?"

"Sorry, babe," Dahlia said to him as she wrapped her arms around his waist.

He pushed a strand of her hair back, smiling gently at her. "It's okay. I know the drill. That's what happens when I'm about to marry a superstar. I love you. Don't worry."

He kissed her, and I averted my eyes as Tucker grumbled beside me.

Carter moved closer. "Guys, it's fine. I'll sit in a dark corner if it gets too much. I'll just—"

"No, Cart. You're allowed to enjoy the night too. Dahlia and Nick are right. Tuck and I will go up there. I'm sure it's just a silly game they want us to play or a *how well do you know your spouse* kinda stuff. Nothing we can't survive."

A deep frown carved my *groom's* forehead as he heard the plan. "Fuck no. Not becoming your circus monkey again, Wilde. Forget it. Been humiliated enough for the rest of my life tonight. I must have been asked to smile for two hundred pictures by now. My face will be all over social media. If it isn't already. Find other people to play the happy couple with." He folded his arms across his broad chest, every defined muscle bulging, the T-shirt stretched so tight it would get ripped soon enough. Yeah, Tucker Philips was tall and well-built, and it still didn't add up in my head that he worked as a hedge-fund banker. I stared at him for a long second, my fingers itching to trace the planes of his abs, my mouth longing to kiss his pouty lips, and my body aching to feel his hard body pressed against every inch of me. I didn't have any leftover recollections of our time together to hold on to, and now my mind felt obligated to compensate. To make up dirty scenarios. Each time, I wondered if they were fantasies or repressed memories.

"Why do you always have to be such a baby about everything? I thought you liked challenges?" I asked, locking my eyes with his. Something passed between us. I had no idea how to describe it. A buzz of electricity raced over my skin, and I got drunk on his smoldering stare. My stomach tightened. My knees wobbled. No, even though he symbolized all my weaknesses in one man, I wouldn't get all hot and bothered for Tucker 'Player' Philips. I'd resist his charm. I'd resist *him*. I was a strong and confident woman, and men were so twentieth century anyway.

"C'mon up, people. Don't be shy," the guy on the microphone said. "Ladies and gentlemen, please make some noise for the bride and groom."

Beside us, a man pushed Tucker and me forward. "Don't be pussies." He pointed at us over my head because, well, Tucker was too tall, and yelled, "They're here." No way could we hide wearing T-shirts with flashing lights on our backs. Nobody would ever believe we weren't the future Mr. and Mrs. Whatever.

"Wilde, you'll pay for this. Count my words," Tucker threatened me through gritted teeth, jaw flexing and eyes dark. He firmed his back and followed me to the front of the bar. Ire radiated from him.

In some crazy ways, it turned me on even more. Genetic or not, I had a sickness in me. Or I was more fucked-up than I thought.

People wolf whistled as we took the stage.

Tucker's eyes were like twin machine guns, locked on me, ready to fire. A thrill coiled through me beneath the heat of his gaze, and I had no desire to run.

"Nice shirt," a man yelled from the crowd. My *groom's* eyes narrowed to slits. He puffed his chest out, ready to attack, the taut fabric stretching dangerously across his torso.

I watched him and crossed my fingers behind my back, praying it wouldn't give way. Carter was right. Tucker looked like he'd dressed in the kids' section of a store.

I touched his forearm, silently begging him to let it go. He relaxed under my palm, the tension in him evaporating.

We linked our hands together, and I hoped I could infuse him with some courage for standing here in front of all these patrons—with me.

The guy with the microphone neared us, and my *groom* tensed again. "We have something special for the happy couple tonight. First, let's ask the future Mrs. Bride to sit," he said, pulling a wooden chair in the middle of the stage. I avoided looking at Tucker, knowing how upset he must have been right now. Once seated, I wrestled a smile onto my lips, crossed my legs at the ankles, and linked my hands on my lap. Very prim and proper. Things were about to get interesting. I could feel every molecule of excitement sparking in the air surrounding us.

"Now, Mr. Groom, you gotta pick a song for your future wife. Let's see your options." A list of songs appeared on the screen behind the stage. Tucker clenched his hands at his sides, his knuckles turning white. Even upset and out of his comfort zone, he looked adorable. He narrowed his eyes, scanning the room as if trying to find an escape, and I bet he was.

My *groom* was cocky and sure of himself to a fault, but I doubted he ever volunteered to humiliate himself in front of a cheering crowd. Always dressed to impress, no doubt tonight was making him very uncomfortable—naked and vulnerable—and I was the one to blame for every decision. My heart wrenched at his predicament, and I admired his strength for standing by me. Ever since we met, he'd stuck by my side through all my crazy ideas, and now here we were, ready to dive in once more. Tucker walked next to me onstage, ready—or not—to make a fool of himself. For me.

Standing right beside me on my left, he swallowed hard and raked a hand through his short hair, as if trying to shake off the tension. I could almost see the sweat blooming on his nape from my spot, his skin glistening under the golden lights like tiny diamonds. He cracked his neck, and our eyes met.

My smile vanished. With just a glance, he stole all the air from my lungs. A series of knots twisted in my stomach as his uneasiness seeped into me. Why were we so in sync all the time?

Studying my face a little longer, he picked a song, and the man announced, "You'll sing for her, man. With all your heart. You'll have the lyrics on that screen, just in case. C'mon, show us how much you love your woman. Give it all you've got. Show her how much you adore her. This is your chance. Rock her world." The man clapped Tucker's shoulder and handed him the microphone.

My *groom* turned to face me in the slowest slow-motion movement I'd ever witnessed, all colors draining from his face. He shook his head and murdered me on the spot with his heavy, murderous gaze. I yelped but forced myself to look unaffected. Inside, my blood sizzled, and flutters partied around.

"Not doing this, Wilde. I'm dressed for Halloween, and I can't sing for shit. No way am I doing this in front of all these crazy folks. Forget it. I'm outta here," he said, leaning away from the microphone, his voice just loud enough for me.

I stretched my arm to graze his fingers. "Hey, look at me. We're doing this. Together. It's only me. We're alone. It's all pretend. Nobody is listening. We're just fooling around. Another little challenge between us. I'm right here, okay? You've got this. We've got this."

He exhaled, his face twisting as if in pain.

"I'll owe you one later. Do this for Nick and Dahlia, okay? I'm with you. I'm not going anywhere."

The music started playing, and a cheer echoed through

the room, filling the silence that had fallen over the crowd. No doubt it was my best friend, anxious for us but encouraging us all the same. I could feel her eyes on us.

We can do this, I repeated in my head. *We can do this.*

"You okay?" I asked my groom.

He nodded. His Adam's apple bounced in his throat.

Once again, he would go through a situation he disliked. For me. With me. And that trust meant everything to me.

He rolled his lips over his teeth, staring at me with something I didn't recognize.

"Take one for the team, big guy." A wave of fierceness had my body shaking with need.

Tucker shut his eyes for a few seconds, forced his shoulders back, and brought the microphone to his mouth, his jaw so tight that I feared he'd grind his teeth to dust.

His eyes snapped open as the first words left his lips. He had chosen a Carter Hills original. How ironic. The crowd started singing along with him. Everybody knew this country song. It was one of Carter's biggest hits as a solo artist. No doubt my friends were the ones behind the chorus. Their voices buried Tucker's. But still, all I could hear was him. Everything I could see began and ended with him. His eyes were transfixed on me, kindling my body with awareness.

He relaxed his stance, the tension draining from his back. He was ready to play his part. Now there were devilish sparks shining in his irises. He kneeled before me, grabbed my hand, and sang as if we were alone in the crowded bar.

My breath caught in my lungs. Every cell in me danced to his voice. Heat pooled between my thighs. My nipples tingled under the intensity of his smoldering stare as he undressed me with his gaze.

For a moment, I forgot this was all fake.

It looked so real. Felt so real. Enough to turn me into a blazing inferno.

The way Tucker intertwined his fingers through mine. The way he ate me up with his stare as if I were his. The way he held my gaze hostage as my heart jackhammered in my chest.

I had never been on the receiving end of so much intensity. My heart frizzled behind my ribs. How could any of this be fake?

> **...And when you need a hug,**
> **my arms will hold you tight**
> **A girl like you belongs with a**
> **guy like me...**

The song ended, and people applauded. We stood still. As if time had stopped and everyone around us had vanished. Air rushed in and out of my lungs. Why was I panting?

A crooked smile slowly appeared on Tucker's face.

The beating of my heart hastened.

The uplift of his lips reflected mine.

My *groom* used the back of his hand to wipe his forehead and sighed. "Wilde, how did I do? Tell me I didn't make a fool of myself. Tell me you believed it?"

I tightened my grip on the fingers still laced through mine. *Believed it?* A part of me still had a hard time grasping it wasn't real.

"Are you kidding? You were perfect." Adrenaline pumped inside me, the rush addictive.

"Kiss him already," someone yelled from behind us.

"Kiss him. Kiss him. Kiss him," the crowd chanted.

We'd go to hell for this.

I didn't care.

Right here and now, all I craved was kissing the man who'd just sung to me the most romantic song ever. Because my head, and my heart, still hadn't comprehended it was fake. That I didn't mean any of this to him.

Without wasting a single second, I wrapped my arms around Tucker's neck and pulled him close. We fixated our gazes on each other, my breathing shallow and my heart thumping so fast I was certain he could feel it. "Just kiss me," I pleaded.

Without holding back, he crashed his mouth onto mine, robbing me of all the oxygen I possessed. Goose bumps bloomed on my nape. Lightning ignited my being —and my soul. Together, we caught fire.

Tucker devoured my lips as if we were still alone up here. Tongues dancing. Hands grabbing. Hips grinding. Nothing chaste or meant to be witnessed by others. A bruising kiss that had my toes curling and left me panting, my entire body aroused.

In that instant, I belonged to him.

He sucked my tongue deeper in his mouth while his hands grabbed a handful of my ass. I purred at the friction of his swollen sex between my legs, begging to be acknowledged. Every swipe of his tongue branded my body. Every cell thrummed with the power of the desire he awakened in me. Tucker was staking his claim, and I surrendered willingly, every part of me drawn to him.

I dug my fingernails into his biceps, requiring his solidity to feel anchored in this world.

"Fuck, Wilde, you taste good."

Unquenchable thirst brimmed in his gaze as he plunged forward and lifted me into his arms, my legs winding around his midriff. He kept a hand over my backside to prevent me from flashing my panties to the patrons.

I held on to him, hypnotized by the pull he had on me. We stared into each other's depths, and like a beacon drawing me in, I slipped my tongue back between his hungry lips, attacking his mouth.

He groaned, meeting me thrust for thrust, tasting every corner of my mouth.

He fisted my hair and arched my head, deepening our connection. I lost the ability to breathe on my own, Tucker being the only source of air I required to survive.

Spellbound in our own world, in the frenzied beating of our hearts and the intimate moment we shared, I relished his tongue against mine and the heat of his erection nestling where it electrified my core.

A symphony began in my chest, and Tucker became the maestro playing with the strings of my desire.

The dark clouds hovering over me for weeks parted. Life didn't feel so flavorless anymore.

I felt more alive in his embrace than I did with any other man before.

Tucker curled his strong hand around my nape, holding me in place as he kissed me some more. His lips, shaped to mine, injected me with something potent and dizzying. I felt wanted and important. Understood and desired.

Last night must have been incredible.

Shivers spread all across my skin at the thought of the events I couldn't even remember.

Our bodies spoke the same language like a well-rehearsed choreography. If right now was any indication of how well we danced together, Tucker and I were a force to be reckoned with. Something great and powerful.

My heart pinched at the realization that I'd never experience the first time with him ever again. That I would never have a chance to know how wonderful it must have been to be loved by him for a night. To be the center of his universe. Even for just a couple of hours.

When Tucker lowered me back to my feet, we were both breathless, intoxicated, watching each other with barely contained lust. My face felt flushed, my lips sensitive and raw, my breasts plumper. Little knots lingered in my stomach. A sirocco swirled inside me.

The man who called us onstage guided us toward the stairs leading down.

More applauses and wolf-whistles.

How long had we lost track of time? I traced my lips with a finger, reminiscing about the kiss that had tipped my world off its axis. It made me believe I could be loved and cherished. One day. That I could feel the same pull with someone else in the future.

My *groom* tugged at my hand and led me offstage.

I breathed easier now that all eyes weren't on us anymore.

People clapped our shoulders as we walked past them. Others congratulated us. Still surfing a cloud of bliss, I had a hard time differentiating reality from fiction. I offered them nods and smiles, sure I had the latter engraved on my face forever.

"Oh my god, this was amazing. You guys killed it up there. Here," Dahlia pushed a shot glass into our hands as soon as we joined them, "drink this." We chugged them before she offered us another one. "Thank you for filling in for us. You were incredible. No way could anyone have suspected you weren't getting married. It looked so real. Even I believed it for a moment. I felt like a voyeur watching a love story unfold before my eyes. It was epic."

The server came to us with a bottle of tequila. "On the house. For the future Mr. and Mrs. You guys rocked. Enjoy."

My friend pointed two fingers at Tucker's eyes, then flicked them toward her, as if to say, "I'm watching you."

I yanked her hand down. "Stop, Dah. This is silly. We were just pretending. Give the guy a break."

Tucker's chuckle at my friend's not-so-subtle threat warmed my insides.

"She asked for it," he said with a wide smirk, showing off his pearly whites. And not one ounce of shame. "I serviced her like she begged me to. Dah, you should thank me for taking care of her needs. Happy to oblige."

I shrugged. "How could I not? It was hot." I fanned myself with my hand to amplify my words.

Tucker winked at me. "Anytime, sweetheart."

"Ohmygod, your ego, big guy," I said.

He leaned forward and pressed a kiss to my cheek.

My body still hadn't comprehended none of this was real because a fresh wave of flutters took over my stomach. My fingers itched to intertwine with his. To anchor myself to him.

"You guys. I swear this is déjà vu. I have dreamed of this scenario. You two teaming together and creating chaos," Nick chimed in, nearing us, unable to hide his amusement. He spun to face Tucker. "Like you'd ever listen to my warnings. I should've known better." He shook his head, his smile reaching both ears. "I thought you would swallow her up there. Are you—" The surrounding noises drowned out his words, and I missed the rest of their conversation.

Dahlia took me aside. "Addi, you didn't have to put on that much of a show. I'm sorry you felt like you had to. But, wow, we could feel the heat even from here."

I shrugged, hoping my flushed face wouldn't betray me. "No worries. Tucker spoke the truth. I asked for it. How could I not want him to kiss me? Have you seen him up there? Even if it was all pretend, butterflies danced in my belly."

"Girlfriend, you'd tell me if it meant something more, right?"

I nodded.

"Are you okay?" she inquired.

"Yeah. I am. The guy is handsome, and he sang to me. It was a one-time deal. Anyway, let me say this: Tucker Philips can kiss."

"That good?" She wiggled her brows.

"Yep. How about some tequila?" I asked, trying to change the subject—and fast—before I exposed my inner thoughts.

"Come on," Dahlia said, linking her arm to mine. "Let's drink to your performance. Or rather, Tuck's performance. And then we'll sing something together. Just like old times."

———

It was four in the morning when we came back to the hotel, all looking like we'd been up for days. Dahlia's hair was a tangled jumble, and no doubt mine was too. She had mascara stains under her eyes. The last time I checked, I did too. Our lipstick had been gone for hours, and our heels hung from our fingers as we shuffled to our rooms.

My best friend leaned in and kissed my cheek. "Night, Addi. Thanks for everything. You are amazing. I'll remember tonight forever. I love you."

I squeezed her arm. "I love you too. See you later."

Nick kissed my cheek and hugged Tucker before leading his woman away.

In the hallway, I watched them exchange tired smiles, in love with each other.

My heart bled in my chest. Why couldn't I be the one stupidly in love for once?

Dahlia deserved her happiness. She'd been through so much. Somewhere deep inside me, I couldn't help but pray for the same thing. To feel something close to how I felt on that stage earlier. Someone's most precious person.

I nodded before returning my gaze to the lovers moving to their suite.

Melancholy filled me and I sealed my lids, refraining from crying, too tired to sort things out in my head.

"Wilde, are you sleeping on your feet?" Tucker asked from beside me. "If you are, it's kinda disturbing. Just a thought."

I opened my eyes and poked my tongue out, offering him an excuse I hoped he wouldn't challenge. "I forgot you were still here. Got lost in my head. I'm so tired. I'm sure I could sleep upright if I had to. You did great tonight. And you can keep the shirt. It suits you. My best man gift to you. Good night."

Tucker eyed me with an expression I couldn't decipher for a second but added nothing. I melted under the heat of his stare, my heart lurching in my throat. His brows furrowed as he gave me a once-over, then shook his head and sauntered away, shoulders dropping, hands tucked into his pockets. The white lights blinking at the back of his T-shirt were the last sight of him as he turned the corner, and I found myself alone in the hotel hallway.

Forcing my gaze away from the direction he left, I resumed my breathing and fumbled with the keycard.

Once in the safety of my room, I pressed my back against the closed door. Exhaustion and alcohol made it harder for me to order my thoughts. And my feelings.

The kiss Tucker and I shared had been replaying in my head since the moment we broke apart on that stage.

Hours later, I still believed it was as real and breathtaking as it could get. I couldn't let the attraction between us affect my judgment—not if I wanted to avoid trouble. That much I couldn't deny. Resolved to move past tonight's episode, I shut my thoughts, ready to crash into bed and for the weekend to be over.

The soft knock on the door behind me rebooted my lethargic brain. I spun on my heels, and using the wall as a support, I cracked the door open.

My heart leaped in my chest when I spotted Tucker standing on the other side of the ajar door.

He scratched his nape with his fingers and looked unsteady on his feet as he said, "Wilde, lost my card. It was in my shirt… I-I think. The one that got shredded to pieces." He paused and rubbed his eyelids with the heels of his hands. "Can I sleep in your room? Please, help a guy out. I'll take the sofa. Let me lie down before I crumple into a heap on the floor."

My eyes found his exhausted ones. He was a breath away from collapsing.

"Yeah. Sure. Okay."

I let him in, and his hand connected with my lower back as he kissed my cheek, shooting warmth through me. "Thanks."

He walked past me, and I followed him with my eyes, missing his comforting touch.

Without even taking the time to undress, he crossed the room and fell face-first on the cushioned piece of furniture.

To remove what used to be makeup off my face, I took a quick shower and padded back into the room, dressed in a nightshirt. No way would I sleep naked with Tucker around.

Ready to escape into my dreams, I slid under the pillowy comforter of my bed, but sleep evaded me, even when it tempted me. I tossed. Then I turned. And counted sheep. I drilled my fingers into my ears, trying to tune everything out. Nah. Not happening. No matter how tired I was, this didn't do the trick. Tucker's snoring was all I could hear. It sounded like an old truck's muffler.

I cursed under my breath as I left the cocoon of the bed and neared him. With my finger, I nudged his arm. "Wake up, big guy. You snore. Real bad. Turn around or something. I gotta sleep too. Please."

He groaned but didn't budge.

I balled my hands.

Why did I agree to let him sleep here? Such a bad idea. Whichever way I spun it around in my head, it didn't sound better.

"C'mon, Tuck. Move," I said, shaking him with both hands now.

He tilted his head, already gone so far away from here, his eyelids heavy with sleep. He almost fell off as he flipped to his side, watching me with a confused frown.

A few swear words left my mouth, and I hated myself for an instant. "I'll regret this tomorrow," I muttered, mostly to myself, before pulling at his hand. "Let's get you into bed. You'll be more comfortable. The couch is way too small for you anyway."

He grumbled something in his sleepy haze but soon rose to his feet as I helped him up.

"You gotta brush your teeth first. My room, my rules."

He growled something I didn't catch.

In the bathroom, he removed his Groom T-shirt and dropped his pants on the tiled floor in one movement, leaving him in only white boxer briefs. Damn it. Why did he have to look so good? All ripped chest and muscled thighs. I had him all to myself last night. This was unfair. I should be able to remember our night together. Everything he did to please my body. His expert hands and very capable mouth.

A heat wave washed through me.

With a sigh, I pushed the disturbing thoughts away before they could affect my imminent sleep and slid back under the covers.

Once Tucker finished brushing his teeth, he circled the bed to climb onto the king-sized mattress from the other side. The warmth from his body enveloped me even from a few feet away, and this time, with nothing to disrupt my sleep, I dozed off in seconds.

Chapter 7

Addison

When I woke up the next morning—was it noon already?—a cart filled with food waited for me by the side of the bed. A large smile spread across my face. With half-lidded eyes, I scanned the room. No trace of Tucker anywhere. Did his presence exist only in my dreams? Or did he leave already? My heart hiccupped, as Dahlia would say. Tension curled in my gut, and I breathed out. For a silly reason I couldn't explain, I wished he were here, snuggled up against me.

I rolled onto my other side and breathed in the pillow next to me, his ocean-breeze scent filling my nostrils. Yes, he had slept here. So, why did he leave without so much as a goodbye?

With no answer to my question forthcoming, I went to freshen up and wash away the lingering effects of my alcohol binge. My hair was a web of knots, and I gathered it in a messy updo at the top of my head, not in the mood to comb it. I splashed cold water over my face, trying to wake myself up a little more. I looked like hell, but after the fun we had last night, it was a small price to pay. I glanced one last time at my reflection, fixed my nightshirt, only to find Tucker sitting on the edge of the mattress as I made it back to bed. Wearing designer faded jeans and a dress shirt, he appeared refreshed and ready to get on with his day. Did Tucker know what regular clothes were? Couldn't he just wear sweatpants and a worn T-shirt like the rest of us mere mortals?

And what happened to his hangover? Right now, I doubted he was even human.

I rubbed my heavy eyelids, chasing away the remnants of sleep, and plastered a smile on my face.

"Good morning, sweetheart. Hope you're hungry. Didn't know what you liked, so got you a little of everything. And black coffee. Just the way you like it."

His dark eyes brightened the room.

"You noticed?" I asked, my voice still croaky from all the singing and cheering of last night.

Tucker nodded, his gaze fixated on mine.

I died right there.

I was wrong all along. I possessed no control. Tucker Philips was the one having power over me. Always had been. More than I'd ever care to admit.

"I've got a few hours to kill before my flight home. I thought we could spend them together. Nick and Dahlia are with Jack at her parents' place. They already left. They asked me to tell you they'll be back in the morning to pick you up. For now, it's just the two of us, Wilde. What do you wanna do? You're the Nashville expert here."

His grin, warm and mesmerizing, tipped something inside me.

I blinked. Once. Twice. Dozens of times.

Why couldn't I escape his magnetic field? Why was I so attuned to every little thing about him? His smell, his heat, his heartbeat.

All traces of my hangover disappeared.

I closed my eyes, trying to ease the drumming of my heart and to block Tucker out. It wasn't working. He was all over me. He didn't have to touch me for me to feel him everywhere. I clenched my thighs together. The twirl of scorching desire pooling in my belly meant nothing.

It means nothing. It means nothing. It means nothing.

How many times would I have to repeat the words to make myself believe them?

Tucker shot me a panty-melting grin. I trembled. God, I was so weak.

Last night played on a loop in my mind, no matter how bad I tried to lock it somewhere I'd have no access. My body vibrated with need.

He eyed me with a frown, and I stayed rooted to the spot, taking him in, the idea of playing tour guide for the day not enticing me at all right now.

I had better use of our time together.

Heat pulsed through me, from the top of my head to my toes.

Tucker quirked a dark brow up, his gaze heavy, and I lost it.

Without second-guessing myself, I fisted the hem of my nightshirt and lifted it over my head before discarding it.

His eyes rounded. His Adam's apple bobbed. The piece of croissant he held in his hand fell from his grip.

We stared at each other, neither of us saying anything.

His gaze set my flesh on fire. He studied me, unable to hide his approval. His pupils dilated. He traced the seam of his lips with his tongue and enveloped his junk with one hand. I followed the movement, the swell in his jeans unconcealed and impossible to miss.

My mouth watered at the sight of him, aroused and not shying away from it.

In that instant, I craved Tucker Philips, like I'd never craved anyone else before.

With confidence in my steps, I strode forward, pushed his firm chest with both hands, and straddled him, thrusting my naked breasts into his face.

His chocolate irises traveled the length of my upper body, leaving a trail of fire in their wake.

My pulse throbbed in my temples.

Lust dripped from Tucker's gaze, coiling around me.

I could bask in it. I wanted to soak it all up.

Nothing he said or did could stop me from achieving what I desired. This little game between us needed to go up in flames, burning us in its heat.

He leaned forward, admiring my breasts, and his warm breath tickled my skin, turning my nipples into stiff peaks. His hand moved to rest on my naked thighs, his fingers featherlight on my skin but enough to melt me into a puddle of need. Every cell in my body pulsed at the soft touch. My vagina was on high alert, dripping wet. I tilted my head back, moaning when his thumb pressed into my flesh and moved up, dangerously close to where I yearned for him the most.

With his expert tongue, he toyed with one diamond tip, robbing me of any rational thinking. My body begged to be at his mercy.

Tucker molded one breast to his other palm, and I trembled against him.

His finger pushed past the crotch of my soaked panties, spreading my arousal, and I thought I'd faint from his touch only.

"Fuck, Wilde," he said with a husky voice. "You're wet. Jesus, we can't do this. I promised—"

I returned his fiery gaze, bewitched by the intensity I noted there. The guy wore his desire like a second skin.

Before he could think it over, I pushed my tongue into his mouth, famished and craving the taste of him. Unapologetic. Our lust spread like a conflagration, and we were its willing hostages. It swallowed us whole, my body ravenous for his. And his hungry for mine.

He cupped my cheeks with his hands, and after hesitating for a beat, he deepened the kiss, battling my tongue and sucking on my lips.

Shivers worked through me. The air surrounding us thickened.

Tucker yelped when I bit his tongue and left indents on his bottom lip, but never pulled away.

My hands traveled over his clothed body, memorizing the ridges and planes, desperate to touch every inch of the skin I'd admired the night before.

He brought his palms back to my breasts, shaping them to his touch, before leaning back, breathless. Moving his muscular hands to my shoulders, he pushed me back a bit, keeping me at a safe distance. "Stop. Wilde, we can't do this. I told our friends I'd stay away from you. My words are important to me. They mean something. Why are you always trying to lead me astray? This is really a bad habit of yours."

I held his hands in mine, knitted my fingers through his, and brought them to my bare chest. I shuddered when his rough skin scraped my sensitive flesh. My back arched when his tongue teased one nipple and his teeth closed around it, tugging and twisting the hard tip. Pleasure and pain mixed together.

"And yet, you can't resist." I writhed in his embrace,

purring like a kitten in heat, hooked to the man kneading my breasts.

His dick hardened underneath me, and I rubbed my aching center over the bulge, eager to feel its fullness in my fist.

I increased the rolling of my hips, and with one hand around me, Tucker erased any space between us, pressing me harder against his erection, his groans permeating the air.

"You kept your word," I cried out, about to come just from the overpowering friction. "They didn't ask anything from me." A loud cry passed the rim of my lips. Desire engulfed me. I had to focus just to hold a conversation. "I'm the one who initiated this. I'm not some delicate flower who requires protection. I'm my own woman. And I know what I want. Right now, it's you. Oh God, it's all of you." A painful gasp tore from my throat when the pad of his thumb pressed against my clit. He drew circles over my bundle of electrified nerves, and I covered his hand with mine to increase the pressure. "Harder," I begged. My thoughts jumbled inside my head, and my voice quivered. "See? It's all me. Oh...yes. *YESSS*. Don't stop." I swallowed hard, about to come undone but not ready to let go just yet. "Like that. Yes. You were right. I'm the one perverting you. Every single time. Faster. Fuck me. With your finger, your tongue, your dick. I don't care. Just do it."

"Jesus, sweetheart, you're burning me alive. You're a wildfire." He shut his eyes, struggling to steady his shallow breathing.

My entire being pulsed, and I dug my fingernails into his shoulders to anchor myself to this world.

"Stop fighting this. I want you." I licked the corner of his lips. My voice dropped to a plea. "Show me how good you feel." I bit his earlobe, and his eyes sprang open, his mouth returning to mine as he devoured my lips. I descended my hand to his crotch and massaged him, enjoying how his dick throbbed against my palm. I worked him faster, eliciting another groan from him. Deeper. One that vibrated through me. "And you can't deny you want me too." As if it could hear me, his dick twitched in my fist. "See?"

Tucker leaned back, his pupils now fully dilated, his gaze dark and menacing. Gone was the amusement from his features. He wet his lip with his tongue, and I crashed my mouth on his, frantic with need.

We kissed like our lives depended on it. We blended together. Oil and flames.

With a strangled grip around his length, I stripped him of all rational thought.

His hips jerked up, and I increased my fondling.

I squeezed him tighter, relishing every growl and one-syllable word he uttered and every jolt of his sex in my grip.

With my hair snared in his hand, holding me there, Tucker pulled my head back, his teeth marking the skin of my throat and nibbling on the flesh of my collarbones.

I screamed my pleasure, the sensations he provided my feverish body exhilarating.

"Wilde, I'll go to hell for this."

"Then I'll go with you. We'll rock that place. Together. In the meantime, show me what I missed the other night." His tongue followed the column of my throat. "Come on, big guy, stop stalling and fuck me. I have all these scenarios filling my head, but only the real thing can help me determine which are fiction and which are reality. I can't live without knowing any longer."

He unbuttoned the top of his shirt, and craving to feel the heat of his skin on mine, I took control and peeled it off him. Outlining the ridges of his abs with my fingertips, my hungry tongue followed each caress. Every piece of him seemed as if it had been carved in stone. High cheekbones. Square jaw. Chiseled chest. Sculpted abs. The intensity of the desire coursing through me reached new heights. With the tip of my tongue, I tasted every inch of his exposed flesh.

"Stroke me bare, Wilde," he ordered through clenched teeth. "Fucking do it."

With not-so-steady fingers, I unbuckled his belt and unfastened his jeans.

"Hurry up. I'm about to explode if you don't release some tension."

This bossy side of Tucker Philips revved me up.

His body tensed as I slipped my hand into his boxer briefs, fisting the heated part of him. I drooled at the sight as I freed him from the restraint of his clothes.

We both breathed out in sync. Lust sharpened his features. His face tautened as a new surge of need grew inside him.

His shaft pulsed as I worked it from base to leaking tip.

"Faster," he urged me. "Jerk me off. Don't end me, though."

"So big," I exclaimed, pumping him and relishing the steel rod beneath the velvet skin as my hand moved up and down his shaft.

"You've seen nothing yet. Wait until I'm buried inside you, pounding you hard. We'll see how deep you feel me. Then I'll fuck that dirty mouth of yours. And show you who's the boss now."

I bent forward to take him into my mouth when he wrenched me away from the taste of him. His glistening cock saluted me when I released it.

"Not yet, Wilde. I'm not done with you yet."

I batted my eyelashes. "Tuck. Please."

"You begged for it. Now stand."

He grabbed a handful of my ass with one hand when I stood before him while the other ventured back between my thighs.

Demanding fingers pushed the crotch of my panties to the side in a rough flick that tore the seam. I gasped when a thick digit slid without hesitation between the folds drenched with my arousal.

I dissolved under his attentive caresses.

"What took you so long? Fuck me," I said.

Still seated, Tucker hastened the pace, pushing two fingers inside my moist channel. He leaned forward, his teeth grazing my clit.

"Yes. *YESSS.*" I rolled my hips over his hand, holding his head in place, about to come from his coarse stubble rubbing over my bundle of nerves every time his mouth played me.

"This is what you want, sweetheart? Dirty? You want me to rub you raw with my finger and my dick, pound into you hard until you can't walk a straight line?"

A tingling sensation rose all over my skin at the sound of his low tone and filthy words. I nodded, wondering how I'd resisted the pull between us until now.

Ruthless, Tucker moved to his feet, holding me against him, the hypnotic and addictive back-and-forth movements of his fingers never faltering. With two steps forward, he pushed me onto my back. Fire in his eyes, face gripped with need, desire sculpting all his features. He was no longer the man I knew. I held my breath as a thrill seared through me.

"Think you can keep up?" he asked, challenge coating his words.

I nodded again. Faster this time. "Will you fuck me

already, or are you waiting for me to do all the work?" I asked. "Come on, don't tease."

"That dirty mouth again. I can't wait to fill it up. Jesus, I wanted to bend you over my rental yesterday and ram into you to shut you up. Because you drove me nuts."

"You should have. I prayed you'd bang me in that empty field. Because fighting with you over directions was hot."

His eyes darted to mine. He breathed out. The muscles of his jaw flexed. "You're something else. I can't wait to have my way with you. Now spread those legs wider. I need my fix."

I lost the use of my voice at the sight of the promises shadowing his eyes. My throat clogged with anticipation.

A scorching fervor flared over every inch of my bare skin when he kneeled on the mattress between my legs and ravaged my center with his tongue. Tremors started at the tip of my spine and crawled along each vertebra.

With measured movements, I rolled and pinched my hard nipples between my thumbs and forefingers, increasing the desire throbbing in me.

"God, you're hot," he said, panting. He stared at me, and seeing him between my thighs, his lower face glossy with my imminent release, broke me apart, then revived me.

Tucker pressed his digits deeper inside me, gliding them back and forth and turning me into a blaze. Waves of unleashed pleasure built in my core.

A million unknown sensations rushed through my body.

Loud cries filled the suite when his mouth joined in and he sucked on my clit. He worked me until he transformed my body into a pile of molten lava. My insides seared. He wouldn't stop until I combusted to ashes.

My pelvis levitated from the bed, Tucker's intoxicating strokes the only thing keeping me grounded.

He played my center with his tongue, giving me no time to catch my breath.

My walls clenched around his fingers. I would detonate in no time.

Flames licked my insides. My hips thrust up to take more of his fingers inside me.

His movements quickened, and stars appeared in my vision.

Tucker was right. We'd go to hell for this. Because right now, I knew it down to my bones that this wouldn't be the last time. It couldn't be. We were just starting, and already I knew I'd never stop longing for Tucker Philips's fire.

Chapter 8

Tucker

I slid my tongue inside Addison's warmth as I moved my hands down to grab her hipbones. Scorching heat filled my balls. Not being buried inside her became almost unbearable. She shuddered violently in my arms as I slid my tongue deeper into her moist heat, hitting the right spot, while I played her engorged clit with the pad of my thumb. Every moan exiting her mouth increased the inferno burning inside me. "Wilde, you taste like forbidden, and I want more. I crave more," I said after I caught my breath and plunged right back in, circling her throbbing mound with the tip of my tongue and nipping it with my teeth.

Cries of pleasure left her mouth. Her moans made my cock grow harder until it was painful and I was ready to burst. This girl would shatter me, and I didn't care. She pressed her fingertips into my skull while she thrust her hips and sought her climax. Her pelvis buckled from the mattress. I assaulted her pussy with faster strokes of my tongue.

With her desire coating my fingers, I inserted my pinky into her tight hole. A high-pitched whimper left her mouth. Opening her legs wider, she relaxed, granting me access. The erotic view triggered a new surge of arousal inside me, and I pushed my digit further in, relishing the tightness surrounding it.

Accelerating the pace, I thrust my fingers in and out of her pussy. Every mewling she let out brought me closer to my own release. Moving to sit on my ankles, my hand still working her, I gripped my cock with my free hand, pumping myself. Even if I tried, I couldn't avert my eyes from the perfection of Addison's body undulating before me. I leaned back in between her legs and sucked on her clitoris. Her walls clenched around my fingers. She was close. I could feel the orgasm building, about to crash through her.

Her eyes, half-masted with longing, met mine as I hovered over her and captured her lips in a kiss.

"More," she muttered, pulling away, her head sinking into the pillows.

She licked the seam of her reddened lips, then bit down, her teeth bound to leave permanent marks, just as she went rigid beneath me. My own body tensed, about to rupture to shreds. It took everything I had not to explode. I returned my hand around my dick, pumping it with zeal and chasing additional relief. In vain. Addison Wilde, spread on her back, naked and at my mercy, only multiplied my hunger for her. Sweat glistened in the valley between her breasts. Staring at me, she arched her back, offering herself to me—utterly and completely.

"You really like it dirty, sweetheart?" I asked as I tilted

my head back, desperate to breathe some fresh air while I watched her abandon herself to my fondling.

Bliss was etched into every line of her face and sparked something primal inside me—pride, power, and a second wind. She was a beautiful woman, but right now, she was drop-dead gorgeous with her flushed cheeks and gleaming eyes every time she locked them on mine.

Something passed between us. The air thrummed with the charge of a million volts.

Addison trembled, and with my mouth back on her, I resumed the slow, deliberate strokes of my tongue, savoring every drop of her release when she convulsed against my mouth.

The sounds emanating from her were a melody I could never get enough of.

My dick twitched. I couldn't ignore him anymore.

"Condom?" I asked through gritted teeth.

Addison pushed herself up on her elbows until our faces were aligned. "I think we're way past that, Tuck. Now get this monster dick of yours where it belongs."

"Just remember…you asked for it."

Removing my hand from between her legs, I moved on top of her until my knees rested on each side of her chest. Lifting her into a semi-seated position, I fisted her hair and pulled on it, forcing her neck to arc. I pushed my cock into her mouth in one fierce thrust. My hand held her head in place while I jerked my hips back and forth, my body refusing to be ignored for another second.

Surprise lit up her eyes, morphing into elation. And lust.

A gurgling sound escaped her mouth as I filled her deeper, and soon she splayed her hands on my ass cheeks, increasing the rhythm of my thrusts and pushing me further down her throat.

Her moans of pleasure mixing with the suckling sounds of her mouth drowned out everything else, becoming my undoing.

"Oh, you like it naughty too, sweetheart?"

She bobbed her head. Fast.

All my restraints deserted me. "Don't worry. Soon you'll feel me everywhere. I swear."

Her cheeks hollowed, and I cursed at the ceiling.

Not ready to shoot my load just yet, I inched back, forcing her to release me.

"But—" she tried to argue.

Before she could complain, I jumped to my feet and discarded every piece of clothing left on me.

Positioned between her legs back on the bed, the tip of my cock teased her entrance. Addison stopped me with one hand before I could enter her. "Put your finger back in my ass, Tuck. I love it when I'm full." Damn. This woman. It was as if she knew how to break me with just her words.

I leaned over her and smashed my mouth against hers, relishing the taste of her on my tongue, unable to resist those pouty lips any longer. Our tongues fought, hungry and desperate, before finding their pace. I caressed every curve and dip with my hands, memorizing them feverishly. I couldn't seem to get enough.

Still propped on her elbows, Addison curled a hand around the back of my neck, keeping me in place while she licked a trail from my lips to below my earlobe, then across my jaw.

I returned my fingers inside her, to their rightful position, enjoying how she writhed underneath me, insatiable.

"Tuck, yeah, like this. Oh God... Yes, please. Keep going. No. Stop. I need your dick. Now. Oh... Yes, yes, *yesssss*."

Her words made me hard for everything that she was.

Leaning forward until I could feast on her slender neck, I continued my exploration, biting her flesh. Her collarbones. The crook of her shoulder. I left fresh marks with my teeth. The swell of her breast. The curve of her neck. I devoured everything and missed nothing. I licked her, easing the sting I left behind. I laved one rosy nipple with my tongue, sucking the areola deep into my mouth. Her hips jerked up from the bed as a sigh of contentment slipped past the rim of her lips.

Every cell in me combusted.

I opened my mouth wider, savoring her flesh. Returning my focus to her pebbled nipple, I twisted the tip between my lips, tugged at it with my teeth, cherished it with my tongue.

"Wilde, you taste so fucking sweet."

Her eyes glazed, proof of the pleasure consuming her.

I increased the tempo of my fingers, spreading her arousal all over her folds, readying her to welcome my eager length.

I closed my lips around the second peak, and the mix of her pale skin and my dark one was intoxicating as I kneaded her round flesh with my palm. With her fingers still around the back of my neck, the vixen underneath me drew me closer to her. Needy, she searched for my mouth as I circled her clit with the pad of my thumb, pressing and rubbing. She mumbled something against my mouth that sounded a lot like "Fuck me," and I couldn't wait any longer. I longed to be inside her, buried so deep I could anchor myself there for days.

My dick pulsed, standing tall and proud, squeezed between our bodies and begging to join in too.

As if she could sense its despair, Addison grabbed it in her small hand with a firm touch and gave him some unyielding attention. A guttural sound rumbled out of me.

The one I couldn't hold inside anymore. She positioned me at her entrance, and in one push, I filled her.

Giving her a moment to let her body adjust to mine, I stayed still, watching the expressions playing on her face.

Surprise. Elation. Desire. Pleasure.

I gritted my teeth as she shifted around me, my control dissolving with each breathless second I let her take the lead.

Leaning forward and balancing on one arm, I claimed her mouth with slow strokes of my tongue. I took my time, soothing the urge until she was ready. "You okay?" I asked.

"Yes. It fills good…. It feels good. Whichever pleases you." On her back, she sucked in a breath. "Gimme a sec," she said, her lips a dark shade of pink and her eyes pleading for me to give her my all. "You're pretty big." She moved her hips in slow, steady rolls, adjusting to me inch by inch. "Okay, Tuck. Give it to me. And don't stop. I want it all. The good, the bad, the dirty. Just fuck me like you mean it. Like you should have last night after you sang to me. In case I need to say it again, it was fucking hot, by the way."

My balls firmed at the request leaving her mouth. The tip of my spine tingled. I could come right now, but it would never be enough to satiate myself. Sealing my lids and inhaling through my mouth, I braced myself, not ready for it to end before it even began.

My dick pulsed inside Addison, and removing my finger from her rosebud, I leaned back and used both hands to spread her wider, so I could lodge myself even deeper. With her folded legs on each side, I lifted her hips from the mattress and rammed into her, wanting to lose myself inside her. Each time I shifted, my hips slapped against hers, her body clenching around mine, making it even harder to prolong the pleasure with the rawness of our bodies connecting, the sound of flesh on flesh compelling me to move faster. She fisted the sheets on each side of her, thrashing beneath me and matching my rhythm. Her lips tightened in a silent plea, and before long, her eyes rolled back as her control slipped away.

The phantasmic vision sent discharges of scorching heat through me.

I shivered, every nerve alive, my heart thundering—a brand-new, thrilling sensation, I was experiencing for the very first time.

Addison pushed her chest forward, and a pleasing gasp resounded through the room. Followed by a dozen more.

My cock quaked, addicted to every one of her whimpers. To every movement of her voluptuous body.

"Sweetheart, look at me," I begged, breathless, resolved not to miss a second, a look, or an emotion taking over her face as I brought her over the edge. My jaw flexed. "In or out?"

"Don't care. Just mark me, Tuck. Make me forget the idea that all men should burn in hell. Make me believe this could all be real. You and me. Just for a day."

I blinked. Addison Wilde was everything I had an obsession for. Fearless, gorgeous, and crazy in her own way. I never slept with the same woman more than a handful of times before, but right here, I knew I could never follow my rules with her. I had a feeling she was like an addictive drug, making me dependent on her brand of loving.

Leaning in, I licked the pearls of sweat adorning her flesh, trying to etch to my memory the feel of her.

She breathed in, and when our eyes connected again, I knew something had shifted inside me….an experience impossible to define with words. I felt it down to the marrow of my bones and to the boundaries of my soul.

"Wilde—"

"I know."

Two words. It was all it took to anchor me back to the moment.

Balancing on my hands, I pounded into her. With purpose and abandon.

I smacked her flesh with mine, drawing whimpers from her.

Every sound escaping her luscious lips brought me closer to a release.

Her hips buckled, and she pressed her fingertips into my thighs, strong enough to leave bruises. Our movements flowed like a perfectly rehearsed choreography.

I looked at her, really looked at her. The sight of her blonde hair like a halo of light and her face suffused with pleasure fucked with the rules I had set for myself over a decade ago. It did. Now I knew for sure.

All my life, I had concluded that sex was just an exchange of pleasure between two people. Nothing else. Nothing more. That's what I'd always believed. Until now. I closed my eyes. It had to stay that way. For my sake. For both our sakes. Because no, I'd never get attached to another human being more than I should. I loved challenges but would never put my heart at risk.

Declining to be entranced by Addison's angel face any longer, I withdrew my dick and flipped her around on her all-fours. With her back to my front, I was safe from her long dark eyelashes and the bottomless blue ocean of her eyes.

The view of her backside was delectable, and I gripped a handful of her plump butt with one hand. I followed the curve of her spine with my tongue, from her tailbone to between her shoulder blades.

"Bend down," I ordered.

Her head descended onto a pillow, her ass pointing upward in my direction.

With a jerk of her hips, she pushed her ass closer to my crotch, and I sank into her to the very core in one rough stroke.

I held onto her hipbones, guiding her movements.

Molding my torso to her back, I leaned forward, my hands searching for her breasts, shaping them to my palms. Whatever I did, I couldn't prevent myself from touching her.

She cried my name each time I hammered into her.

Addison turned her head and captured my gaze. The look she gave me fused every bit of me back together. Pieces that had been broken a long time ago.

Cast under her spell, yet determined not to be bewitched, I averted my eyes.

"*Tuuuck.*"

The word died on the tip of her tongue, but I heard it. And my name, pronounced in the breathless way she did, unlocked something deeper inside me.

I fought hard to stay detached.

My breathing eased once I felt I was regaining some sense of control.

Everything Addison was could be summed up in two words: addictive and forbidden. Tasting her seemed like my birthright and connecting with her my prerogative.

Our bodies moved in a dance we mastered so well.

I gave her everything, and she took it all, meeting me thrust for thrust.

I smacked the bare flesh of her ass, and she let out an aphrodisiac moan. Still on her knees, pushing on her hands to lift her body up, she returned to an all-fours position. Leaning back, I leveled us into a tantalizing variation of the reverse-cowgirl position, my legs folded and Addison's front leaning against them. With my hands fastened around her, I rammed into her from under, her ass bouncing up and down my thighs, her arousal coating my testicles.

With both hands, I lifted her and withdrew from her until I could slide my body down the mattress. Once her center aligned with my face, I lowered her over my mouth. I played her bundle of nerves with my tongue, pressing and sucking, nibbling and teasing.

She tried to bend forward, her hand reaching for my hard-on, but I clamped her thighs, preventing her from shifting position while anchoring her to me.

I continued my assault on her clit, inserting two fingers, then a third one into her channel and crooking them to hit the spot that would get her to come undone.

Resolved not to miss the look on her face as she came, I detached my mouth from her flesh and flipped us around until I set myself between her legs while she lay on her back. Her ankles locked around my waist. Her arms looped around my neck, keeping me close, and her mouth devoured mine, shooting me with promises I didn't deserve. I felt precious in her embrace. Special. With my eyes shut, because I refused to see the depth of hers and be taken hostage against my will, I kissed her back. Her tongue enticed mine as my hand found the back of her neck, acting on instinct.

She cradled my cheek with her small hand, and when I re-opened my lids, she forced my focus back to her—to us —as if she sensed I could get lost in her. That she had to bring me back to the present as my thoughts spiraled uncontrollably inside my head. "Tuck, I'm right here."

We stared at each other for a beat, frozen. Each intake of air burned the lining of my lungs.

Addison kissed me with ardent abandon.

Panting, we kept moving together, new waves of pleasure building between us, more potent. More galvanic. The air around us tensed, ready to blow up.

I flashed her a wide smirk. "Still thinking you should take charge, sweetheart?"

"Nah, I kinda love it when you boss me and flip me around."

I rested my hands on her folded knees, and for a minute, we both got engrossed in the movement of my dick plunging into her.

I grunted and jerked my hips faster. "Now. Let go," I ordered, squeezing my jaw tight, about to detonate inside her. Her long legs wrapped tighter around me and secured the physical bond we shared.

Addison's hips undulated, and she cried out her orgasm, her head tilting back. I lifted my eyes just in time to see the bliss taking over every one of her features. There. The sight of her cracked an iron layer of my heart. Her inner walls milked my dick, but I got it out just in time to come all over her creamy breasts as I jerked myself once. Twice.

Her gasps, loud and primal, acted like a thousand volts dashing through me.

She wrapped her hand around my manhood, and she finished me to the last drop, my release branding her in a possessive manner. Something I had never done before. And somehow, the sight of it pleased the bestial side of me.

Once we both came down from the rush, we stared at each other, our chests reeling fast with every breath we drove in.

Without breaking eye contact, I watched her as she took in the white display I painted on her body.

Her eyes, darker than usual and glued to mine, validated how this little marking session turned her on too.

Challenge filled her gaze as she traced a line through my semen.

A smile broke free on her face.

Did she even have any idea how hot she looked right now, covered in my seed?

With a mischievous glare, and just when I thought I'd seen it all, she brought a coated finger to my lips, urging me to suck on it.

I blinked, flabbergasted, unsure if I'd landed back from the orgasm that tore through me seconds ago. With a swirl of my tongue, I cleaned her digit.

"Lick me, Tucker." She glanced at me with expectant eyes. With anybody else, I would've refused, but Addison possessed a pull on me that very few people had ever had. Without questioning her request, my tongue found her hard nipple, drawing circles around it, tasting the saltiness of her sweat and my release mixed together. It was as intoxicating as the woman it now belonged to.

I pinched her puckered tips between my fingers and moved upward until our mouths collided.

There was no going back. I caught fire, and now I craved her heat.

With one hand, I brushed her damp hair away from her forehead, searching her eyes. "I'll push my flight back. I need a do-over. Or a thousand. Fuck, you're the most amazing woman I've ever met, Wilde. I can easily get hooked onto your brand of crazy. Can't wait for more."

"You can't leave me like this," she murmured. "I'm still not fully satiated."

"Consider this fixed. I'd never leave you not fully satisfied. This is my promise to you."

She nodded, and I kissed her some more. With my arms secured around her, her closeness the only thing I wished for at the moment, we rolled to our sides. I pulled her naked body closer, my heart beating to her rhythm as we fell into a deep slumber.

———

Addison bent forward in the large white-tiled shower, and I entered her from behind, her pussy tight around my wooden cock. We'd been going at it for a long while, and until now, I had resisted the urge to come. We stopped counting her orgasms after five.

None of this made sense. Never in my life did I have that much stamina. Addison had woken up something in me, and I feared my dick would fall once we broke apart. It wasn't normal to be jacked up for this long.

With one arm around me, she dug her fingernails into my ass as I speared into her. Her cries reverberated between the glass walls.

"Wilde, if this fuck marathon is a dream, then let me die a satisfied man and never wake up from the euphoria."

I circled her waist with one arm and pushed into her with a purpose, feeling her body vibrating underneath mine. My pulse raced. Addison rose to her tiptoes and wiggled that sexy ass of hers. If I let her, I knew she could end me.

I was dying to kiss her nape, to trail my teeth over the softness of her flesh. To make her mine. Here. Now. Forever. But that wasn't a game I was interested in. Our eyes locked over her shoulder, and something shifted in the air. A curve embraced the corner of her lips. My heart jumped in my chest cavity. Aware of her. Painfully so. No matter what, my heart would never enter the equation. It had to be kept safe...from feeling too much. A handful of times in my life, I'd almost failed my own rules, but sanity always had reached my brain just in time, preventing me from going into a territory I refused to visit. *Love.* It wasn't in the plan. Not now. Not ever. And so far, I had succeeded in keeping my emotions separated from sex.

But Jesus, the ravishment on Addison's face sent mixed signals to my head. And to my heart.

"Wilde, I'll come soon," I warned, catching my breath, as I rammed into her, using her hips to balance myself, my legs wobbly.

She pushed away from me and turned around. When she dropped to her knees and engulfed my dick in her warm mouth, I cursed under my breath. Her eyes flared as they met mine. Giving me the most torrid show, she pushed her head back and twirled her tongue around the tip, licking and sucking me as if I had gifted her with the tastiest treat. An overload of sensations filled me. Something in the depths of me tore open. My body was anchored here, but I was floating around.

Unable to stay still, I pressed both arms against the shower walls. No way would I miss any second of this. The vision of this girl sent high voltage to my balls.

"What are…wait…fuck..." All the words lodged in my throat.

Addison gripped my ass cheeks and pushed my length further down her mouth until I hit the back of her throat.

She raked her nails over my ass, and I came before I could even comprehend what was happening. How did she do this? How did she control my body as if it belonged to her?

I tilted my head back, letting the pleasure race through me.

I was doomed. From now on, every woman I fucked would be compared to Addison Wilde. Whoever named her chose wisely.

My entire self got drunk on her, and I caressed her hair when I unloaded inside her mouth.

She spat my cream on the shower floor. "Not swallowing," she said, meeting my eyes.

"I'd never ask you to."

She returned to her feet, and with my arms around her, my chin pressed to the top of her head as we surfed the aftershock together.

"The next few weeks will be hell without you," I said as I got dressed, ready to leave, an hour later. My midnight flight was leaving in less than two hours, and it was not like me to be running so late. "Breaking the rules had never felt so good. Maybe my dick needs a rest after all. I'm pretty sure it'll be raw for the next few days." I held onto the woman who'd rocked my world so many times in the last ten hours that I'd lost count. With a finger, I tipped her chin up and kissed her. I branded her lips with a promise of more. I'd be back. For round two. Or six. I had no idea anymore. This couldn't be the end.

Today, we had become two parts of a whole. Yin and yang. I had no idea how to explain it, but I sensed it. In every cell of mine. There was a force, stronger than our combined wills, pulling us together. As if we were supposed to be united. The word attraction didn't cut it. What I felt could only be described as an addiction. It resembled nothing I'd ever experienced in my life.

Addison dissolved in my mouth. She drew a line across my torso with a finger, sending shivers along my spine, from my skull to my toes. "No strings attached, Tuck. It was clear from the start."

I shrugged, grinning against her pinched lips. "I know. I don't do relationships, remember? And I never implied I expected more, sweetheart. Still, we'll see each other again at the wedding. Who said we weren't allowed to have a little celebration of our own that weekend?"

She pushed back, and her smile stole my breath away. "I'm not sleeping with anyone else until we meet again. I like you bare inside me."

"Oh, Wilde. No way will I be able to think about anyone else, knowing I'll see you again soon. I still have to tap this pussy of yours. Over and over again."

"So gentlemanly."

I burst out laughing. "Sorry. You like it dirty, woman. I'll give you dirty. Until you beg me to hold you because your legs are too weak."

"You're not a cuddler, big guy."

"Nah, but I could make an exception. For you. For an hour or two."

"I'll take your word for it." She kissed me one last time and led me to the door as I shouldered my bag. "Dream of me, Tuck. 'Cause I know I'll dream of you every time I touch myself."

I pivoted to face her. "Don't say things like this, or I'll never make it to the airport on time."

I leaned in to kiss her, but instead, she licked my cheek from my jaw to my temple. Then she nibbled on my earlobe as she whispered, "Until next time, big guy. I bet you'll come running back long before those six weeks are over."

"I can resist you."

"Impress me then."

She pushed me out of her suite, grinning. Before I could speak a word, she slammed the door in my face.

Realization hit me. Hard. Like a train at full speed. Straight in the chest.

Nick would be disappointed in me. No. Dahlia would murder me. My dick softened in my pants. Our friends' warning was a ruse. To keep us apart. To prevent us from imploding and leaving destruction in our wake. They must have known who I'd be dealing with. They had to know Addison was a vixen.

I sighed.

Maybe they only tried to avoid wedding hurdles. The maid of honor and best man screwing could complicate things. A disaster bound to happen.

As long as neither of us developed feelings, it shouldn't spoil anything, right?

And yet, a little voice in my head told me it would be more complicated than that.

Chapter 9
Tucker

With a tumbler of whiskey in hand, I sat at the bar across the street from my office, studying Sabrina, the girl I had a date with tonight. She'd been talking about something for the last fifteen minutes, but kill me now, I had no idea what it was about. Not. A. Fucking. Clue. We'd agreed to this date before I left for Nashville, and now I was stuck somewhere I had no reason, and no interest, to be.

Since I'd been back from Tennessee almost a week ago, and no matter how much I tried to forget about that weekend, my thoughts always drifted back to Addison Wilde. All the time. As if she'd imprinted herself on my brain, and on my body, and had control over it even from a thousand miles away.

Two days after I returned, I'd even been tempted to call her. Yeah, so unlike me. Tucker Philips didn't reach out to women, except for booty calls. My self-preservation made an appearance just in time, thwarting me from giving in to my own unbreakable rules. No commitment. No relationship. No love. Those were the three adages I'd been living by for as long as I could remember.

My friends called me Chicago's number one player. By my own definition, I wasn't a player. I was only preserving this heart of mine from being hurt like my old man's. He'd sacrificed his vital organ a long time ago, and I was the witness to his descent to hell. No, I wouldn't suffer through the same ride as he did. I was smarter than him. And a whole lot stronger.

Sabrina caressed my arm, and usually, I would already have brought her home, spread her on my bed, and devoured her in a dozen different ways. But not tonight.

I wouldn't admit it to a living soul, but my game had been off lately. For the last couple of months, I'd found myself not attracted to most women crossing my path— Addison being the only one my radar had picked up. I blamed Nick for all of it. He had made her a forbidden fruit I couldn't taste, and my ego decided she was worth the chase. And the risk.

I took a sip of my drink and managed to nod, pretending to be interested in what my date was chatting about.

What a snooze fest.

The morning after we first hooked up, when I told Addison I'd been on a dry spell, I wasn't kidding. If anybody else had asked me about it, I would have denied it, even under torture. After all, I had a reputation to preserve. Lately, it was like I had lost interest in the fuck game I'd been playing for a decade. All women I met looked the same, smelled the same, were the same. Only their names told them apart. In the last six months, I'd slept with three different women named Vanessa. Even if they didn't look alike, they still had too much in common. Big tits. Fake laughter. And too willing to open their legs on the first meeting.

Been there. Done that.

Nothing challenged me anymore.

Addison had been the first person to add a little zest to my life. To get under my skin. To play with my sanity and entice me all at once.

The idea I'd lost my touch, my magical seduction power, concerned me.

I'd never been off my game. Not a damn day in my life.

With a series of nods and what I hoped could pass as smiles, feigning interest, I brought my glass to my lips and took a long sip.

Sabrina—was that even her name? For an instant, I couldn't be sure anymore. Yeah, something was off. I never mixed women's names. Ever. I was a womanizer, but not a heartless jerk. I had manners. And values. Whatever people around me claimed.

Maybe I should go to the doctor. Get a health check. Blood work. A CT scan. Anything.

I had met my physician two weeks ago, and he'd said nothing was wrong with me. Perhaps he missed something, some super rare condition, and I should get a second opinion.

I sighed, burying my face in my hands, my elbows propped on the table.

"Are you okay?" the woman—now I refused to call her Sabrina in case it wasn't her name—asked.

I shrugged. "Yeah. Sure. Tired. And a lot on my mind." *A siren who lives in Georgia. And some of the most amazing sex of my life.*

She moved to her feet, adjusting the straps of her white

dress, offering me a full view of her indecent cleavage. Nope. Even that didn't do the trick. My old Tucker ways were dead. Something resembling panic swirled through me, tying my stomach in knots.

The woman bent at the waist, her breath caressing my earlobe. "Oh, I know the remedy to that. I'll freshen up and be right back." She winked and flashed me a grin before turning the corner toward the restrooms, batting her fake—I would bet on it—eyelashes my way.

As soon as she disappeared from my sight, I exhaled in relief. I dragged a hand over my face, trying to comprehend what it all meant.

With my other hand, I cupped my junk. No. Nothing there either. My dick had forfeited the game too. Was this how depression felt? Like you had no more interest in what impassioned you before?

I swallowed the emotions that raged inside me.

If this girl believed I would follow her, she'd have to wait for me forever.

Before I could think about it twice, I fished a bill out of my wallet, placed it on the table after chugging down the rest of my drink, and got the hell out of there.

Yeah, jerking off to relax and get rid of my angst felt like a better idea than having that girl's lips all around my dick tonight.

Addison's last words before we parted ways replayed in my head. *I'm not sleeping with anyone else until we meet again. I like you raw inside me. Dream of me, Tuck. 'Cause I know I'll dream of you every time I touch myself.*

I had to admit, maybe her words carried more wisdom than I first thought. Right now, they sounded like a solid plan. One I decided to live by too.

———

Dragging my feet, I sauntered back home in no hurry to spend my Friday night all alone. Since my best friend left town a little over a year ago, I'd been compensating for his absence with women. More than usual. Not that I complained at first, but soon it became old news, and I missed male bonding. To make things even more pathetic, my other best friend, Jace, the most pussy-whipped guy to walk the face of the Earth, was almost never available to hang out. Even our weekly Wednesday poker nights hadn't survived Nick's departure. Whenever they were in town, I spent more time with the Busters players than with my own friends. Sure, Barry Hamilton was a decent guy and a good friend of Jace and mine, but it wasn't the same as hanging out with the two guys I'd grown up with.

The high-rise building by Lake Michigan appeared in my peripheral vision. The best place money could buy. Yes, I'd done pretty well in my career so far. I got recruited in college because I was gifted with anything related to numbers, and I'd secured a six-figure salary within two years of graduation. I worked crazy hours and never took vacations, but hey, I was at the top of my professional game at twenty-five. People had it worse than I did.

"Good evening, Mr. Philips," the doorman greeted me.

"Hey, Leo. How is it going?"

"Great. Have a nice night, Mr. Philips."

"You too, Leo." I nodded to him as I entered the elevator car. The box felt smaller than usual, suffocating me. Trying to ease my breathing, I loosened my tie and released the first two buttons of my shirt.

I slumped against the wall, leaning my head back and emptying my lungs, the weight of my thoughts unnaturally heavy.

How had my amazing life turned so depressing? I couldn't pinpoint exactly when it started being a bummer, but this playboy existence didn't have the same appeal it used to. Now that my friends were all about to be happily married and had drifted away from our bachelor lifestyle, I could feel the burden of loneliness pressing down on my shoulders. They had moved on. From this. From me. And I got stuck here. Alone. As if the world had spun at double speed around me, the seasons changing and time ticking, while I stood here, immobile, frozen in the evolution of my own life. A heavy stone I couldn't see but could feel in every bone of my body. A scream rising from somewhere deep within me begged to be freed. To compel me to move on. But I had no idea how to and what the implications of letting go would be. Or how far the restraints I'd imposed on myself a decade ago reached.

With the intention of chasing my grumpiness away, I changed into my workout gear and reached the second floor. A session on the treadmill and a few rounds of weightlifting relieved the crippling sensation coiling inside me. It usually did the trick to snap me out of my funky state.

An hour later, energized and with a more restful mind, I jogged up the stairs to the twenty-third floor, then rode the elevator to the forty-sixth.

My heels dug into the Brazilian walnut wooden floor the moment the door clicked shut behind me. My condo had an open-floor design, so I could see the entire place from the entryway. The living and dining rooms were on the left side with floor-to-ceiling windows offering the best view of Lake Michigan and the buzzing city stretching out below. The kitchen lay in front of me and consisted of a broad island and stainless-steel appliances. On one side was a door to the master bedroom and en-suite bathroom. And on the other side were doors leading to the two guest rooms, a bathroom, and a library I used as a home office.

With high concrete ceilings and exposed brick walls, it had the old factory charm people raved about while being less than five years old.

"Hey, man. What are you doing here?" I asked, taking in the man sitting on my modular Italian leather couch, his feet stretched on the matching ottoman, a tumbler of whiskey in one hand. Not a care in the world about squatting in my place during my absence.

He smirked and I unfroze, walking in his direction. A matching grin stretched my lips as I pulled him into a hug once he got to his feet.

"I had some things to deal with in town. Thought I would crash here for a night or two. If I remember correctly, the day I left Chicago, you said I could come here anytime since I was now homeless, according to your standards."

He winked as I shook my head.

My hug around Nick tightened. "You serious?"

My friend stepped back and brought his drink to his lips and nodded. "I still have to sort out my stuff in the storage unit. I found some place to give most of it away. For a good cause."

"You're in town for two nights?"

Because out of everything my friend had said, that was all that mattered to me at the moment.

"Yep. You heard me right. So, what's the plan? Hitting the bar? Poker night?" He scanned the room. "Wait? No ladies hidden anywhere or waiting for you in the shower, right?"

I shook my head. "Not tonight. A guy needs to recharge his batteries once in a while." I offered him my best cocksure smile, refusing to let him see the truth beneath the mask I'd created when I was still a teenager. Hiding my fear of love under the pretense of fucking around to keep my heart safe from heartbreak. It was crazy, the shit you could get away with when you hid it under boundless confidence. Even from the people closest to you.

"What do you have in mind?" Nick asked. "For tonight." He moved to the bar in the corner of the room and poured me a drink.

"Since I had no idea you'd be in town, I have no plan."

"Think we can bribe Jace for a poker night? I've missed those."

I snickered. "Help yourself. Since you left, Pam has tightened her grip on his balls. Last I heard, she wanted to get pregnant. Imagine the hell she's putting him through."

Yeah, Pamela White was possessive of her man. Years later, I still couldn't comprehend why both my friends had fallen for her. They were genuinely intelligent guys. So, it made no sense they fell for her charade. Nope.

"Let me call him. We'll see how it goes," Nick suggested. He clapped my shoulder. "Glad to be in town, man."

Without saying a word, I pulled him into a tight hug, hoping he knew the feeling was mutual.

———

Slouched on the couch, waiting for Jace to get his ass here, I ordered food through an app on my phone. "Wings or pizza?" I asked.

"Wings. Dahlia isn't the biggest meat eater. Buffalo would be great. Or the one with the hot sauce they added on the menu before I left."

"Hell's Heat, they called it. I'll take a bit of every-thing. Tonight calls for a celebration. Your being back in town is a rare event nowadays." Once I was done, I brought my attention back to my friend. "You came by yourself?"

"Yep. Something felt off the other weekend. I thought you might wanna talk about it. Or maybe just need a shoulder to cry on." He winked.

I shrugged.

"I'm listening if that's the case," he added sincerely.

I sipped my drink, hoping he wouldn't be able to read through my bullshit.

"Seriously, you were there for me when my life fell apart. You helped put me back together when I was broken after Derek, when I thought I'd never be able to rise from the ashes I'd been reduced to. If you hadn't believed in me back then... I don't know. Green Mountain was your idea."

Each word he spoke filled me with the memories of the tragedy I hadn't visited in over a year.

"All I'm saying is, I'm thankful. I wanna pay it forward. Whatever is going on with you, tell me, and I'm here, okay? No matter the time or distance, I'll be on the first flight, sitting on your posh couch, wiping your tears or kicking your ass. I'll always be there for you, man."

Everything he said hit me square in the chest, resonating where it mattered.

I averted my gaze for a moment, ordering my thoughts. "It's nothing," I finally said. "Or nothing a vacation can't fix." No matter how hard I tried, I wasn't ready to open up to him. To tell him how lost I felt. How it hurt to see everyone around me moving on with their lives while I stayed rooted in the same spot. First, I had to figure out if I was worrying over nothing, if it was just a phase—a small hiccup in my journey that would right itself—or if it was truly alarming.

"You sure? You'd tell me if it was serious, right?"

I nodded. "Yeah." I nursed the drink in my hand. "Just

tired, I guess. I got that new account at work. It's big, man. And I've put a lot of night shifts in it. I'll be all right."

Nick leaned forward, his back straight, and his elbows resting on his knees. He watched me for an instant. "Got an idea. Why not come to Green Mountain for a few weeks? You could stick around after the wedding. It could be fun to spend more time together, and a change of scenery might be just what you need. To lift your spirits and clear your mind."

"Aren't you guys going to be on your honeymoon by then?"

"Not right away. We're waiting for Carter to wrap up his tour so Jack can stay with him. I know there aren't lines of barely-dressed women waiting at the town bar or super exciting nightlife, but... I don't know. Dahlia's old house hasn't hit the market yet since we just moved into the farmhouse officially two weeks ago. And Carter is thinking of buying it for that new rental business he's got going on. It's yours if you want it. For as long as you want it. Think about it."

The version of Tucker Philips I'd always been would have refused the offer outright. Living in a small town, hard pass. But this version of me—off his game and lonely—thought that spending time with his friends might do him good. Even in the middle of Crack-Nowhere, Tennessee. And that version won the mental battle.

"Sure. It could be nice. Let me think about it." No, I wasn't about to blow my cover and let him worry about me. If I agreed too quickly, he'd suspect something. Nick already had enough on his plate. My uncle Mike's construction business he'd just bought, moving into a new house, the wedding.

I swallowed, hoping I sounded convincing enough as

he gave me a pointed look. "Let me check if I can clear my schedule first, okay?"

His face lit up. "Sure. The invite won't go anywhere."

The concierge rang my phone, announcing someone was downstairs, cutting our discussion short, and I thanked the delivery guy in my head for his perfect timing.

———

Nick retreated to the guest room around midnight, an hour after Jace left. Boys' night had been everything I'd wished it to be. And more. Fueled by friendship, whiskey, poker, beer, and laughter. It made me forget all my problems for a night.

Incoming text messages filling my phone screen caught my attention as I exited the shower, a towel tied around my waist. I dried myself off quickly and slid under the covers, my device in hand, curious about who would write to me at this time of the night. I prayed it wasn't some drunk chick looking for a quick hookup since I was on a self-proclaimed sabbatical.

A grin spread across my lips as I saw the name on the screen and the five messages waiting for a reply.

ADDISON

Hey Tuuuck, miss me already?

Just kidding. Maybe not. Do you, though?

Have you forgotten?

Forgotten? Forgotten what? I scratched the side of my head, racking my brain, trying to remember if I had agreed to something and it had escaped my mind.

ADDISON

We don't have much time left. I'd like to be done with it by the end of next week. Can you make it happen? Counting on you here.

Don't ignore me. I thought we had a deal. And you haven't delivered yet. I'm still waiting.

What deal?

Just when I was about to ask what it was that I'd somehow forgotten, another message came in.

Fuck. Jesus. Damn it.

My entire body stiffened. And for the first time since I had left Nashville, even my dick had a reaction. A very hard and a very thick reaction.

I swallowed, taking in the picture on my screen.

Addison. I knew it was her, even though I couldn't make out her face, in lacy lingerie, offering me a view of her upper body. I recognized the chameleon tattoo under her left breast.

"I love the idea we all can change colors and adapt to a new environment when we have to," she had said when I had asked her about its meaning.

Another message came through.

ADDISON

Do I have your attention now?

My thumbs typed fast.

ME

Hey, Addison. What's up?

ADDISON

Finally. Thought I had the wrong number for a moment. Some other dude would have had a great surprise.

My lips curled into a crooked smile, and I decided to mess with her.

ME

What surprise? Did you send me a package or something?

ADDISON

…

No. I checked. It was delivered to your number. Unless you're telling me you're not Tuck…

ME

How would you know? I could be anyone right now.

ADDISON

Are you?

ME

Maybe.

ADDISON

Stop playing dumb. We texted in Nashville. Remember, Groom?

ME

But it might not be me typing right now.

ADDISON

I'm pretty sure you don't have female company over. Dah told me Nick was with you. Unless it's him I just sent that picture to. And if it was, he would have called me on it by now. Sorry, man. I'm not some dumb bimbo you usually date who you can fool.

ME

I thought that's what we did the other day. Fool around. And if I remember correctly, you were pretty good at it. Just saying.

ADDISON

Gotcha. I knew it was you. Loved the pic, Tuuuck?

Just the mention of it sent waves of heat through me.

ME

I might.

I fucking did. It's like you have a special power that appeals to me, Wilde. And the key to my usually impressive libido.

My hand returned to my junk, loving how my body responded to hers, even from across multiple states.

ADDISON

Wanna play a game with me?

I swallowed. Hard.

How did she do that? Have me wrapped around her finger?

ME

Depends. What are the rules?

More warmth traveled through me. I loved that she always managed to challenge me when I least expected it and could get a reaction out of me every single time.

ADDISON

No rules.

ME

That sounds like something I'll regret then.

ADDISON

Did you regret fucking me, Tuuuck?

ME

Never.

ADDISON

Then you'll like this game.

The girl was a walking aphrodisiac, even if I couldn't see her.

I pumped myself a few times under the sheets, enjoying the effect her words had on me. She was good. I had to give her that.

ME

Try me.

ADDISON

Call me.

I pressed the video chat button instead, but she refused the call. What now?

ADDISON

No video. We're not allowed to see each other playing this game.

ME

I thought there were no rules.

ADDISON

I changed my mind. Call me now.

Why did the words *call me now* sounded like *fuck me now*?

I adjusted myself under the covers, never releasing the grip on my dick, and pressed the dial button.

She answered after the second ring, her voice gravelly and full of lust.

Shit. This was bad...for me.

"Hey, Tuck. So I guess you wanna play my game?"

I swallowed and swept my bottom lip with my tongue. "I love games, remember? But yours are dangerous...for me at least."

"Oh, I recall a lot of things. And you're a great player. Don't sell yourself short."

Okay, kill me now. I could come at the sound of her sultry voice alone.

She continued before I could muster a reply. "I was lonely tonight and wanted to get laid. But then I thought about you, raw inside me, and the promise I made before you left. So, I decided since you created this problem, you should be the one fixing it."

"Tell me more," I said, my cock swelling a little more with every word she spoke.

"Fuck me, Tuck. I need to come. And I don't wanna do it alone. So, you'll do it for me."

"Woman, you're evil. This is torture."

"You're only allowed to use your voice," she said.

I cleared my throat. "That's another rule."

"I make the rules. Always," she said. "Now get to work. Tell me what to do. Tell me how to fuck myself, thinking it's you."

I moved the pillows around and lay on my back, pushing the sheets away, combusting underneath them, and placed the phone on my chest. I angled one arm under my head, never letting go of my pulsing erection.

My heartbeat pounded in my skull.

Addison's words kept me anchored to the present. "I'm soaked."

At this pace, I'd come undone before we even started.

"Touch yourself, Wilde. Push two fingers inside that tight channel of yours. And moan. I wanna hear you pleasure yourself. Don't hold anything in." I repositioned my hand below. "Glide them in and out of you at a lazy pace. Again. Are they slicked enough yet?"

"Mm-hmm."

"Put your other fingers into your mouth. And lick them. I wanna hear you."

Whimpers and sucking sounds resonated on the other end of the line.

"Now roll those pink nipples of yours between your digits. Hard. Until they're so sensitive they ignite every nerve end and your back arches under the intensity."

"Oh, Tuck. *Yesss.* It feels so good. So, so good. Keep going."

"Wilde, are you aroused for me? Are you dripping wet? Are your fingers coated with your pleasure?"

"Mm-hmm. They are… I am…"

"Good girl. Press on your clit with the pad of your thumb."

"Like this?"

Oh. Little vixen. She was doing it on purpose.

"Harder. Like I'd do if I were there. Now rub it. Fast and slow. Let me hear you."

"Ohmygod. *Tuuuck.* Yes. Like this. Oh yes. Don't stop talking. I'll do anything you ask me to. A-ny-thing… Oh, God. More. I need more." Her cries of pleasure made her voice falter.

A surge of scorching fire licked my back.

"Keep moving those fingers in and out of you. Don't stop. Imagine these are *my* fingers. Long. Hard. Experienced. They know exactly what you need from them. They feel you. They know how to bring you to orgasm. Yes, slide them deeper in. Ride your hand like you'd ride my cock if I were there."

The tip of my spine tingled, and before I exploded all

over my abdomen, I released the grip on myself for a moment, catching my own breath, and lengthening the pleasure.

"Tuck… I… Oh…"

"Let go, sweetheart. I'm right here."

A symphony of purrs resonated from her end, and I resumed the movement of my fist around my steeled erection.

"Do I feel good buried ball-deep inside you?"

She cursed her reply.

"Faster, sweetheart. Push those fingers deeper. Take me all in."

She moaned louder.

I increased the pace of my own pleasuring.

My pants mixed with hers.

We were about to convulse together.

A high-pitched sound cut through the silence of my bedroom, and as if my body had been waiting for it, I came in powerful jolts all over my abdomen.

I couldn't think of any other time I'd come for so long in my life. As if I had infinite sperm reserves. "Now suck on those filthy fingers, Wilde," I said once my breathing returned to normal. "Suck on them like I'm the one doing the honors. Like I'm hungry for you. Because right now, I'm dying to taste you."

I heard a pop sound through the phone, and a lazy and satisfied smile lifted the corners of my lips.

We both caught our breaths.

My racing pulse finally eased. "How do you feel, sweetheart?"

"Better." I heard the contentment in her one-word answer.

"Good," I said, lifting myself on my elbow to grab a box of tissues from my nightstand.

"Thanks, Tuck." Her voice sounded relaxed. It had lost its previous lustful tone.

"Can I see you now?" I asked, spread on my back, spent.

"Nah, it would ruin the fantasy. Night."

I blinked. This woman. She was unbelievable.

"Wait. What were your texts about? Me forgetting something. About a deal between us."

Addison yawned, and I echoed her right after. "Oh, that? The video I'm making to go with Carter's song. For the wedding. You agreed to send me baby and childhood pictures of Nick so I can make a montage for the wedding reception. I'll add clips from the ceremony and reception afterward, so they'll have a keepsake of their special day. I'm swamped at work, so I'd like to get it done sooner rather than later. This new client of mine is a jerk."

The gears of my brain worked, trying to remember the conversation. In vain.

"You forgot, right?"

I breathed out. "Yeah. Sorry. I have some and Jace does too. I'll call Mrs. Peterson tomorrow and see if she can send some over and try to forward them to you in a few days. Would it work?"

Enthusiasm returned to her tone. "Yes. It would be perfect. I'll call you in five days or so to make sure you don't forget again. Thank you."

"Wait." Her earlier words came back to me. "Want me to give that client of yours a little reality check?"

She snickered. "I don't need saving, Tuck. I'm a big girl."

Yeah, I know you are, sweetheart. But, for some reason, the idea she had to deal with that dickhead bothered me. I emptied my lungs to vent my annoyance. "If you change your mind, gimme a call. I'll kick his ass to another state. Night."

"Night, Tuck. Sweet dreams."

We hung up, and after I cleaned myself up, I returned to my previous position under the sheets, my eyes trained on the ceiling. For the umpteenth time this week, I wondered what was going on with me.

In Nashville, Addison Wilde had woken up something in me. I didn't know how to describe it or what it was made of, but I knew, with absolute certainty, that it was real.

My phone chimed with an incoming text message.

ADDISON

For the record, I took that pill.

ME

Are you okay?

What else was I supposed to ask in this situation? It felt selfish to leave her to deal with our fuck-up all by herself.

ADDISON

Yeah. Felt sick for a day. All good now.

Good night.

ME

Night.

I put my device away, uneasy at the thought that she might have gotten sick because of me. That our night of pleasure had unintended consequences.

My lids grew heavy, and sleep claimed me, my dreams filled with images of the girl I wasn't allowed to fantasize about.

The one I'd promised to never touch. And failed.

Big time.

Chapter 10
Addison

"No, this isn't working. We've been over this three times already. I can't use the pictures from the opening night for the new ad campaign. They're blurry. Nothing I can do to fix them." I paused and rolled my eyes. At least the people on the other end of the conference call couldn't see me. I breathed in to calm myself. Soon, I'd strangle them through the phone if I had to.

"You sure none of them are salvageable?" the client asked. Again.

My eyeballs almost bulged out of their sockets. Okay, what didn't he understand? Pressing my lips together, I adjusted the sleeves of my cream ruffle blouse, then took a deep breath in before letting it out. Nope. It didn't work. I pressed my palms together under my chin, summoning my inner strength to calm my temper. Yeah, better than using the same hands to murder this guy who, by now I was sure, was deaf. Or dead if he kept arguing with me over a damn picture of his not-so-handsome face. He and his team were just a bunch of morons.

Breathe in. *One. Two. Three.* Breathe out. *Three. Two. One.*

"As I informed your assistant, your director, and yourself multiple times already, no, we can't. You'll have to provide us with high-definition shots, or we can organize a photoshoot at your convenience."

"Stop," the jackass said, his twangy voice irritating every fiber of me. "You don't understand. I want those pictures. I love how I look in them."

How could he be so obsessed with his own face?

Anger radiated from me. Yeah, the client was asking for my wrath. I usually possessed a more balanced mood at work, but we'd been arguing about this issue for far too long already.

I cleared my throat, trying once more. "I understand, but it's not possible."

"But—"

"Let me finish," I cut him off. "Next time, hire a professional photographer instead of a kid with a cheap phone if you wish to use those pictures for advertising purposes or anything digital. Or if you're under the delusion that you want your face plastered on billboards in the future. There are other ways to cut costs," I said, not bothering to hide my arrogance under pretty words, while I moved to my feet, adjusting my neon-blue pencil skirt with my fingers.

The walls of the conference room closed in around me as my blood boiled with annoyance. I'd had enough. Enough of that jerk. Enough of this circus.

The pictures weren't good. That was it. I was a graphic designer, not a freaking illusionist.

"Give us a second, Mr. Reinart," my boss Joseph said, pressing the mute button on the device set between us on the table. "Addison, where do you think you're going?" he asked, his attention now fully on me.

"My office. I'm done dealing with this guy. If he thinks he's that good-looking, he should go to a model agency, not own a used car dealership. I have work to do, and I've been wasting my precious time with this dickhead all week. Not anymore."

"Addison," he warned in a stern tone.

I flipped a hand in front of me. "You know what, Joseph? I'm going home. I've been feeling like shit all day." I gathered my messenger bag, the file containing the client's notes and stupid photos, my mug of tea, and left the room. Only the clicking of my heels broke the tense silence as men in silk ties and pressed suits watched me leave.

Joseph must have switched off the mute button, because soon I heard his annoyed voice resume the conversation.

Rebecca, my best friend in town and the assistant to the creative director of another campaign we were working on together, hurried after me.

"Addi, what's wrong? Are you okay?"

I continued toward my office, not slowing down. "Fine. Don't worry."

"Joseph will be mad you left him in there to deal with the egoistic loony by himself."

I harrumphed. "He's not alone. Seth and Callum are there. He'll get over it. You know Joseph barks but never bites. He needs me on the team. I'm the only one qualified here since Marjory quit, so I'm not scared about losing my job if that's what you're referring to."

She took a loud gulp of air in and got in step with me.

She gripped my elbow with her small hand, forcing a halt to my escape. "Talk to me," she insisted.

I yanked my arm free. "Nothing to talk about. I've been waking up in the middle of the night twice a night this week, and it then takes me forever to fall back asleep. During the day, I'm exhausted. It just affects my temper. Nothing an afternoon nap and a hot bath won't fix."

My friend pressed her palm against my forehead. "No fever. Go home. I'll hold the fort for you. Turn off your phone, and go to bed. I'll bring you soup when I get home later, okay?"

I nodded. "Thanks, Becca."

"Anytime. Call me if you need anything."

I pulled her into a hug, feeling a bit emotional. If I were being honest with myself, I was so exhausted—and either pissed or teary, if not both at the same time—that a half-day off sounded amazing right about now. "There are leftovers from Cece's in the fridge under my name. Help yourself. I'm pretty sure you only packed a PB&J sandwich for lunch, anyway. You wouldn't want their famous pesto pasta to go to waste, would you?"

A huge smile brightened my roommate's face. "Thanks. You're the best."

I shrugged. "I know. Can't help it."

———

Back at my apartment, I barely had time to remove my heels before falling face first on the mattress. I never went to bed without removing my makeup, but today I had to make an exception to my usually disciplined bed routine. Too lazy to slip under the covers, I grabbed the blanket at the foot of the bed, tucked it around me, and dozed off in a matter of seconds.

"Feeling better?" Rebecca asked, sitting on the edge of my bed, her hand caressing my hair, hours later.

The sound of her voice brought me back to this world. I peeled my heavy eyelids open one at a time. For a second, the room spun around me, and I tried to remember where I was and what time it was. Through the window, the sun hung low in the sky, so I'd bet early evening.

"Addi, you look like I've woken you up from a grave," my friend said, her voice soft and comforting. "How are you holding up? You have that groggy appearance you wear so well." A warm laugh followed her words.

I sat cross-legged before her and ran a hand over my face to chase away every last trace of sleep. "I feel groggy too. And dizzy. My body weighs tons."

Rebecca's palm met my forehead once again. "Still no fever. Hungry?"

"Nah." I scrunched up my face. "My stomach won't accept anything."

"Rest some more then. I brought soup if you change your mind later."

"Thanks." I lay down on my back, bringing the blanket along. Rolling to my side, I curled into a ball, and sleep claimed me in no time.

The next morning, I sat at the small kitchen table, wrapped in a teal plush robe, one foot propped on the chair, an arm draped loosely over my bent knee as I sipped my morning tea.

"Hey, you're up," Rebecca said as she joined me, pouring steaming coffee into her travel mug. "Glad to see you're doing better. Coming to work?"

I gave her a one-shoulder shrug. "I still feel under the weather. For the first time ever, I called in sick. All I can think about is my bed. I just got up because I had to pee.

And shower because I had mascara smudges around my eyes. I looked terrible."

My friend tugged at my low ponytail. "Sure, you looked terrible, Addi. You always do." She snickered, and I joined in. She took a seat before me and studied me with a frown.

"What?"

"Do you think it could be…you know…?"

"Heredity kicking in?" I asked.

"Or something like it. I don't know… You haven't been yourself in weeks. The only time you've been wearing a smile was after you came back from Nashville a week ago. Other than that, since you learned dickhead cheated on you and might have given you chlamydia, you've been off. I worry about you."

I sucked in a breath. My friend knew me too well. "Funny thing. I asked Dahlia if she thought this could be it. Like my family history was repeating itself… She didn't think so." I paused, trying to fight off the thoughts that scared me. "Truth? I can't tell for sure. And I thought I was doing better. I really did… The insomnia is new, though. Maybe it's a phase. I'm over my relationship…been for a while. Even when we were together, in the end, I knew he was never meant to be the love of my life. What I miss the most is the idea of love, you know? Sharing a bed. Not the guy per se. What if I can't find my happily ever after anywhere else? What if I'm destined to end up a cat lady or something? I love being in love. I'm not sure I'm ready to forfeit the whole idea just yet."

"Still thinking about meeting with Felicia? To try to renew what you girls had for an instant?"

"Nah. Maybe. I could. But I like men too much. It's stupid. I should really be over them by now. Forget they exist. Felicia is nice. We experienced some great times together..."

"But—"

"Yeah, there's a but. I won't commit to her. I just can't. She's not the one. That I can tell."

Rebecca watched me, sipping her hot beverage. "Addi, you'll find the one…one day. Not all men are cheaters-losers-liars. Dahlia found a great one. You can't stop gushing about him. And I have a good guy too."

"Ben is quite a catch. You're lucky."

"Addison Wilde, you're destined for greatness."

I reached across the table and gave her hand a gentle squeeze, soaking in her warmth. "Thanks. I hope you're right. Now go or you'll be late."

"You gonna be okay on your own?"

"I promise. I'll call you if I'm not."

Rebecca screwed the cap on her mug, grabbed her purse, and left after kissing my cheek.

After a morning nap, I sat on the couch by the large window, basking in the sunlight pouring into the living room, with my laptop resting on my folded legs. Our apartment was small, but the location was everything. A ten-minute walk from one of the busiest commercial streets in Atlanta. A fifteen-minute walk from our job. I could be anywhere so easily that I even sold my car after my junior year of college since I never used it.

The place was modestly furnished, but we lacked for nothing. Two bedrooms with walk-in closets—those were considered rare gems in the city—an open floor plan consisting of two connected spaces: a dining room slash kitchen and a living room. Wide windows letting lots of sunlight in, tiled flooring, white walls, and bright blue accent in the form of pillows, picture frames, and other decor items.

I double-clicked on the file holding my latest T-shirt designs and got to work. I loved my job, but this, right here, was something that made me proud. The little business I'd started from scratch. In addition to designing shirts, I had also proven myself pretty good at organizing events. Over the years, I had planned weddings, album launches, business inaugurations, and baby showers, amongst other occasions, including Dahlia's bridal store opening and her upcoming nuptials. If I could find a way to make my two passions coexist together, I'd be a fulfilled gal. Be my own boss and not take shit from people like Pierce Reinart ever again.

Hours passed, and I lost track of time until a chime on my phone startled me. I finished applying the glittery purple filter over the wing part of my design and pressed *save* before picking up my device.

The biggest smile I could summon bisected my face as I took in the picture.

TUCKER

Now you can't deny I've always been the best-looking one between both of us.

I cupped my heart with a hand as I studied the two little boys—probably about six or seven years old—wearing shorts, sitting on the hood of a car, eating ice cream cones with matching grins.

"This is adorable," I said out loud before realizing nobody could hear me.

With a shake of my head, I texted my *groom*.

ME

Got to say, you two were pretty cute.

I could imagine Tucker's smirk lighting up his cocky face and snickered as the image formed in my head.

TUCKER

I knew it. You find me irresistible.

Oh God, his ego.

ME

Don't let it go to your head. I never said you were still good-looking, though.

TUCKER

Wilde. Wilde. Wilde. No need to say it. I saw it in your eyes the day we spent locked up in your suite.

I got my confirmation from the multiple orgasms I gave you out of my selflessness.

I tilted my head back, laughing, and dropped my laptop on the couch beside me. I made myself comfortable and typed with both thumbs.

ME

Sorry. Truth be told. I was faking it. I was scared to hurt your lack of modesty.

My face hurt, my lips stretched to their maximum. My heart cartwheeled in my chest, and laughter rumbled out of me. Yes, it felt good to be happy.

TUCKER

Want me to take the next flight and prove you wrong?

I pushed my hair back with a finger, my laughter resuming.

ME

You wouldn't?

TUCKER

Wanna bet on it?

If I leave in an hour, I'd land by dinner time.
Any plans tonight?

ME

Stop screwing with me.

Truth?

TUCKER

Always.

ME

I've been having a few off days. Home
today. My sleep is disturbed so I left in the
middle of a meeting with a client yesterday.
The guy was being a douche.

TUCKER

Whoa. You did that? Same guy you told me
about?

ME

Yes.

TUCKER

Truth?

ME

Always.

TUCKER

You should have let me kick his ass. I'm a
pretty good ass-kicker. Also, you need the
Tucker magic touch. No wonder you can't
sleep. You miss me, sweetheart.

ME

I do not.

TUCKER

Wanna bet?

I poked my tongue out and took a selfie and sent it to him.

TUCKER

Yeah, I remember that tongue. And the wonders it could deliver.

I pinched my shirt, fanning myself. For some reason I still couldn't explain, Tucker Philips had a way of shooting heat through me. In every possible way.

TUCKER

Gotta go. I'll be there at five-thirty. Wear a dress. And your hair down. I love it wrapped around my fist when I'm inside you.

I chuckled. And exhaled. Fervor zinged through me. Somehow, our little conversation had lightened my mood, and I felt better.

ME

Yeah, right. See you at the wedding, big guy.

Tucker never replied. I waited for at least ten minutes but nothing. My smile dissolved, and I got up to warm up some of the soup Rebecca had brought home last night.

Lying on the couch with the remote in my hand, I tried to watch some TV, but nothing captured my attention for more than a few minutes. I huffed and browsed the internet, then decided a nap would do me good.

The pounding on my door brought me out of my slumber.

"Coming," I mumbled, trying to return to the land of the living and escape the lethargic state I was in. "Becca, have you lost your keys again?" I couldn't believe it. The girl lost them at least once a week. Along with her phone. And once, she even lost her purse. The girl would lose her head if it weren't attached to her shoulders.

I unlocked the door and swung it open, only to stare, moving my mouth like a fish out of water, blinking.

"Hey, sweetheart. Are you gonna let me in or not?" Tucker asked, pushing past me and ruffling my hair as if I were a kid. "Where's your dress? Why aren't you ready? Are you still sick? You sounded fine earlier. Do you want me to make you soup or something?" He leaned in to press a soft kiss to my cheek. "By the way, you look beautiful."

My feet stayed glued to the entryway. No matter how hard I tried, I couldn't move, rooted to the spot.

"Wilde? Are you sure you're okay? Having a hard time closing your mouth?"

I bobbed my head in the slowest motion. Tucker walked back to me, closed the door, and with his fingers intertwined through mine, pulled me out of my stupor.

He looked absolutely divine in his gray suit, dark purple button-up shirt, and black tie. Yes, I had to admit, purple looked amazing on him.

I snapped back to the present. "What...what are you doing here?"

He sighed with a shake of his head. "Told you I'd be here at five-thirty. Wait... You didn't expect me?"

"Nah. I thought you were joking."

He pivoted to face me. "Sweetheart, I never joke about taking a woman out on a date. Now get ready. Our reservation at Cosmos is in an hour."

I blinked some more. "Cosmos? I'm sure this is all a dream. None of it is real," I said, gesturing around us. "Please pinch me. Nobody can get a reservation at Cosmos on such short notice. This place is booked months in advance. Even on a Thursday night."

"Well, everyone is not me. Now go. I'll make myself at home while you change." He removed his jacket, hung it on the back of a chair, rolled his sleeves, and slapped my ass in an intimate way when I retreated from the room.

In the mirror by my bed, I took in my appearance. Oh gosh, I looked disheveled. My hair was all over the place, dark shadows circled my eyes, and my clothes were rumpled from spending the day on the couch.

Beautiful? Tucker Philips forgot his prescription glasses. Clearly.

Adrenaline shot through me as I heard him humming something from the living room. *Cosmos.* The guy really went all in for this…huh…date? What should I call it when a guy flew two hours just to have dinner with me in the most romantic and exquisite restaurant in the city?

If anyone else but Tucker had come here tonight, I would've already called my best friend to tell her all about it. But since I didn't want to jeopardize anything before her big day, I chose to keep the news of Tucker being here to myself.

Flutters of excitement ran through me, and I slid myself into an Otto & Newhouse coral sheath I got last Christmas. One of my rare fashion indulgences I bet Tucker would approve of. It gave my boobs all the attention they deserved, without looking too desperate, and ended just above my knees.

I fixed my hair into a loose braid, curled my lashes, and applied two thick coats of mascara, wanting my eyes to look bigger and more awake than they appeared. Foundation, a spray of perfume, a pinch of blush on my cheeks, and coral lipstick. I smacked my lips together, ready to go.

Tucker gasped the moment I stepped into the kitchen, hopping on one foot to put a heel on.

"Wilde, wow," he said, his gaze slowly drawing over my

figure with an appreciative nod. "Otto & Newhouse? It's like you speak my language. Looks great on you." His perusal weighed on my skin, causing shivers to appear. "All right, I can work with a braid." He winked. "Come on, let's go." His large hand pressed on my lower back as we made it to the door.

In front of the building, a car with tinted windows was waiting for us.

"After you," my date said, opening the door to let me in.

I angled my upper body to face him when he slid into the backseat beside me. "All of this for tonight?"

He nodded. His eyes swam with a million things I wished I could name.

"Why are you here, Tuck? Tell me the truth."

He stared into my eyes, and my body shuddered from the intensity of his gaze. "Told you. To take you out on a date. You said you've been feeling off. Figured a little something to lift your mood wouldn't hurt."

I smiled while I studied him.

A frown creased his forehead.

"Okay, fine. Truth then." He fished something out of the inner pocket of his jacket. "Here. I wanted to give you those."

I accepted the envelope and opened the flap. Inside lay over twenty pictures of Nick at different stages of his life.

I swallowed, meeting his serious demeanor. "You flew here to gimme pictures? You know you could have sent them in an email, right? Or by mail."

He nodded. "Yes. But I wouldn't have had the pleasure of seeing you in person if I hadn't come here. Don't look so surprised, Wilde."

"We're not sleeping together." The refusal passed my lips before I could think of the words.

A mischievous smirk painted Tucker's face. "I didn't come here for sex if that's what you are assuming. We said six weeks, and I'm sticking to my word. I flew over because I wanted to spend some time with the maid of honor before the big day. Get to know each other better. And because I was starving."

A warm laugh bubbled out of me, and Tucker's baritone joined in.

"Fine. I guess they don't have food in Chicago. Let's feed you then, big guy. And for what it's worth, I'm happy to see you. Thanks for coming over and cheering me up."

My heart flipped in my chest when a genuine smile took over his face, but I ignored the pummeling and focused my attention on the view outside.

He rested his hand above my knee as if it was the natural thing to do, and I didn't push it away, loving the warmth that zipped through me where our flesh connected—and the flutters that leaped in my belly.

When my gaze drifted back to the man sitting next to me, the smoldering in his irises got me breathless. It sent my pulse into a frenzy, and I tried to shut it down before it could shatter my resolutions—and the safety of my heart.

Without a word, he knitted his fingers through mine, and I relaxed in my seat, resting my head against his shoulder while I enjoyed the ride.

Chapter 11
Tucker

Cosmos was exactly how I'd imagined it to be. Dimmed chandelier lights, dark ceiling and walls, ocean-oak tables and flooring. It was both romantic and chic. I pulled Addison's chair, and she flashed me a smile over her shoulder when she sat down—one that could send my heart tipping if I wasn't careful.

"Wine?" I asked when the server brought us the drink menu.

"Huh, one glass. Told you I was having insomnia. Alcohol will just feed it, and I'm desperate for eight hours of uninterrupted sleep."

I turned to the waiter, pointing to a bottle of red before thanking him.

Addison rested her face on her folded hands, watching me. Like the ocean on a sunny day, her blue eyes sparkled under the low light, sucking me in. "Tell me. Why are you really here? You didn't come all this way to have dinner with me and bring me baby pictures of your best friend."

I cleared my throat and tasted the wine when the server poured some into my glass after swirling it. "Perfect." I waited until he filled our glasses and left before continuing. "That's the truth. Heard great things about this place. Never had a chance to visit it before, though. You're my only friend in town, Wilde. So, I thought I could check two boxes on my list with one visit. I won't tell you I've missed you if that's what you're afraid of."

I flaunted her my biggest smirk and winked, and she sighed, bringing her glass to her lips. "Oh, this is good."

"It is, right? Anyway, to answer your question, I barely ever go on vacations, so tonight somehow feels like a little reprieve from work."

"Well, this is sad. I don't get much free time either, but still, everyone deserves to have a break once in a while."

A curve drew on her full lips, and my finger itched to trace the contours. I yearned to savor them one more time, to reminisce about their taste and the feel of them against mine.

She raised her glass to mine as the silence between us charged with unsaid words and the blazing chemistry I shared with no one else. "Let's drink to your night off then."

"To us."

Dinner was exquisite, but right now, I couldn't tell if it tasted better only because the company was appealing. Sitting beside each other, Addison and I ended up splitting all that we ordered, talking about anything and everything.

"Dumbest thing you've ever done?" she asked as we shared a piece of chocolate-swirled cheesecake, her spoon floating in front of her mouth and curiosity swimming in her irises.

"Who asks that?" I teased with a lifted brow. "Usually women wanna know the cutest or funniest thing I've ever done."

"I'm not every woman," Addison said, her gaze fused to mine.

A loud, heartfelt laugh bubbled out. "Don't worry, I've noticed. I've been reminded of it quite a few times already since I met you."

"Thank you." She smiled, and pride poured from every inch of her face.

"You're thanking me? Geez, you're weird. A nice weird, though." I shook my head, unable to hide the stupid grin creeping onto my face. "Dumbest thing... Let's see. One night I was in a rush to get somewhere, followed a crazy girl's instructions, and ended up ripping my favorite shirt, spending my night dressed like a stripper, and throwing away my hotel keycard when I discarded the ruined piece of fabric."

She cupped her mouth and yelped. "Oh God. So dramatic. I hoped it ended better than it started. I bet she was worth it, though."

I exhaled loudly and rewarded her with a boyish grin I was aware ladies loved. "The girl made me share her bed. The next day, we had some of the best sex of my life. So, in the end, I would say she redeemed herself quite amazingly. She's unforgettable."

I brought my wine glass to my lips and took a long sip, never breaking eye contact with my date.

"Still up for some *Wilde* adventures?" she asked, her eyes shooting devilish sparks in the dim light of the restaurant.

"Should I be?"

She stared at me with intent, the sound of her voice

seductive. "It depends. How much do you like to get burned when you play with fire?"

"When the fire is addictive, I could risk my life for it."

We said nothing as we finished our dessert and I paid the check, fighting with Addison over it.

Outside, the summer breeze swept across our faces.

"What time is your flight back?" she asked.

I checked the time on my watch. "In three hours."

She clapped her hands before her. "Awesome. Let me give you a tour of my city. After Nashville and New York, Atlanta is the next best thing."

I moved until I faced her and tipped her chin up with a finger. "Don't you wanna go back home? Get some sleep. You look a bit pale."

"No. You're only here for a few hours, and if this is the only time off you get this year, I want it to mean something. It must count." She laced her fingers through mine, and some sort of electrical discharge stirred in me from where our palms met. Addison blinked, and I'd bet she felt it too. Instead of releasing her grip on me, she tightened the connection. "Follow me."

My gaze drifted to her heeled feet. "You're not seriously thinking of walking all over town in those, are you?"

"Nah. I'm much more technologically advanced than you think, big guy. We're taking those."

I followed the direction of her pointed finger.

"You're kidding, right? Tell me you are."

She nodded. With conviction. "*Truth always.* Remember?"

I perused my surroundings and forfeited the idea of a better option.

"Fine. But those things are way too small for a guy of my height."

She chuckled, her fists resting on her hips. "Stop trying to find excuses because you're afraid."

She used her credit card to rent the scooters, and we each hopped on one.

"You're gonna ride in this dress?"

"Watch me."

This woman. She would never cease to amaze me.

We rode for over an hour as she showed me where she worked, her favorite park, some tourist attractions, the college she attended. The entire time, my attention was riveted on her as if she were a magnet and I was trapped in her field.

"See? You aren't injured. All safe and sound," Addison quipped.

"It's actually fun," I conceded.

We continued our tour, exchanging heated gazes and loaded grins.

Minutes later, she stopped in front of a fast-food place so suddenly, I almost bumped into her.

"What the hell, Wilde. Are you still hungry?" I asked as she fumbled with her scooter.

"This thing is broken. Or the battery is dead. Either way, it won't restart."

"Let me check." I failed at fixing it too. "Use mine. I can walk. I'm in good shape. I should be able to catch up with you."

She glanced at me. "I know. That's not the point. It won't be nearly as fun," she said with a pout. She blinked, but soon her eyes lit up with a mischievous twinkle. "Got an idea. I'll hop on yours." She approached my scooter. "Make room for me, big guy." With her arms secured around my midriff, she pressed her front to my back, molding our bodies to perfection.

The sensation of her warmth against every inch of me awakened the electric tingles I'd felt earlier.

It affected every string of my composure.

When we stopped on the sidewalk in front of her apartment building sometime later, I breathed easier the instant she peeled herself away from me.

With the discarded scooter long forgotten, I cleared my throat as I checked my watch, Addison standing a foot from me. My eyes caught the movements of her chest, her breasts rising with each breath, enticing me. "I'll have to go soon." My words sounded huskier than intended, and I cleared my throat.

I ate the gap between us with a stride and used my hand to tuck wild tendrils of her hair behind her ear.

Her lips trembled as she met my eyes, her expression shadowed by the streetlamp above her.

Our eyes fixated on each other for a long minute, neither of us brave enough to break the enchantment that had settled between us.

"Can I kiss you?" I asked, enraptured by her lips.

She shook her head but leaned forward at the same time.

Addison Wilde was a tall woman, even more with those heels on. I didn't have to bend too much to claim her mouth.

She sucked in a breath when my lips grazed hers, and my heart skipped a beat at the contact.

The mere connection sent a gazillion shivers along my spine.

My fingers tangled in her hair of their own volition, angling her head to deepen the kiss.

At this moment, I felt alive. And fucking amazing. As if only her mere presence removed the dead weights that had been pressing on my chest forever. As if I could fly along with her.

My entire dark world brightened with colors.

I really had to see that doctor. Now I was certain something was wrong with me. No more doubts. Women never had this kind of effect on me. We used each other for pleasure—or companionship for a limited timeframe—nothing more.

My body hardened.

Before I got in too deep with her and couldn't leave, I ended the kiss. Scratching my eyebrow, I muttered, "Sorry."

Addison averted her eyes, adjusting her sinful dress. The one I'd been longing all night to peel off her, hugging her curves like a second skin.

"I should go," I said. "Let me walk you to your place."

She bobbed her head. "Sure."

"Hey." I framed her cheek with my palm and forced her to look at me. "If we keep doing this, I'll never be able to catch my plane. You know how it went down last time." Hurt along with something else danced in her eyes. "I've always been honest about this. Bachelor parties and wedding flings with you are one thing, but we can't just fuck around for weeks without emotions getting involved. And I don't do relationships, Wilde," I whispered, the weight of my regret crushing my chest when I spoke the last sentence.

She reeled her hurt in without even blinking. "I knew the specifics of this arrangement when I seduced you in Nashville. I'm not some innocent woman, Tuck. I can take care of myself. I'm not looking for a relationship either. Well, I am, but not with you."

Her words, even if they echoed mine, stung. They pierced a layer of my heart I never knew existed before.

That doctor's appointment couldn't come fast enough. While I was at it, I should also book one with a neurologist. Perhaps I'd hit my head at some point without realizing it. I seemed to have inflicted some serious damage to my skull, and now the side effects were strangling my rational thoughts.

"Truth. The thing is, I'm not looking to get my heart broken. I'm playing with you because you're a safe choice. I know better than to fall for a womanizer like you."

I arched one eyebrow.

"Okay, and because you're insanely hot. But no need to blow your ego out of proportion." She squeezed my hand, still pressed against her cheek. "And I'm the one who made the no-sex rule first tonight. I'll just have to relieve myself on my own, I guess."

"Wilde… I'm… We-we don't…"

She placed a finger over my lips to silence me. "I had a perfect night. Let's not spoil it with false promises neither of us can stick to."

I nodded because I was at a loss for words.

"I'll still walk you upstairs."

"I wouldn't expect any less from you."

At her door, I leaned forward, and skimmed her cheek with my lips. I sucked in a sharp breath to calm the turmoil inside me and molded one hand to the crest of her hip, holding her in place, anchoring her to me. The desire to touch her was overwhelming, and I couldn't seem to resist it, no matter how much I told myself to keep my distance.

We breathed each other in for a short moment.

"Thank you for doing this with me tonight, Wilde."

"Thanks for flying here to spend a few hours with me. I had a great time."

My hand drifted to the small of her back, and I tugged her to me. There was no way she couldn't feel how strongly my body was drawn to hers. Addison ground her hips against mine, stoking the fire kindling between us and the million sensations swirling inside me.

"Tuck—" Her voice, a breathless murmur, played with my self-control.

"Let's do this again some other time," I whispered, my lips buried in her mass of blonde locks.

She swallowed. "Let's not."

I let out a warm chuckle. "See you around then." I stepped back and spun around before she could close the door in my face. "Sweet dreams, Wilde."

———

For the next week, Addison and I either talked or texted every night, sharing about our days, our jobs, or nothing in particular. Our little night chats had become the highlights of my days. Yes, I'd turned into that kind of guy. The heaviness of my work and my lonely existence didn't matter anymore every time we were together—in person or hundreds of miles away.

Fresh from the shower, I changed into a pair of lounge pants and a long-sleeved T-shirt, grabbed a beer, and perused the time on my watch, waiting for it to strike nine. Sitting on my bed, my legs stretched before me, I peeled the label off the bottle.

Seconds later, Addison's name appeared on my screen, and I picked up the call, unable to stop the curl growing on my lips.

"Hey, Tuck. Miss me already?" she asked as a greeting, the smile in her voice contagious.

Even if I were tempted to say no, I knew I wouldn't be able to lie to her. "Always, sweetheart. How was your day?

That fucker Reinart giving you trouble again, or did you manage to ditch his account?"

She sighed. "He actually came to the office today."

"Whoa, he did?"

"Yep. And decided to flirt with me. As if that would convince me to work with him."

I fisted my hands at my sides. Stupid used-car guy. I wished I could tell him what was on my mind right now.

"Did it work?" I chastised myself when the words left my mouth, but no way could I take them back without sounding like a jealous asshole.

Her chuckle filled the line and my heart at the same time. "Nah. Too late for playing nice. I'm so over that account. I have better things to do with genuine clients who respect me as a graphic designer. And as a woman."

That's my girl.

Fuck. Did I really say that? I shut my lids, wishing I hadn't spoken aloud.

"Your girl?" Addison asked after a few infinite seconds.

Yep, I did say it out loud. It wasn't just one meaningless thought popping into my head—I had so many of those these days. Daydreams about her sporting a happy grin or watching me with a devilish glint in her eyes. Addison spread underneath me, ready for me to ravage every inch of her sinful body with my tongue. Or her in my arms at night or locked around me as I pounded into her in the shower. Things I wished to tell her, or asking for her thoughts about both trivial and life-changing decisions.

I covered my slip-up with a nervous chuckle. "You know what I mean. Don't make a big deal out of it. Anyway, I'm just proud you gave him a run for his money."

"Yeah, well. How about your day? Did that meeting go as expected?"

I cleared my throat. "Yeah. But it will mean more

work for me." I paused. "It's a good thing, though. I love my work, but some days, I wish for a simpler life. Huh… I'm about to get a big bonus, so there's that." I grimaced when I added, "It just doesn't have the appeal it used to."

"Perhaps you could try something else. Just a thought."

"What would I do?"

"Anything. Dahlia told me how gifted you are. You could try your hand at anything. Like the sky is the limit. Not a lot of people have that chance in life."

I reflected on it. "I guess. Still, I've never imagined myself doing anything else."

"What would you do if you could reinvent yourself?"

I didn't even have to think about it. "I'd do something that brings people together. Whatever it means. I never really put too much thought into this."

"Like what? Organizing events? That's actually what I would love to do. Right after designing T-shirts."

"Quite impressive. Nah, I was thinking more like hosting events instead of organizing them. Or…really, I have no clue. I'd need to ponder it a bit more." I shifted on my bed. "How's the video montage coming? Think I'll be able to see it before the wedding?"

"I'm almost done. There are some changes I wanna make first. Give it a week or two at the most."

"Don't deceive me, Wilde," I teased, unable to hide the amusement in my tone. "I expect great things from you."

"Please don't expect too much. I am trying my hand at it."

"I won't," I said, the teasing clear in my tone. "After seeing your creativity back in Nashville, I'm sure I'll be impressed."

We talked for a little longer, switching to video chat at some point.

"What would you choose as a superpower if you could pick any one?" she asked.

I considered the question for a full minute. "Fly."

"Why?"

"So I could come to see you right now and make sure you're really okay and not pretending for my sake."

I winked, and she appeared flustered. The pink hue looked good on her cheeks.

Addison bared an exaggerated, all-teeth smile, and I couldn't contain my laughter.

"Fine, you're not faking. I can clearly see it right now." We both burst out in chuckles. "We should hang up. It's almost eleven. Time flies with you, Wilde. And I'm not helping you kick your insomnia to the curb by keeping you up late most nights."

She didn't formulate a reply. Instead she watched me with a soft smile. My skin tingled, and my gaze got lost in the blue lasers trained on me.

"Thank you," she said after some time.

"Why?" I asked, almost breathless from the intense connection we shared.

"Just for being you. Night."

Her soft voice blanketed the loneliness that had been visiting me in these last few months, a protective feeling that I cherished.

"Night, sweetheart."

For the next hour, I lay on my bed, unsure of what I had experienced tonight, but longing for a repeat because my body and soul were now at ease.

———

The next day, I was about to leave for work when the concierge met me at my front door, holding a kraft paper package. "For you, Mr. Philips," he said, handing it to me. I looped the strap of my messenger bag over my shoulder and, curiosity getting the better of me, tore open the wrapping to find a folded piece of purple cotton inside. Instinctively, I knew it was one of hers. A T-shirt Addison designed. Bracing myself for whatever message it conveyed, I unfolded it, her scent reaching my nose. The devil had sprayed it with her perfume. I couldn't help the crooked tilt of my lips as I flipped it over.

Official Atlanta Scooter Club. Honorary member.

This time, at least, the size seemed just right.

A badge and a certificate fell on the floor, the latter signed by "Addison Wilde, President." My lips stretched wider. She had gone all in, Wilde-style, on this.

I tried to call her but hit her voicemail. Instead, I sent her a text.

ME

> Got the delivery. I can't wait to show my colors to the people of Chicago. Think we could start a chapter here?

ADDISON

> Oh, you're jealous of my president title, is that it? Let me think about it. I'm not against monthly meet-ups. Securing my position as the head of the club.

ME

> If you're the president, I'll be your vice.

ADDISON

> You would agree to rule under me?

ME

> Anytime, Wilde. That ass of yours is etched on my brain forever.

Gotta go or I'll be late. Traffic is a bitch.
Tonight at 8 still good for you?

ADDISON

Yep. Later. Show your colors, big guy. Make
me proud.

Instead of dropping the piece of clothing back in my apartment, I shoved it into my bag after I took a whiff of it, the scent coiling into my heart in a way I never expected. Today, I decided to bring a piece of her along with me to work, not a care in the world how lame it might seem.

My phone rang at seven eleven that night. Forty-nine minutes before the time Addison and I had set for tonight's phone date.

"Hey you," I greeted her. "Everything all right?"

She usually called me at the time we pre-set, never late or early. The hitch in her breath hinted that there was actually something bothering her. She remained silent. My pulse picked up at the thought she might be sad or upset.

"Wilde, talk to me or I'm booking the next flight to Atlanta and not leaving until you spill it."

She inhaled a shaky gulp of air. "You'll think it's silly," she whispered.

"Maybe. But you're not the type of woman to hide behind silliness and other people's opinion. Speak. I'm all ears."

I switched the call to video chat.

"Forget it, I'm not answering that."

"Who's the baby now? Come on, let me see you."

She sighed but ended up agreeing to it.

My mouth curled at the sight of her. Disheveled hair. Reddened cheeks. Dark outlines under her baby blues. Her face was a mix of cuteness and exhaustion.

A shadow lingered over her expression, and I squared my stance, worry tinging my blood.

"Sweetheart, what's going on?" I asked, unable to hide the edge in my voice.

"I told Reinart to go fuck himself today. In person. In front of everyone." The air she let out sounded painful.

"What did the fucker do?" I growled, ready to jump into my phone screen, my words clipped.

"He cornered me and palmed my ass. Called me *baby*, trying to seduce me while making me feel like a powerless piece of meat."

Fury, raw and blinding, rose inside me, blackening my vision. I breathed faster, clenching my free hand at my side, the other one too busy strangling my device. "Listen, don't ever say harassment is silly. The guy had it coming. He deserves every shred of your wrath. And telling him to go fuck himself is not enough of a punishment for acting like a jackass and manhandling a woman." I controlled the rage revving up in me with noisy inhales and exhales. "If it were up to me, his ass would be hanging from the Grand Canyon right now. Thanks to my strong foot, I've got a sick right kick."

Addison's shoulders relaxed, and a small curve of her lips graced her pretty face. It suited her much better and eased some of the murderous thoughts invading my mind.

She continued before I could finish plotting this guy's fallout. "These days, I don't recognize myself anymore. I'm either full-on happy or ready to kill with my bare hands. That's if I'm not about to bawl my eyes out or pass out from exhaustion. When Reinart got handsy, I froze. I'm usually a scary and feisty opponent when someone pushes my buttons. Not today. I should've kicked his butt to Alaska myself."

"He deserves more than a *go fuck yourself* from you. The

dickhead has been acting like a jerk for weeks, and you've been putting up with him the entire time. I would've loved to witness you giving him a run for his money, though. Don't feel bad, but you've been working a lot lately. With the last-minute wedding planning details and everything else, you deserve a break."

"I'm just... I don't know. Disappointed in me, more than anything else. Fighting back and delivering upper-cuts the Southern way is more my thing."

I mirrored her lopsided smile. "Please never let me be on your bad side. I'd be scared for my life….and my balls. No way I'm ever stepping into the ring to fight you. Still…I kind of enjoy it when you play dirty."

She relaxed her posture, and some color returned to her features. "Thank you. For having my back. And calming my mad self."

"I did nothing."

She shook her head. "Nah, you did everything right. You listened to me and made me feel less shitty about my day."

Pinching my lips together for a moment, I asked the question burning the tip of my tongue. "Why didn't you call Dahlia to vent about it?"

"She doesn't know about Reinart. She's in full wedding-preparation mode. And truth? You're the first person I thought of. It sounds stupid, but I knew you'd understand and not blame me for not ripping his balls off." She paused. "Dahlia would have driven here to give the guy a piece of her mind. It would've been ugly." A soft laugh bubbled out.

"Nah, that I don't believe. Dahlia's isn't scrappy like that."

"Don't underestimate her, big guy. We're Southern

girls. We're tougher than we look. Don't forget she already threatened you."

"Yeah…that. You've got a point. She was scary enough."

"See? Told you. Anyway, Becca offered to tag along tonight and get drunk after work. In the past, I would've done that, but… I don't know."

"What changed?" I asked, holding my breath.

"You. We happened. I wanted to tell you. Don't ask me why. It makes no sense at all."

"Maybe it does," I ventured.

"Maybe. Anyway, thanks for listening to me and giving me the space to vent."

"Always, Wilde."

We remained quiet for a long while, our gazes lingering, our silence speaking louder than words.

"By the way, thank you for the shirt. I'll start recruiting after the wedding. I'm pretty sure our Chicago chapter will put yours to shame. Just saying. Be prepared, sweetheart."

The tension vanished from her features, the knowledge calming the jitters I'd experienced earlier.

"Hey, Tuck?"

"Yeah."

"I really like this friendship thing we've got going on. It's important to me."

"Me too. It's actually nice to have you in my life. Never thought we would end up here, you and me. I never had any girls as friends before. You're the first one."

"I'm your first *girlfriend*?"

I sighed. "You know what I mean. Also, don't let it go to your head, Wilde."

We both burst into a fit of laughter.

"Gotta wake up early tomorrow. Night, Tuck."

"Good night, sweetheart. Hope your dreams are filled with me."

She giggled. "We'll see."

We hung up, and I stared at my phone screen for longer than necessary afterward.

"I miss you," I said to the blank screen. Then I shook my head, trying to push away the words I just spoke. Because they made no sense. And even though they sounded foreign on my tongue, they felt right.

An invisible clamp crushed my stupid heart at the thought. More knots twisted my stomach.

I'd been lonely for a while, and now it weighed on me. Damn me and my stupid mind for mixing everything up.

Chapter 12

Addison

Rebecca shook me out of my slumber two days later. "Hey, Addi. Are you still feeling off? You've been sleeping all day."

I lifted myself on one elbow, trying to blink my drowsiness away, so out of it that I felt like I'd just landed after a very long trip.

With a slow browse, I perused my bedroom. It felt both foreign and familiar as my brain rebooted at a lazy pace. I registered the vintage dresser set I had bought in college and repainted in a teal hue. The full-length mirror framed with reclaimed barn wood Dahlia had gifted me when we were teens. I blinked again. My focus adjusted, and I brought my attention to my roommate.

"Been talking to Tucker till late last night. We were playing a stupid twenty-questions game and couldn't stop."

My roommate shot me a puzzled stare. "You two have been spending an awful lot of time together since he came here a week ago. Anything I should know?" She waggled her eyebrows in the annoying way she always did.

I shook my head. "C'mon, Becca. We live a few states apart. Nothing's going on. Don't make up stories. Fake news is so last year. We're just getting to know each other. Best man and maid of honor thing. It's easier if we work together than fight all the time."

"Oh God, you're attracted to him. Big time. You're blushing."

I pressed my hands over my burning cheeks. "I am not. Stop. Don't create a story that doesn't exist."

She raised her hands between us. "The next thing I know, you'll be each other's plus-one at the wedding."

I cleared my throat.

"Oh, you already are? Are you kidding me?"

I waved a hand. "It's easier that way, you know. No distraction. Better teamwork. We're doing this for Dah and Nick. It's nothing."

"Yeah, yeah, it's nothing. If you say so," she said, barely able to reel her smirk in.

"I'm not seeing anyone, and Tuck hasn't invited anyone yet. Why shouldn't we simplify our lives for once? Inviting other people means babysitting them for the day. Hard pass."

"Whose idea was it?"

"Mine. His. Who cares?"

"I do," my traitorous girlfriend said. "I'd pay a lot of money to be in your headspace right now."

"Enough. Let's not talk about the wedding. It's in a month. A lot can happen by then. Let's do something fun tonight. You and I."

Her amusement dissolved. "Nah, I can't. Ben got tickets for the ballet in town. I gotta get ready soon."

"Oh."

"Sorry, Addi." She winced. "Can I take a rain check?"

"Yes. Don't worry. I'll try to catch up on my sleep. I've been working nonstop, and my insomnia isn't cured. I still wake up in the middle of the night and toss and turn."

She clasped her hands. "You need your *non-friend* Tucker to rock your nights, girl. You've been having insomnia since you met him. So maybe he holds the secret key to the cure. Like he induces it and then has to heal it." She allowed the idea to settle in my brain for a beat, then added, "Yes, I bet it'd work."

"Ohmygod. Do you hear yourself? You speak nonsense."

"Do I? It sounds perfectly sane from my end."

I nudged her side. "*Blah, blah, blah.* Just go get ready now. Ben hates being late."

My roommate left, and her words replayed in my head. *He induces it and then has to heal it.* What if her words rang true? What if Tucker was the answer to my sleepless nights? To my restless body and mind?

Without thinking, I opened my laptop and browsed the web for a few minutes until I found what I was looking for, then closed it with a thud before retreating to my bedroom to gather everything I might need.

Four hours later, I landed at Chicago O'Hare Airport with only a small carry-on and my courage.

Pretending I had to send back the pictures through the mail, Dahlia gave me Tucker's address, and I recited it to the cab driver.

I kept my back straight the entire ride, hoping my plan would not fail me, or my humiliation would just skyrocket into space. Not that I cared normally, but I didn't want things to be awkward between us. Also, I was trying to forget I was riding in some stranger's car. Cabs were gross. Who knew what had happened in this backseat before?

"Lady, you look nervous," the driver said in a strong accent.

I rolled my shoulders back. "No. I don't do nervous. I'm rather excited…or something close to it."

My stomach was tied in knots. Excitement wasn't the right emotion. My insides turned into a ball of nerves the closer I got to my destination.

I paid the fare, grabbed my bag, and with my chin high and back tall, I entered the impressive building that matched the address I'd noted on my phone.

A man in his sixties greeted me. "Good evening, miss. May I help you with something tonight?"

"Hi. Sure. I'm here to see Tucker Philips."

"Who should I announce?"

Nervous jitters awoke inside me. No, I didn't want this man to call Tucker and ruin my surprise arrival. Our daily phone talk was scheduled in less than ten minutes. I needed to up my game not to miss my opportunity window.

"Sir," I said, using my most convincing tone and smiling sheepishly. "Tucker is the groomsman at our best friends' wedding. We have things to discuss. It's kind of important. I was hoping to surprise him. I'll have him call you as soon as I'm up there, or you can ride the elevator with me to make sure I'm not some crazy ex-girlfriend."

"Oh, so you know Mr. Peterson?"

Feeling Lady Luck on my side, I added, "Yes. Nick is marrying my best friend. We're about to become this one big family, the four of us." An idea crossed my mind. I opened the photo app on my phone and swiped to the pictures of the bachelor-bachelorette party night. I flipped my phone to show the man pictures of the four of us and of Tucker and me in our matching T-shirts.

He studied me for a long beat. "It's not in the building

rulebook to let anyone not on the list go up unannounced. Mr. Philips is a nice guy. And he's quite private too."

"He is," I agreed. "We're working on a video montage together. He's providing me pictures of Nick as a child. Do you have kids?"

The man's lips twitched, and he grabbed his phone from the inner pocket of his jacket. "Two. They're adults now. My daughter just gave birth to our first grandbaby. Lela. She's two weeks old." He thumbed the screen and showed me the picture of a little pink-swaddled bundle.

"Oh, she's beautiful. And tiny. You must be proud."

"I am. She's an angel." He put his phone away. "What's your name, miss?"

"Addi."

"Listen, I'll make an exception this time and let you go up. In a couple of minutes, I'll call Mr. Philips to make sure everything is fine with you being here. You seem like a nice young lady, but I'm old and have witnessed a lot of craziness in my life. If you bullshit me, I'll have security remove you faster than you can spell my name."

My eyes darted to his name tag. "Your name's Leo."

"Exactly."

"I promise I'm one of the good ones, Leo. I flew here to talk wedding business. And see Tucker."

He nodded, and after I thanked him, I moved forward to drop a chaste kiss on his cheek before entering the elevator, ready for the next phase of my plan.

———

When the doors opened on the forty-sixth floor, I held my breath, desperate to calm the thundering of my heart. I didn't do nervous. No, I wasn't programmed to feel anxiety like the rest of humanity. Until now. For the first time in my short existence, my organs were playing pinballs inside my body.

In ways I couldn't explain, Tucker always sent my heart into an exciting yet fearful dance.

I stopped in front of the mirror in the hallway to fix my hair, touch up my lipstick, and adjust my loose white top. Paired with denim cut-offs and ankle cowboy boots, I looked Southern-sexy. And hot enough to seduce the man living a few doors down.

With a white-knuckled grip on my bag, I padded toward the door number I'd memorized. I checked my phone, and it told me Tucker would be calling in... *Five, four, three, two, one.* Okay, he wasn't that punctual, but close enough. I waited for the device to ring and brought it to my ear after accepting the call.

"Hey, big guy. You're late," I teased.

He hesitated for a second, no doubt checking the time.

"Three minutes. I wouldn't call it late."

"Three minutes is three minutes. I could've decided not to wait for you."

He let out a chuckle that made my insides flutter with warmth. "Keep telling yourself that, Wilde. I'm certain you're addicted to me by now."

"You wish."

A grin took my face hostage as I knocked on the door.

"Can you gimme a minute? Someone's here. Must be the concierge."

"Sure."

He yanked the door open, his eyes searching the surrounding space before settling on my silhouette, as if to make sure I wasn't a figment of his imagination.

"Hey you."

His throat worked, and I found the movement enticing.

"What are you doing here?" he asked, a frown carving lines into his forehead.

"Thought you'd like some company."

His dark irises surveyed the length of me. "How did you get here?"

"Plane. And cab. The usual."

Tucker blinked, his frown deepening. "Wait. You took a cab? On your own? To see me?"

I shrugged.

"I thought you said cabs freaked you out." His eyes searched my face. For a hint. Or anything he was dying to read there.

"They do. So?"

"Fuck, Wilde. I'm touched. You braved your fear of gross vehicles for me." He rested his hand over his heart, looking as if he were genuinely impressed with me.

I huffed. "I wouldn't call it a fear, but you're right. I did. In the heat of the moment, I almost forgot about it."

He stashed his phone in his back pocket and reached me in a single stride. He wrapped his muscular arms around me, lifted me up, and pressed me against him. In that instant, I felt so special. To him.

When he put me back down on my feet, my front brushed his strong torso, and my body electrified at the contact. For a minute, we stared into each other's eyes, neither of us breaking the charged silence.

Until he cleared his throat. "Wilde, are you here to invite me on a date?" he finally asked, the husky sound of his voice reverberating through me.

I shook my head, my smile anchored to my lips.

"Are you here to give the pictures back?"

I shook my head again.

"Are you here because you missed me?"

I offered him a one-shoulder shrug. "Maybe."

His ringtone broke the moment. We both ignored it. But soon, it rang again.

"Oh. It must be Leo."

"Leo?"

"The guy downstairs. He's meant to check with you to make sure I didn't force myself into your apartment—and your life—like some lunatic."

Tucker frowned. "Wait. Why?"

"Just answer. I'll explain later."

"Now that you mention it, how did you get up here?"

I offered him my most irresistible smirk. "I have my ways." I pretended to zip my lips with my fingers.

He chuckled before answering his phone. After exchanging a few words with the doorman, he brought his attention back to me, and intertwined his fingers with mine. He reached for my bag with his other hand. "Let me show you around." He stopped and turned to watch me. "Are you spending the night?"

"It depends."

"On what?" he asked, his gravelly voice now sending shivers through my entire being.

"You."

His throat rippled, and something glinted in his eyes. He said nothing, but seconds later, I found myself standing in his bedroom. He dropped my bag on his bed without an explanation. "Let's talk about it later."

I nodded and followed him to the kitchen.

"Had dinner?"

"Nope. But I heard from a respectable source that Chicago can't feed its people. I'm scared I'll starve tonight."

"That's a shame. I wouldn't want you to go to bed famished. Remember, I have plenty on me I can feed you with. Too bad you're picky. If you change your mind, all you have to do is ask. And I'll stuff your mouth." He lifted his dark brows, a smirk tugging at his lips.

Barely keeping a straight face, I gasped for show, feigned surprise, and delivered a comeback. "So generous and selfless of you, Tuck. Feeding Chicago's people with seeds and love juice, one woman at a time. Yeah, I can see the appeal."

"You don't know what you're missing, sweetheart." He bumped his shoulder against mine playfully. "Let me fix you something then, or we can order in. See? I can be a gentleman."

"Who said I came here for a gentleman?"

He smirked. "Touché."

We exchanged smiles, and I went along with him while he showed me his place.

"The view is magnificent from here," he said as we stared through the giant wall of panoramic windows in his living room. "But after a while, it loses its appeal because I don't see it anymore. My eyes are used to the sight. It's a shame, though."

"I can't wait to see it in daylight. I'm sure it's beautiful in the morning."

"So, you *are* spending the night." It was more an affirmation than a question.

"I guess I am. Careful though, I always sleep naked."

A groan left his lips. "I can work with that. Barely."

"Great." I couldn't stop grinning like a fool.

———

We sat cross-legged on the floor by the window, the city lights below trying to catch my attention. The entire time, though, my gaze rested on Tucker. He had changed into normal-people's clothes, which meant a T-shirt, the one I sent him—which sent giddy flutters to my stomach—and a pair of what could pass as sweatpants. No Esteban Fu or Jaxon Arison in sight tonight. In my opinion, he looked even more incredible than in his usual dress-up attire.

"Why are you here, Wilde?" he asked as I battled him for the last chunk of chicken from the Chinese takeout we'd ordered. At first, we passed the containers back and forth, but now we were sitting side by side, our chopsticks becoming swords, reaching for the best pieces.

"Are we playing the same game we did when you came to visit me the other night?" I asked with a lifted brow, plastering the most innocent look on my face.

He shook his head with a loud sigh. "Why won't you just tell me?"

"Because it's more fun this way. When you know nothing about my devious plans."

"Devious?" He mirrored my expression. "Will it get me into trouble? Again?"

"Maybe. Maybe not. Are you willing to find out?"

His Adam's apple bobbed, and I got entranced by the movement, missing his answer.

"What?" I asked, my voice so rough I had to cough to clear my throat.

"Am I so handsome it's distracting you, Wilde?"

"Nah, keep dreaming, big guy."

He pointed at my face with a finger. "Tell that to the flush on your cheeks."

"Not blushing."

"Oh, you're just bothered. Fine by me." He waggled his dark brows before moving in, his lips looking too freaking delicious for his own good—and all mine.

Tucker Philips emanated an energy that was too powerful to ignore. At least, my body had a hard time staying indifferent. For once in my life, I enjoyed not being in control and being chased after.

"Addison, why are you here?"

Oh my dear God. Goose bumps blossomed on my arms at his mere whisper of my name. No way could I resist this man. Was Rebecca onto something after all?

I swallowed, trying to grasp the remaining threads of my composure. "See, my roommate has this theory. About you."

"About me?" he echoed.

"Mm-hmm." I paused, calming the skittish hormones that were desperate to get him naked. "She says you're responsible for my insomnia. That you induced it. After our little Nashville adventure. And that if I want to cure it, well, you gotta fuck it out of me."

"Fuck it out of you?"

I nodded.

"Is this true? Do you need me to fuck away your insomnia, Wilde?"

Jesus, why did he always have to be so damn sexy every time he opened his mouth?

"I traveled all this way so we could test her theory. What do you say?"

"You know we're not supposed to have sex, you and I, right? We agreed."

I nodded again.

"And you know I'll get in deep trouble with your best friend if we get caught, right?"

I nodded half a dozen times. "Does it mean you won't do it? My sleep schedule is all over the place. I'm a tired shit show during the day and can't find a soothing position at night. Tuck, help a girl out. Desperate times call for desperate measures. Please. Fuck that curse out of me."

"Did I say I wouldn't do it?" He shot me a cocky sideways grin.

"Nope."

"So, Wilde, ask me again. With that dirty mouth of yours that always gets me hard as a rock."

"Tucker Philips, would you please get me naked on the floor and fuck this state of insomnia you 'might have induced' out of me? Over and over again for the rest of the weekend?" I used my fingers to air-quote the words.

"When you ask it like this, so charmingly, how can I refuse?"

I grabbed the hem of my shirt, about to peel the fabric off me, when he stopped me with a hand.

Tucker inched closer, his breath caressing the shell of my ear. "Wilde, not so fast. I wanna seduce you first. We always skip the foreplay." He cupped my face, his gaze heavy on mine. Hot air filled every bit of space between us. Full of sexual tension and lust sparks. He traced the contours of my lips with his thumb, his focus on my mouth.

"No. You took me on a date. We have daily hour-long chats, and we had a picnic just now. It counts for something. Told you already I'm not here for a gentleman."

He pushed back, scooting away from me. "I'm a gentleman. I always am."

My breath caught midway to my lungs. "Show me then. Rock my world." My voice quivered. My senses heightened at the sight of him. The sexual energy emanating from him fueled my brain.

Tucker removed the bottle from my hand and placed it on the floor beside me. The hammering of my heart filled my ears as it rebounded off the walls of my skull. "You're gorgeous, Wilde. Just so you know, if you were my girl, I would never hurt you. You're too precious."

His words, even though I knew we would never be a couple, made an impression on me. They meant something to me. Maybe not all men were heartbreakers—or cheaters—after all. For a second, I wished Tucker Philips was available. Because the friendship we had developed in the last two weeks was something I cherished. And something that did not occur often in a lifetime.

He gripped my waist with his big hands and pulled me to him, his loud intake of air vibrating through me.

"How do you seduce a woman, Tuck?" I asked, breathless.

"Somehow, it's different with you. You're not just a girl I'll forget all about in the morning. You are…*you.*"

"What does it mean?"

"You know things about me I've never told anyone. Even when we're doing this, it's not a game to me. Because I would never use you this way."

My words lodged in my throat. The sincerity of his words affected me in a deeper way than I would've ever thought.

After swiping on his phone for a moment, soft music began playing from a sound system I couldn't see, and Tucker tightened his grip around my body.

"Dance with me."

My palm found his, while his other hand kept me pressed to him. I was so under his spell that I almost failed to recognize the song. My lips curled up as I leaned back to watch him. "Our song," I whispered.

"It'll forever be," he confirmed with a sexy wink. One I bet could set my panties on fire if they weren't already drenched.

Gosh, he was good at this, I thought to myself. I was the seduction queen, but right now, this man facing me was throwing me out of my own game.

**...Because all I wanted was to
call your name
All I wanted was to claim you
as mine...**

At this moment, I forgot our arrangement was just that
—an arrangement—between two consenting adults. I
believed I could be all these things, and that someone
could love me, like really love me, for who I was. For me.

Tucker's mouth descended over mine, and he brushed
my lips in the gentlest of caresses. I shivered from head to
toe. A guttural moan escaped my mouth before I could
leash it in.

He released my hand and pressed his against my warm
cheek, grazing the corner of my mouth with the pad of his
thumb.

"Fuck, Wilde. Why are you here again?"

"So you can fuck my insomnia out of me," I whispered, breathless, overwhelmed with foreign sensations.

His hands traveled down, and he traced the length of
the junction between my thighs with a finger. I sucked in a
shaky breath. Oh dear freaking God.

A moan tumbled out of my mouth. This man. He had
a way of making my body sing every time he touched me.

Unable to contain the desire pooling low in my belly
and radiating to all my cells, I rolled my hips over his hand,
now rubbing me over the fabric of my shorts.

Tucker spoke next to my ear, his words a murmur
against my skin. "Just like this, sweetheart. Come on, chase
that pleasure." His breathing hitched, his movements
growing faster. "Yes, like this."

A moment later, I tilted my head back, my eyes
closed, bitting my bottom lip, as elation built deep inside
my core. Then I pressed my forehead against his hard

chest, barely able to drive some oxygen in. All the sensations swirling inside me captured my body and took me hostage as ribbons of pleasure coiled around me. My knees buckled as an orgasm hit me. Powerful and unchained.

My toes curled.

A loud whimper left my lips.

Tucker growled, holding me with both hands, as I tried to regain my control, weakened by the relief he provided me.

"Better?" he asked, his lips claiming mine in a dance I could easily lose myself in.

I nodded, unable to express anything in words.

His hard erection pushed against my lower belly, and I palmed it through his pants.

His hand entwined in my hair as he kissed me with purpose, eating my lips, savoring my tongue, starting a fire deep within me.

We would combust together.

Right now, none of this felt like a fling or something we could wake up from. Because I had never felt this good in my entire life. As if I belonged in his arms. As if our minds, our bodies, and our souls were one, and nothing could come between us.

I grabbed the hem of his T-shirt with trembling fingers, ready to discard the piece of fabric, when he stopped me with a hand.

"Addison, stop."

Something in his words—or was it his tone?—jolted me, and I jumped back.

Tucker blinked, and my heart skipped a beat at torment written on his handsome face.

"What?" I asked once I found my voice.

He rubbed his nape, shook one leg to relieve the

tension tenting his pants, and exhaled. "We can't... I can't... We said..."

"Can we make one exception? For tonight only. I'm so tired all the time."

"Wilde—" Uncertainty shadowed his face.

I blinked. A lump grew in my throat, and a rock pressed against my chest. The roots of rejection spread to every inch of me.

I ran a hand over my face, my eyes brimming with tears. I should've never come here tonight. This was a mistake. We said no strings attached and no sex, and then I traveled two hours to get fucked by a man who would never be more to me than a few nights' stand.

I pivoted on my heels, ready to bolt out of there and forget all about this stupid idea of mine—or Rebecca's. Yes, she was the one who put those ludicrous thoughts into my head. Why did I follow her advice? What was wrong with me? Nothing made sense in my life anymore. Did I fail myself so badly in my relationships with losers that I forgot who I was along the way? Had I become so desperate?

Exhaustion hit me and chased away the last flecks of lust still lingering inside me.

"Sorry. I should go," I muttered, not turning around to glance at Tucker one last time. I would never let him see the pain spreading across my face. No. I was Addison Wilde, a strong and independent woman. I didn't need men to feel complete.

I hurried toward the master bedroom to fetch my bag. I'd never been to Chicago before, but I was sure I could find a hotel downtown and spend the next two days either locked in a room, throwing my stupid self a fueled-by-ice-cream pity party, or play tourist. I'd always wanted to see the Bean and eat a deep-dish pizza. Here was my chance. Yay.

I crossed the threshold of the bedroom, using the back of my hand to wipe the tears welling up in my eyes.

Two muscular arms wrapped around me from behind, halting my escape. "Wilde, wait." Just the sound of Tucker's voice appeased something deep inside me.

"Let go of me. I need to get out of here," I said, carrying no conviction in my voice.

"Wilde, look at me. Are you crying?"

I cringed. How could Tucker always read me like an open book?

I spoke through clenched teeth. "I am not."

Instead of releasing his grip around my waist, he tightened it.

"Tuck, let me go. Please," I begged. But soon my words twisted into sobs I couldn't contain.

Without saying anything, he spun me in his embrace, his arms circling my heaving shoulders and holding me against him.

He murmured into my ear, "Shhh... Shhh..."

Tears I didn't even know I'd been holding back spilled onto his shirt, while he ran his hand through my hair and kissed the top of my head.

Once my sobs quieted, he took a step back. Using both palms to cradle my face, he erased the traces of moisture left on my skin with his thumbs.

"Addison, I didn't push you away. I was just trying not to put at risk what we have and destroy what we've been building for the last two weeks. I want you. God knows I do. Every inch of me does. But I made a promise to my best friend. And failed to keep it twice already. And I made the promise to you that I can keep it in my pants for over a month. This isn't me.

I'm the guy people trust. No matter how strong this pull between us is, I'm sure we can wait till the wedding. Doesn't mean I want you gone, though. You're my first girlfriend. Huh? Why do I always say it like this? You're the first girl I'm friends with. It means something to me. I feel different around you. Good different. And by the way, your brand of crazy has grown on me, but we said no strings attached. The last thing I want is to hurt you. I've never slept with a girl I considered my friend before. This is all new to me. And truthfully, I'm not sure how we should proceed because I still wanna be your friend after the wedding. Even if it means no more sexual benefits from it. Let's not fuck this up. We agreed we'd have sex the weekend of the wedding and then stop."

I snorted.

Why did my first rebound have to be a nice guy?

Chapter 13
Tucker

"Y ou should have been a jerk," Addison said, her voice throaty now after all the tears she cried. "Then it would be easier to just move on and never talk to you again. Why do you have to be nice to me? It's fucking everything up."

A warm laugh broke the tension that had settled between us as it left my mouth. "Sweetheart, don't repeat that. I have a reputation to uphold. Don't ruin it for me."

Her eyes were still glistening, but a grin made its way to her lips. It eased some of the uneasiness that had taken over me after she'd run away from me when I stopped our make-out session. Still, I had a hard time justifying why I did it. All I craved was to fuck her the way she asked me to, till the morning, and start all over again. But something inside me—call it the voice of reason, surprisingly sounding so much like Nick's—nagged that it was a bad idea. That I'd regret getting too close to her. Too comfortable in our relationship. Also, I meant everything I said. Our budding friendship was important to me, and I refused to jeopardize it because once the sex part was done and over with, our relationship would suffer, no doubt. I really appreciated the bond we shared now. It was unique. Nothing I'd ever experienced before. Easy and entertaining all at once.

Jesus, what was happening to me? First, my dick went on a sabbatical, and now this. Where did the voices in my head come from? They toyed with my mind, uninvited.

All my life, Nick had been my best friend, my brother, but also my confidant and family. I rarely opened up to people, but when I did, he was my go-to person. But somehow, in a matter of weeks, Addison Wilde had become the person I wanted to confide in. The one I wanted to call when I had doubts, needed advice, or a kick in the ass. Or the last voice I wished to hear before going to bed.

It made no sense, but hey, at this point, I had stopped asking myself why. We both had trust issues, and I could recognize a lot of myself in her. Or perhaps most of our friends were in serious relationships, and we, single people, had to stick together. No matter what, I relished her company and was in no hurry to get rid of her anytime soon.

"Don't go," I pleaded. "Stay. You can either sleep in the guest room or share my bed. I won't have sex with you, but I could…huh…hold you. I've never really done that before, but my gut is telling me this is what you might need from me... What we both need."

Addison looked away. "Huh, I don't know. Not sure if it's…if it's a good idea."

"Think about it."

She yawned, and I followed suit.

"Tired?"

"Exhausted."

"Let's go to bed, okay? You need a good night's rest. I'll watch over you. To make sure the insomnia stays away. What do you say?"

She offered me a small shrug.

"I'll take that as a yes." I tipped her face in my direction with one finger. "Were you serious when you said you sleep naked?" I asked with a wink, trying to bring back the flirtatious ease between us.

Addison burst into a fit of laughter, and the sight filled my heart with peace. Yeah, we would be okay.

"Maybe. Now you'll never know."

"Stay here. I have an idea." I went to my closet, grabbed a T-shirt, and handed it to her.

She quirked a brow, watching me with suspicion swimming in her vibrant blue eyes.

"Wear my T-shirt."

"Tucker Philips, you own mortal clothes?"

"Shhh, I told you already not to spread rumors about me. But truth be told, I am human. Since we're having a sleepover, it's only fitting that I lend you clothes. This way, you won't have to sleep naked, and we can share a bed. It's been forever since I had a friend over for the night"—I studied her face—"in my bedroom." The color had returned to her complexion.

"In this case, I'm flattered to be *the one*."

She started toward the bathroom, and I clutched her elbow, stopping her in her tracks. "Are we good? Tell me the truth."

She nodded. "We are… We…we will be… My emotions are all over the place right now. It's the…huh… the lack of sleep. Sorry for being a train wreck. I'm usually not offended by many things." She smoothed the T-shirt I'd given her, rubbing the worn cotton between her fingers.

"Thanks for this." She brought it to her nose and took a whiff before disappearing into the en-suite and leaving me on my own, wondering what I would do with her for an entire weekend.

We had already crossed lines in the past, and now I had no idea how to act, my usual game not helping at all.

Once she emerged wearing only panties and my T-shirt, it almost knocked me off my feet. *Fucking fuck.* God had to help me here. I prayed to a few saints in my head, pushing down the tautness taking over the lower half of my body.

Addison paused in the doorway, one hand on her hip and the other resting on the frame above her head. "What do you think? Suits me?"

I swallowed. Hard. She looked too freaking hot. The half-mast down below was now a raging boner, taking permanent residence in my boxer briefs, as my eyes traveled all over her gorgeous body. My fingers itched to reacquaint themselves with each curve and dip.

Soft waves of her hair bounced and shimmered with every step. With her makeup removed, her natural beauty was even more alluring. I didn't dare blink, not for even a heartbeat, afraid I'd miss a single second of her dewy, irresistible look. Her legs—satin-smooth and sculpted to perfection, the kind I ached to have wrapped around my waist—affected me more than I cared to admit.

"Perfect," I croaked. The rest of my words got stuck in my throat.

I rushed and locked myself in the bathroom. Any longer and I'd be tearing through my trousers, desperate for her hands on me. Once under the scorching stream of the shower, I fisted my cock, desperate to jerk off and relieve the tightness winding through me, strangling my voice of reason.

My mind drifted back to Addison waiting for me in my bedroom, and the gesture felt wrong. All kinds of wrong. My dick softened in my fist, and I showered quickly.

Something was happening to me, shattering years of existence and everything I had ever lived by. First, I refused sex with a gorgeous woman I was definitely attracted to, even after she begged me to. And now, I refused to come into my fist—or rather my body did—because of said woman. Banging my forehead against the wall, I cursed myself and all my *they make no sense* resolutions.

When I exited the bathroom, Addison was already in my bed, buried under the comforter, looking like she belonged there.

Another surge of misplaced longing spread through me.

"You've decided to sleep here," I teased, drawing the towel snugger around my waist. My penis and my logic fought each other, and I had no idea which one to listen to.

"Yes. Unless you've changed your mind…"

I hated the indecision I could read on her face. Turning my back to her and using the time to give my raging hormones a pep talk, I slipped my ass into a pair of boxer briefs and sprang on the mattress beside her.

"No, I haven't changed my mind." I flicked the switch and shifted onto my side. "Now come here, so I can hold you and scare that insomnia away."

And just like that, Addison Wilde had tamed the wild part of my existence—and my heart—in the most natural way.

———

The rumpling of sheets woke me up in the middle of the night. I pulled the woman in my arms closer to my front, but she writhed away from my embrace. "Hey, Wilde. You awake?"

She rolled to her side until she faced me. "Sorry. Did I wake you up?"

"Don't worry about it. How long have you been up?"

She traced the length of my chest, just between my pecs, with a fingertip. A shiver zinged down my spine and stole my breath. "No idea. A while."

"Why didn't you wake me up?"

"You were sleeping peacefully. I love hearing you breathe. It quiets my mind."

I untangled myself from her and moved to my feet. Grabbing two hoodies from my closet, I handed her one.

"Huh? What are you doing?"

"Come on. Wear this and I'll show you."

She rose to her knees, sliding her arms through the sleeves as I closed in and pulled the hood over her head.

"Don't want you to get cold."

When I inched back, I noticed how perfect she looked dressed in my clothes, and some invisible clamp tightened around my traitorous heart. The thought sent my pulse into a frenzy and my mind spinning.

Her voice grounded me, pulling me back to the present and keeping the panic at bay. "You know I'm still half-naked, right?"

I shrugged. "Just a sec." I offered her a pair of sweat-pants, way too big for her.

"Tuck, I can get some from my suitcase."

"No. I want you to wear these." I helped her into them and tied the drawstring at the waist as much as I could. I rolled the waistband and pant legs until she could walk without tripping.

Once satisfied, I held out my hand for her to grab and pulled her toward the living room. I grabbed the blanket from the couch, added a few pillows, and led her into the hallway.

"Where are we going?" she whispered.

"You'll see."

We took the emergency staircase and climbed four flights of stairs until we reached the fiftieth floor. Then we took another door that brought us to the rooftop.

"Whoa, this is… Wow," Addison exclaimed, her eyes drinking in the city skyline. A soft breeze swept across our faces as I tugged her toward my favorite spot.

I set the pillows and blanket on a wooden deck next to where a few tenants were growing plants and herbs, and we lay on our backs.

"Pretend we're stargazing," I said as we stared at the inky sky, the lights from the city preventing us from seeing anything other than their glow.

We remained silent for a long while, Addison's hand nestled in mine, the sound of our shared breaths blending with the noise of the busy streets below.

After a moment, she flipped to her side, and with her arm propped over my chest, she rested her chin on top of her hand. Her blue eyes bore into mine, and her eyebrows furrowed as if she was trying to read something I couldn't guess.

She sighed and motioned around with her free hand. "I'm sure girls love it when you bring them here. It's magical."

As if stung by a bee I jolted upright and sat bolt straight, making her jump in surprise. "Wilde, you're the first person I've ever brought here. It's my secret spot. My *I need to think* zone. Nobody has ever come here with me before. Not even my friends…" I shook my head and sighed, lowering my voice. "You're the first one."

Her eyes rounded, and she blinked a few times. "No, can't be. You're joking, right?"

I shook my head again and decreased the distance between us, pushing strands of her hair behind her ear. Sparks flared at my fingertips and I yanked my hand away, rubbing it on my pant leg. "Nope. I would never lie to you. When I can't sleep…huh…I come up here and let the calm of the night push my worries away. I thought it could do you some good too."

A pink hue colored her cheeks, making her look younger and more vulnerable in the low light of the night. "You serious?"

"Dead serious, sweetheart."

We watched each other for a fraction of a second, and it was enough to increase the tempo of my heart.

Addison moved to her knees, and looped her arms around my neck. She pressed a soft kiss to my cheek, her lips soft and warm against my skin. "Thank you, Tuck. It means a lot. I'm happy you trust me enough to share your special spot with me."

We settled back into our earlier positions, on our backs and our fingers knitted together as our eyes returned to the dark sky.

After a long stretch of silence her voice sounded tentative when she finally spoke. "Can I ask you something?"

I nodded.

"What happened in your life that made you decide you're not worthy of love?"

I stiffened at her words and shut my eyes, trying to wash away the barbs piercing my heart. How could this woman read me so well? How did she secure a key to my soul?

I cleared my throat, coughing to hide my discomfort. "Sweetheart, you're wrong. It's a choice I've made. And so far, I haven't regretted it. I don't feel like putting my heart out there. I prefer it safe and sound inside my chest. Not crumbled because someone else chose to smash it."

Thorns sprouted down my throat, and I breathed around their sharp edges to avoid choking. Would my simple explanation convince her to let go and not pursue the topic?

Addison said nothing and tightened her squeeze around my fingers. She brought our joint palms over her heart.

"Okay, fine. Don't tell me. Sorry I asked. You already know my story. Parts of it at least… I thought maybe you'd wanna share yours too. You're clearly not ready, so when you are, remember I'm here. No judgment, just a listening ear."

She kissed my knuckles without letting go of my hand, a quiet reassurance that she was there and that I could trust her. All I had to do was lower my guard and she would truly listen. In that moment, I realized what we shared wasn't just physical. It was a genuine friendship, something rare and worth cherishing. Something I had never experienced with a woman in my life. The sweet touch of her lips filled my heart with a warmth difficult to define, but powerful and soothing all at once.

"My dad," I finally said.

Addison said nothing, but I could tell by her alertness that she was listening.

"My parents… They met at seventeen and fell in love hard. Then they had me… My mother was my dad's entire world. God, how he loved her… I was just a kid, and it was so evident to me."

I swallowed. I hadn't told that story in—well, never. Nick and Jace knew most of it because we grew up together, and I couldn't hide what happened from them.

Yet, they never got to know every detail. The entire picture. Even when they asked, I would stay mute about it or change the subject because it hurt too fucking much to relive that year of my life.

Addison shifted closer, until her full length was pressed against my body. Everywhere our bodies touched, her warmth diffused through me, reminding me I wasn't alone and that she cared.

"A few months after I turned twelve, my dad caught my mom with Ron, our neighbor. They were having an affair. It had been going on for a couple of months… I-I didn't know the specifics. Nobody told me, and I never asked. Anyway, it shattered my dad. Like I said, he loved my mom so much that he would have given her the world if she'd asked for it." I paused, reliving the most hurtful memory of my childhood. "Instead of kicking her out, my father… huh…tried to patch things up and give their marriage another shot. My mom…she...wouldn't stop seeing Ron and asked for a divorce three months later. That day, my dad offered her two choices. Be a family, the three of us, or not to fight him in court for my custody if she decided to leave him… Leave us."

I paused, trying to put some order into my emotions.

"But the truth was, she had just learned she was pregnant…with twins. And… Well, the babies were Ron's. She'd kept it a secret at first, but when my dad offered her those two choices, that's when she dropped the baby-bomb on him. It fucking ruined everything. In the end, she chose her other family over me and my dad, leaving him heartbroken. Leaving *us* broken."

"Oh, Tucker. I'm so sorry." Now propped on her side, Addison cupped my cheek with her hand, her chin resting in the crook of my shoulder.

"Afterward, I saw her for a month during summer

vacations and four days during the holidays. That was about it. After a while, we lost touch. She hasn't been my mom in a long time."

"And your father? What happened? Did he ever remarry or something?"

"He started sleeping around. And drinking more than usual. Sometimes, he wouldn't come home at night. When I turned fifteen, I learned he often fell asleep at the bar he visited a few too many times each week. They started calling me when he was passed out to take him home. When I turned nineteen, we had a chat. I told him I couldn't deal with his shit anymore. I was tired of being his dad, making sure he had clean clothes to wear to work and a stocked refrigerator. He finally accepted help and emerged victorious from his self-destructive cycle. He has a girlfriend now. Has been with her for almost three years. I can tell that even though he loves ever, she's not my mom and will never occupy the same place in his heart. Or maybe my mother fucked with his ability to love again."

Addison buried herself deeper into my embrace. I wrapped my arms tight around her, holding her, wishing we could stay like this forever. "I'm sorry it happened to you, but you gotta remember you're not your dad. What your mom did was wrong. I can't believe she pushed you away. No mother should ever do that to her children…to her own babies. It's not your fault she messed up or that he hit rock bottom. You deserve to stop hurting over mistakes that were never yours to begin with. This whole situation had nothing to do with you. You can't live your life expecting the worst to happen all the time. I've had my share of shitty relationships, and my heart has been broken too many times to count, yet I still consider love precious. I'll never stop believing I deserve it too, because once I find the right person, it will mean that all the past struggles and pain have led me to the one I'm supposed to be with, and none of it was in vain. Just some part of my journey."

I placed a kiss on the crown of her head, letting it linger. Every word she spoke resonated in me. My heart banged loudly against my ribs. I blinked, chasing a foreign emotion away, not ready to assess its meaning. "Thank you. It means a lot. Your words and the fact that you listened to me as I rambled about my childhood."

"Tuck—"

I silenced her with a finger pressed to her lips as she tilted her head so we could look at each other, past our bodies and into our souls. "Just so you know, I've never told the story to anyone before. Not in detail, at least."

She sucked in a sharp breath. "For real? I'm your first again? Color me flattered." She paused, regrouping her thoughts. "Why did you then?"

"Because whatever happens between us in the future, I consider you my friend. You once told me I had trust issues with women, and I denied it. You weren't so wrong after all… Except for Nick and Jace, you're the first person who has figured me out. Whom I have let in. I-I can't explain it, but it feels right. I really thought I was doing a good job hiding that broken part of me."

"Sorry I unmasked you, big guy."

"Sure you are."

"Maybe I missed my vocation."

"Shrink? I'd come for a consultation, but you'd have to wear glasses. They'd look high-school-principal kind of hot on you."

She nudged my chest. "Pervert." She hesitated for a second. "I had a boyfriend I really loved in college. Shawn. I saw myself going the distance with him. He got me. We talked about moving in together, traveling the world, all those crazy dreams you have at nineteen."

"What happened?"

"One day we were touring apartments, and the next he said I was suffocating him. He left for Asia to backpack all summer, fell in love with someone else, and I never saw him again."

"I'm sorry."

"Don't be. Most of my relationships have had tragic endings…for me. I got left behind and lied to more times than you can imagine."

"Oh… Now I get your anger toward men," I said.

"It's not really anger. Wariness would be a more accurate description. One day, I'll find *the one*. I just haven't met him yet."

I dropped a kiss on her forehead, and we lay there on the rooftop of my apartment building a bit longer. My confessions swirled around us. Some parts of me relaxed, and others got tensed. That always seemed to be the case when I was spending time with Addison.

"My parents separated when I was young. Phoenix and I—he's my twin brother—we barely saw our dad for two years because he was dealing with stuff. Eventually, he sought help, and my parents got back together. Phen…he lives in Europe now, so we barely ever see each other. My parents spend a lot of time there to help him out. He has twins of his own… One day, I hope we'll find our way back to each other. I miss him." She paused. "Guess, we have something else in common."

"What?"

"Twins run in our families."

We both remained silent.

"I know your weekend here is nothing like you planned, but I'm glad I told you about my parents," I said. "It was about time I got it off my chest so that it stopped eating me from the inside. Thank you for trusting me with your confessions too."

She tipped her head back to watch me with something akin to affection—or an emotion not far from it.

Braced on my elbows, I kept my gaze fixed on her. Neither of us said anything, the depth of our heartfelt confessions saturating the air. After a while, I said, "You know what? This little trick of yours—having me open up —helped me get rid of a pile of rocks that had been sitting on my chest for as long as I can remember. Thanks for being my friend, Wilde. I'm grateful."

We hugged a little longer until she moved to her feet and held out her hand. "Come on. Let's go to bed."

Hand in hand, we made our way back inside.

A new layer of our relationship had blossomed in the last hour. Now we'd forever be linked by the revelations of our pasts.

After we repositioned ourselves under the covers, Addison whispered, "Thanks for being my friend too."

Her breathing evened, and once I made sure she was asleep, I followed her, hoping we would meet again in our dreams.

Chapter 14

Addison

Four days later, I hurried home after work, excitement running through my veins. Once I showered and changed, I took my time, making sure Tucker would have enough time to receive my surprise delivery before I dialed him. Our daily phone call was all set, but today would be a special one. He just had no idea.

He answered after the third ring. "Hey, sweetheart. Why did I receive a Chinese food delivery under your name just minutes ago?"

I sat on my couch and grabbed the box of orange-glazed chicken and a set of chopsticks I'd picked up on my way from work.

Switching the call to video chat, I set my phone on the throw pillow. "I thought we could have dinner together."

"You thought well," he said, unwrapping his food. "I'm starving. You just got home?"

I let a long breath out. "About twenty minutes ago. I'm so tired. These extra hours I'm putting in are draining all my energy reserves."

"And your insomnia?"

"Still having a blast disturbing my nights. Anyway, that's not why I wanted to ask you on a date tonight." I chewed on a piece of chicken and almost orgasmed from the sweetness.

"Jesus, don't do that when I can see you, Wilde, or I'll take the next plane out of here."

I snickered behind my hand. "You won't. It's not what we've decided."

Tucker shook his head like he couldn't believe he agreed to this. "Now is the time to remind me that I'm the stupidest man you've ever encountered."

"Oh, Tuck. I'm fluent in stupid men, and let me tell you they look nothing like you. You're caring and funny and generous. They are not. See? Two different universes. Back to my surprise. Give me a minute."

I opened the browser on my computer and attached a file I sent via email.

"In a minute or two, you'll receive an email with an attachment. Don't open it until I tell you to."

"Is this some kind of torture you're inflicting on me? Or a plan that will put me at risk?"

I gestured *no* with my head, unable to restrain the stretch of my lips. "None of those. Just something I did and wanted to share with you. Listen, you're the first person I trust to see this. Consider yourself a beta tester. All constructive criticisms will be considered and evaluated afterward. I'm open to new ideas. There will be another version coming in about a month with updates. Ready?"

"Always."

For the next three minutes and forty-seven seconds, we watched the video montage I made of Dahlia and Nick for their wedding. It included an acoustic version of a new song Carter had written and scenes of him as he sang. He filmed it a few months back and sent me the footage. After the wedding, I would update it with pictures and clips from that night.

The song ended, and the last frame was a picture of the future newlyweds and Jack hugging under a tree with the words I added, followed by their wedding date.

To Dahlia and Nick

You two are examples of courage, determination, and love.

Being around you guys makes each of us a better person because you never stopped dreaming and moving forward even when things got rough. That's what makes you two the role models we should all aim to be.

We wish you years of happiness. You deserve the best. Always.

We love you with every bit of our hearts, and we are happy to be a part of your special day.

Tucker and Addison -xx-

"You signed my name?" Tucker asked, his voice sounding huskier than usual.

"Do you want me to remove it? I thought the words

suited for both the best man and the maid of honor since they are our best friends. And have been for so long."

"No. Don't remove it. I'm just touched you thought of including me since you did all the work, which, by the way, is incredible. Better be ready for people to shed some tears. This song…it's perfect."

"It's not ours, but Cart did a great job. I know it's not easy for him to see Dahlia getting married again, but he's come so far emotionally since her last nuptial. Gosh, it's not my story to tell, but he was so heartbroken. It affected all of us to see him hurting so much. He's moving on… Slowly."

"Poor guy. I can't relate because I've never been so in love that it tore my heart open, but I can see how hurtful it can be. They share a special bond. Even I could see it the first time I saw them together."

"I think his latest album was some sort of therapy. To let go of the past and move forward. He deserves greatness. Anyway, let's watch it again, and this time press pause when you have comments or suggestions. Bring it on, big guy."

―――――

Closing my office door behind me, I shot Tucker a quick text. It'd been a few days since our video date, and I crossed my fingers he was still in the mood to spend time together. Because this proposition I had for him was one nobody in their right mind could ever refuse.

Also, I was well aware I possessed something of great value in his eyes.

ME

Hey, groom of mine. Miss me already?

He answered mere seconds later.

TUCKER

Do you want me to miss you, Wilde?

Flutters swirled in my belly. I could picture him sporting a cocky smirk and a glint in his eye, sweeping my body up and down with a slow glance. I shivered as images formed in my mind. *He's a safe choice, Addi. He is unavailable. Just enjoy the company. For now.*

ME

Any plans tomorrow night?

TUCKER

For you, I'll free my schedule. Wanna snuggle? I bet you miss my chest pressed against your back or my hard-on molded between your ass cheeks. Am I right?

I snickered despite myself. Tucker Philips, Chicago's womanizer, offering to cuddle with me. Nobody would believe me if I told them.

ME

Careful, big guy. This could ruin your reputation if I start to blog about it. Are you willing to take the risk?

TUCKER

Yeah. I'd love to be your dirty little secret.

Your place or mine?

ME

Somewhere else. More exotic.

TUCKER

Talk. Now.

I switched the call to video chat, and he accepted within seconds.

Tucker flashed me a ten-thousand-volt grin as he sat behind his desk, unwrapping a sandwich.

"Hey you," I greeted him.

"See?" He motioned to the space around with his finger. "Sitting and ready for any news you're about to deliver."

He curled his lips, showing a row of pearly whites, a contrast to his dark skin. The pink dress shirt he wore, rolled up at the elbow, showcased his corded forearms and the golden watch around his left wrist. Tucker Philips possessed everything to make any male model envious. Pierce Reinart, my jerk of a client, should take a page out of his playbook before thinking he had a shot at piercing this industry, pun intended. Where Tucker was all masculine and projected confidence and oozed sex appeal, Pierce was the cheap used model with no magnetism, a chip on his shoulder, and a condescending attitude.

My eyes were trained on Tucker, and as if he could

read the naughty thoughts swirling inside my head, his grin grew bigger. And more devastating. For me.

I cleared my throat and tried to recall what we were talking about before I started ogling him.

He spoke, and his voice killed my fantasies. "Wilde, what did you wanna tell me?"

With my fingers, I combed the loose tendrils of hair blocking my vision, doing my best to bury the butterflies invading my stomach.

"Oh yes, sorry. Got lost in my head for a second," I muttered. *Smooth, Addi.*

Another smirk shaping his lips threatened to send me back to where I had just escaped from. Damn him. Why did he have to be mouth-watering handsome?

I shook myself free from the new trance that was about to capture me again. "You. Me. Tomorrow. Hockey game. Playoff. I got tickets. Nashville versus Chicago. My hood versus yours. Are you in?"

He blinked, put his lunch down, pretended to unplug his ears with his fingers, and adjusted his tie. "Playoff tickets? Are you for real?"

I nodded. "Got my hands on a pair for the game in Nashville tomorrow. What do you say? I know it's last minute, but we can't waste those. They're worth a little fortune, and I got them as a thank you for a few hours of work I put in."

His nostrils flared. "Tell me they're not from that fucking useless car guy."

"Nah. A friend from high school. Mark. His dad owns a radio station in Nashville. Gave Cart and Dah their first break back in the day. Anyway, I reworked their logo and branding. Guess they were happy. Are you coming with me?"

"This is serious shit. You can't make jokes about tickets like those. Are you tricking me right now?"

I shook my head, unable to keep my face straight at the excitement pouring out from him. "It's real." I watched the awe taking over him, and a chunk of my heart swelled at the sight. "You have exactly two minutes to decide, or I'll invite Nick. Dahlia doesn't care about hockey, even if hockey players are stupidly hot."

Tucker moved his phone so close I saw his face in high-definition. "Keep Nick out of it. I'm your guy."

I clapped my hands together. "Perfect. I knew you'd never be able to resist my charm."

I winked, and he burst into a warm laugh.

"Woman, you're a temptress. You don't need tickets for me to notice you. Let me clear my schedule for tomorrow, and I'll get back to you with an offer of my own. Still on for our chat tonight?"

"Sure. Gotta go, anyway."

We hung up, and before I could resume my work, my phone pinged with a text message.

TUCKER

Don't book transportation just yet. I wanna check something first.

I typed fast as a new set of jitters awoke inside me.

ME

Okay.

For the rest of the day, I worked on a dealership mid-year sale banners and social media campaign, humming Carter's newest song that was released yesterday. The one from his latest album, whose cover and promo material I had designed.

Rebecca knocked on my door after five when I was

gathering my stuff, ready to bolt out of here. Tomorrow I'd work from home before leaving for Nashville.

"Hey, girl," she said. "Don't wait for me tonight. I'm spending the next couple of days at Ben's."

"Soon you'll announce you two are moving in together. You're barely ever home these days."

She shrugged but couldn't contain her enthusiasm. "Yeah, I wouldn't be against it. I think he's the one."

"He is," I agreed. "You two are a perfect match. I'll be in Nashville this weekend, anyway."

She waggled her eyebrows. "Did you get those tickets?"

I danced a little jig without saying anything.

"Oh, and am I wrong to assume you invited Mr. Chicago to join you?"

"Nope. Not wrong."

"Addi, you have no idea what you're doing, right? I can predict him breaking your heart if you're not careful. I see it in your eyes. The yearning. You're not good at hiding your feelings." She stepped forward and hugged me. "Just be careful, okay? I don't want to see you hurting."

"It's just a hockey game, Becca. Don't put too much thought into it. And I'm a big girl. My heart is safe because I know Tucker isn't available. We're allowed to be friends and to enjoy each other's company. So, this is what it is. A friend-date. I heard Nick once say how much Tuck was a dedicated hockey fan. I can't waste these tickets on someone who won't appreciate their value."

"For hockey fans, tickets like these are equivalent to what a marriage proposal is for others. Don't you think he'll assume there's more to your feelings?"

"He is a no-relationship type of guy. Stated it many times already. The ticket is just that. A ticket."

She grabbed my hand in hers, and I followed her through the door. "Just be careful."

"I will."

The gleam in her eyes told me she didn't believe me, but I believed myself—or was trying really hard.

We parted ways on the sidewalk after I promised to send her pictures because Ben was also a huge hockey fan.

Eight o'clock arrived, and Tucker called me on the dot.

"Be ready. Tomorrow, I'll pick you up after lunch. You and I, we're going on a road trip. Dress the part because Chicago is coming to your city, and we'll crush Nashville. The Honky-Tonks aren't good enough to defeat the Busters. If I were you, I'd skip the purple and dress in red. The color of victory."

Laughter shook me, and I wiped my damp eyes with my fingertips. "Oh, you've clearly never been to a game with me, big guy. Let's see who's the biggest and most loyal fan."

"Deal," he said in a deadpan tone. "And by the way, pack a bag because we're spending the entire weekend there. I never got a tour of the city last time. You owe me, Wilde. And I'm cashing out on it."

———

Tucker knocked on my door the next day, dressed in jeans and a Busters red jersey. He looked so different from the way I was used to seeing him, but this playful outfit suited him perfectly.

"Nice jersey," he said as I twirled, showing him my purple Honky-Tonks top with number seventeen printed on the back, and fixed the cap on my head.

"You were saying?" I teased.

"You win, Wilde. Even if you're not wearing the right colors, the cap looks good on you." He leaned in to kiss my cheek. "Ready to go?"

"Yes. Just let me get my bag."

"Let me." He entered my apartment and went straight to my bedroom to grab my stuff.

"Thanks," I said, following him to his rental.

After he criticized all the songs I played on my phone and I disagreed with his musical choices, we let the radio pick the music for us.

"Top three best childhood memories?" I asked after we grabbed takeout and settled ourselves for the four-hour drive.

"Let's see." He reflected on it for a beat. "A vacation at the lake when I was about nine or ten. We rented a cabin. Nick came with us. My parents had to force us out of the water." The memory played in his mind. I could see him getting lost in thought. "Once, on Halloween, Jace, Nick, and I had decided to dress as one big sea monster. We worked on our costumes for months. Jace's mom helped us sew some parts. Anyway, we won the school's best-costume award. It was epic. We received a gallon of candies as the grand prize." He paused. "For a semester, I was part of the soccer team. Not that I wasn't good at it, but I was more into geeky things like reading and numbers than team sports. However, I did enjoy the workout part and started running every morning before school for fun. When my family fell apart, the daily exercise was what kept me grounded and focused. Months later, I entered my first official sponsored run and gathered like two thousand dollars for a charity that helped kids with special needs. My cousin has a syndrome, something about his chromosomes. Anyway, the pride I felt after that day equals nothing else."

"Wow, that's impressive. I can picture you as a teen in my head. I have similar memories of Dah. She left on world tours twice, then got pregnant, married, and became a widow in a span of a few months, and we grew distant for a while. I was still in college, trying to figure out my future and remain active on the party scene, while Dahlia became an adult overnight. Growing up, I was the one not following the rules, always up for a good time. She was the mature one, the old soul. One decision changed the rest of her life. At twenty, she had plenty of money, but that came with a lot of obligations. I had student loan debts and an adventurous mindset. She's my best friend…forever has been. We've always found our way back to each other. She's more like a sister to me. Even when she was on another continent, she was still there for me. All the time. She's my favorite person."

"What's your best memory?"

"There are too many to choose from, but the day she walked onstage for the first time and sang with Carter is a moment I will eternally cherish. They were just seven years old. I was a witness to every stage of their career. When she walked onstage at Green Mountain Fest years later, I knew she'd make it big. We did everything together growing up when she wasn't with Carter. Bonfire. Shows. Breaking curfews. Sleepovers. My memories of us are infinite."

I twisted on my seat, my back now pressed against the passenger door, and admired Tucker's profile.

"What are you looking at?" he asked.

"You," I said.

"Why?"

I shrugged. "Because I like to. You're perplexing, yet transparent at the same time. It's a combination I wanna crack." I paused. "And also, I'm wondering why you're not wearing the right jersey color. Purple is your color."

"It is?"

"Yep. When you took me on that date, you wore a purple shirt. My ovaries overheated at the sight."

His lips drew up into a smirk. "Glad to know I had an effect on your ovaries."

"Well, I'm not allowed to fall for you, but I have no control over certain parts of my body."

"I'll remember that. Can I ask you a question?" I nodded. "Why are you dating guys who don't deserve you? Is it some sort of punishment you inflict on yourself, or do you enjoy the pain of a broken heart?"

"When I love, I love hard. And so far, my heart has led me down the wrong paths. It's difficult for me to know when people have a hidden agenda. I'm a pretty open book. From now on, I'll be careful with who I let in. Hurting isn't something I like."

He squeezed my hand, and I turned my palm over so we could knit our fingers together.

"Thanks for the ticket, Wilde."

"Thanks for the road trip, big guy."

A comfortable silence settled between us.

"Would you mind if I shut my eyes for a little while?"

"Wilde, I'd be upset if you restrained yourself for me. Sleep all you want. I'm watching over you. You're safe. I'll make sure of it. Gather your energy. Tonight will be the opportunity of a lifetime, and you won't wanna miss any second of it."

"I'm glad we're doing this together."

"Me too."

And before I could speak another word, sleep claimed me.

Chapter 15
Tucker

Before the game, we did not have enough time to go to our hotel, so we met Mark, Addison's high school friend and the one who got her the tickets. He and his buddies were having a pre-game happy hour at a bar on Broadway. The music was loud, the beer flowing, and the chicken wings spicy enough.

"Addi, you brought the enemy," Mark sneered, draping his arm over her shoulders and sitting way too close to her for my comfort, pointing in my direction with his chin. I scanned all around me. Yeah, I was the only one sporting Chicago's colors. But I'd never betray my team. The Busters were not only my friends, but also people I respected and the best team in the league. No argument could change that. "I can't believe you wasted a precious ticket on Chicago's fan club."

I sipped my beer, smirking behind my glass. "We'll see who ends up crying themselves to sleep later, man. I'm pretty sure my guys will crush yours before they can even understand the game has started."

His hand fucking lingered on Addison's back, and a seething rage erupted inside me.

On my feet, I moved into her space, my mouth an inch away from her ear. I heard her sharp intake of breath. *Move to another target, Marky-boy.* "Want another drink?" She'd been sipping the same lemonade for the last hour.

"Please." She raised her empty glass, sucking on the cherry she had plucked from the bottom.

Mark studied me, his eyes narrowing into slits, clearly trying to find answers to the questions popping into his head.

I shrugged and averted my eyes, bringing my attention back to the woman who was oblivious to what was in front of her eyes.

Feeling cocky and wanting to give this guy a warning without being too obvious, I dropped a kiss on her forehead. "Be right back, sweetheart."

His stare followed me, and I felt the burn on my back.

For some reason, I hated that guy. I was generally someone who enjoyed the company of most people crossing my path, but so far, Mark had rubbed me the wrong way. His obsession with my date didn't sit well with me.

An hour later, we crossed the street and mingled with the crowd marching toward the stadium, chanting, a contagious cheerfulness soaking the air.

Addison intertwined our fingers, hopping with every step. "This is amazing. I've never been to a playoff game before. It hasn't even started yet, and I'm already pumped."

I fastened my hand around hers, and my heart

hummed in my chest from the happy vibes radiating from her.

We ordered snacks, soda for her and a beer for me, and took our seats. This day was surreal. Chicago hadn't played in the series for two years, and history was being made in Nashville. Exhilaration reverberated around us.

"Thanks for doing this with me," she said from my right.

People jumped to their feet, clapped, and wolf whistled when both teams entered the ice, and for the next hour and a half, we screamed and sat on the edge of our seats, the game in front of us wild and entertaining.

The Honky-Tonks mascot, a raccoon, came to us during the first intermission and kissed Addison's cheek. The episode played on the jumbotron, and the entire stadium erupted in cheers. The stupid animal pointed to my Chicago jersey and faked fainting, then returned his focus to the beautiful woman at my side. A crimson tint spread across her cheeks as she sipped her soda, flashing a smile at the cameras.

During the second period, people—mostly assholes—walked past us, offering her beers. She tucked them under her seat with thankful nods after they asked her on dates or suggested meeting up later. *This woman is a catch. I'm well aware. Get in line, dickwads.* I curled a possessive arm around her shoulders, but they were either idiots or blind because none of them seemed to be deterred by it.

"Tuck. Do something. It's getting uncomfortable," Addison begged with rounded eyes after the ninth person hit on her, this time proclaiming his love, slurring his words.

I brushed the length of her jaw with my fingers, my body electrifying at the simple contact, and before she could argue, I claimed her mouth, sucking her bottom lip between mine. Her entire being stiffened, then relaxed as she locked her arms around my neck and drew me to her.

I tried to break away, but Addison wouldn't let me, pushing her tongue into my mouth. All hell broke loose, and with the permission she granted me, I kissed her like I'd been yearning all evening.

A throaty moan crossed her lips, and I broke the kiss, afraid I'd humiliate myself if we kept going, the bulge in my lower body pressing hard against the fabric of my jeans.

Breathless, we pressed our foreheads together. Too caught up in making out, we hadn't noticed our faces on the jumbotron. The mascot to our right cupped his heart, shoulders slumping with exaggerated despair. People around us laughed at his theatrical display.

Only then did I realize the game had stopped.

Second intermission? Did we miss most of the second period?

Addison buried her face in her hand. "Oh gosh, we always end up giving everyone a show."

I lowered her hand and kissed her temple, tucking her under my arm. "Can you blame them? I'm pretty good-looking."

She slapped my stomach and rested her head against my shoulder. "With anyone else, it would've been super awkward. Thanks for being here," she said, her body warm and comforting against mine as we watched the third period.

With VIP passes on lanyards around our necks, we joined Mark and his father near the press box after the game.

The fucker kissed Addison's cheek—again—and splayed his hand across her back. "How did you like it?" he asked, way too close to her face for my liking.

She beamed, flashing me a wide grin, her eyes sparkling with glee before turning her attention to him. "Best. Experience. Ever. I'll gladly do any future rebranding you guys might need for tickets like these. Thank you so much." She wound her arms around her friend's neck and hugged him.

The fucker had the audacity to wink at me over her shoulder as she did.

As soon as he let go of her, I laced my fingers through Addison's and tugged her closer to me, kissing the crown of her head, just for good measure.

"Addi, we're having a private party later," Mark said. "Would you like to come?" He meant her—only her. Not, *you two* or *you guys*. He dismissed me right in front of her, not even trying to be subtle about it.

"Sorry, man. We already have plans," I chimed in, without giving her time to answer. I led her away, but she came to a stop and spun to face me once we were far enough away that the guy couldn't eavesdrop.

"Tuck, what the fuck. Couldn't you let me reply? I think I can speak for myself. Don't ever do that again. It was rude and unwarranted. We wouldn't be here if Mark's dad hadn't offered me the tickets. And if Mark hadn't vouched for me in the first place to do the job. So, play it cool. And respect my friend. Don't go all caveman on me." She angled her face to check on Mark and held up a finger as if to say "Wait a sec." Wrath rippled from her as she waited for me to say something.

I dragged a hand through my hair and shook my head, glancing down, before I opened my stupid mouth. "The guy's in love with you, Wilde. Big fucking much."

She crossed her arms over her chest, her eyes flashing with warning. "No. We've been friends for years. Get your eyes checked. And don't come up with stories to justify your behavior. I'm not buying your shit. You were rude. Accept it. Say you're sorry. And move on."

"No, I am not. Have you two ever dated?"

"What? No."

"He has a crush on you. I'm telling you."

"Stop. You know nothing about Mark."

"You believe you know what you're talking about. That's where you're wrong. I'm a guy, Wilde, and I know how guys think. With. Their. Dicks."

"Not everyone is superficial or led by their hormones," she countered.

"Oh girl, don't play innocent. You're too smart to be that naïve."

She groaned, and this little fight of ours got me hard for her. Right now, I wanted her on her knees and to fuck that devilish mouth to shut her up. Nothing could ever look as hot and dirty as Addison Wilde giving me head.

This woman had a way of getting under my skin. All the time. No matter what she said or did.

"I swear—"

"You swear what, sweetheart? Let me hear you," I pressed.

She muttered something I didn't catch, then added, "Nothing."

"It wasn't nothing. Your eyes are spitting venom, and you're flustered. What is it? Don't be shy."

A scowl painted her face.

"Since when do you shy away from your thoughts?"

"You're acting like a jealous boyfriend. I'm not yours, Tuck. I never was and never will be. Stop acting like a possessive jerk."

Her words rang true, but they sent my stomach spiraling with a foreign sensation. "It's not... I-I'm not."

"Yes, you are. You can't decide who I flirt with. It's not

your call to make. I can fuck whoever I want tonight, and you don't have a say in it. My body, my life, my choice."

Anger rose in my core. Her words made sense. I should be glad she didn't see me as boyfriend material. It didn't mean I had to agree, though. Or accept it. Imagining her having sex with high-school loverboy over there sent chills down my spine. That meant nothing, but I hated the idea with a fervor I'd rarely felt before.

"Wanna fuck him? Go ahead. I'm outta here. See you tomorrow when I drop your ass back in Atlanta."

I whirled around, about to explode, when a small hand clutched my elbow. "Tuck, don't go," she said in a low voice. I turned to watch her once I reeled in some of my ire.

Hurt flashed on her face, but she kept her lips pursed into a thin line, her eyes telling me she wasn't done with this conversation. "Wait for me. Geez. Let's just say goodbye and thank him. That's the least we can do."

We walked back to Mark, and he took his time kissing her cheeks and whispering into her ear. Addison giggled and tapped his chest with her hand. I saw red—blistering fire engine bleeding red.

Without a word, I grabbed her waist to spin her around and kissed her. She pushed away after biting my lower lip hard on purpose, then skewered me with a scalding gaze while faking an upturn of her lips for those watching. A new surge of fury swirled inside me, now matching hers.

This furious version of Addison Wilde set my blood racing and my hormones soaring.

Minutes later, our heavy steps echoed as we stomped toward our rental. Neither of us said a word. At the reception of the hotel we'd chosen for the night, we both took our credit cards out at check-in.

The receptionist's gaze traveled between us. "Just to be sure, was it one or two rooms?" she asked.

"Two," Addison said while I barked, "One."

I angled myself to face her. "Come on, Wilde." I lowered my tone, keeping some of my wrath at bay. "Don't punish me. Don't turn your back on us. We agreed to one room."

"There's no *us*, Tucker. I don't belong to anybody and certainly not to you. You made sure I knew from the start you were unavailable."

She said everything I wished she'd say, but no matter how I tried to process it, it hurt like hell.

"Don't ruin our weekend because *you* failed to notice your friend Mark has a crush on you," I said, fighting with all my instincts that told me to kiss her, make peace with her, and promise her the world.

"We're not talking about this anymore."

"Fine. Let's get to our room. We're meeting the guys from the Busters in less than an hour."

Once upstairs, the tension between us still ran high. After showering, Addison dropped her towel in the middle of the room while she rummaged into her bag for a new outfit.

A groan formed in my throat. The mixed signals emanating from her disturbed my mind. She didn't want us to have sex. She told me she could bang whoever she wanted tonight, but walked naked feet away from me without an ounce of shame or a second thought.

She hummed a song I didn't recognize, slipping her mouth-watering curves into lacy black lingerie, ignoring me the entire time.

I rubbed the column of my throat with my hand, at a loss for words. Did she want me to spread her naked on the bed and have my way with her, or was she just playing me to see how long it would take me to break and make a move on her, only for her to refuse me afterward?

With my dick pulsing against the zipper of my jeans and my brain not working right due to the lack of blood flow, I tried to solve the puzzle that she was, with no right or wrong answer. I entered the shower, the hot stream flushing out some of the angst bubbling up in me.

Refreshed and deciding to give Addison a taste of her own medicine, I walked straight into the room bare-assed, my chest still glistening with pearls of water, like I owned the place.

Our eyes met in the mirror while she applied her makeup, and I could see the tug-of-war waging in her mind. Her little naked act earlier had repercussions she hadn't expected. A pink flush covered her neck and cheeks. Now we were both aroused, but too stubborn to do anything about it. All because I had made a promise to my best friend, and we'd decided we shouldn't get together before the wedding. And also because we were both too proud to put a stop to whatever this was.

We both got ready in our respective corners. When Addison neared me wearing a short black dress that displayed her toned legs and delicious calves, I forgot all about our fight.

"Can you zip me up?" she asked.

I nodded, unable to speak, rendered speechless by the sight of her.

Adding to my weakness, she stood before me looking like a dream, smelling of summer and nights of endless pleasure. God, I was completely screwed when it came to her.

I pushed her hair over her shoulder, my finger lingering on the soft skin of her nape. Shivers licked her spine.

"Would you have preferred to accept his invitation to hang out? On your own? Be honest, Wilde."

"No. Never. We're here together. Who do you think I am? You thought I would just drop you at the hotel and party all night on my own without a second thought? Seriously, Tuck, what is wrong with you?"

I exhaled the remnants of my doubts and looked away. "I. Don't. Trust. The. Guy. Do you need me to spell it out for you?"

Anger laced her words. Addison turned in my arms, my fingers still glued to her neck. "How did it become a trust issue? Did I ever do something to make you doubt me?"

"No," I grumbled through clenched teeth.

"Then stop with the nonsense. I'm happy to meet your friends. I wanna spend time with *you*. If I were into Mark, I would have already been dating him, don't you think? I'm not here with him. I'm here with *you*. I invited *you*. Stop being a jealous asshole. Grow the fuck up and don't meddle in my personal life if it doesn't concern you. I mean it."

"Understood."

We lost ourselves in each other's stares. Like two magnets, our mouths collided, and our hands traveled all over the other. Addison climbed me like a tree, rolling her hips over my hard-on, whimpering into my mouth. I tangled my fingers in her hair, guiding her lips where I wanted them to be while I feasted on the flesh of her neck and breastbone.

"I've missed the taste of you so bad," I said between pants.

"Oh, Tuck. Never stop."

I slipped one hand under the hem of her dress, caressing the lacy fabric of her panties. When my fingers connected with her damp center, she purred so loud it almost broke me right there.

With her body wrapped around mine, I stepped forward until I could press her back against the wall, granting me more room to eat her up the way I couldn't stop dreaming about.

Reality hit me. Like a cold shower dampening the electric passion.

Addison felt it too because she leaned back, her lipstick smudged around her mouth, her eyes glossy with desire, and her chest rising fast.

I let go of her, and she scrambled back to her feet, adjusting her dress that had bunched up around her hips.

"We said no strings attached. No sex until the wedding. We gotta follow our own advice. We can't keep doing this. Crash and burn together. Someday, the burn won't heal, and we'll be left with scars," she said.

"I know. I'm sorry. I had no right to claim you as mine in front of your friend. Or here just now. You have a way of rattling my cage, and my control, Wilde. Two weeks to go and my dick will be all yours. For an entire weekend, you will own this playground. We're almost at the finish line. Let's not spoil it, okay? And by the way, I'd walk through lava to prevent you from getting hurt. I won't let dickheads hit on you without fighting them away."

She hugged me, resting her head against my chest as our breaths slowly returned to normal. The taste of her lingered on my lips. "We just had our first fight...and makeup session. I don't like fighting with you, though. But this was *hot*."

I cupped her face with a palm. "Me neither. I hate that. But yeah, this was pretty intense." I pressed a kiss to her forehead before we broke apart.

Barry Hamilton, the best center in the entire country and my friend, greeted us when we walked into the penthouse the team had booked for tonight. After Chicago's victory earlier, the guys had decided to have a small, low-key celebration since they had a strict curfew and low alcohol consumption rule during the playoffs.

"Hey, man. I can't believe you're here tonight," he said, clapping my back and offering me a beer. "Glad you could come."

"Addison, Barry. Barry, Addison," I said. "She's the one who made it possible."

He turned toward her and kissed her cheeks.

"Great game. Too bad you weren't playing for the other team," my date teased with a wink.

Barry's baritone laughter vibrated through the room. "Guys," he addressed his teammates, "the enemy is in the house. You have an hour to make her a Busters fan. Go ahead, seduce the woman."

We all chuckled.

He spoke into my ear. "I like her, man. Don't chase this one away." He clapped me between the shoulder blades and turned to welcome more people.

"Okay, I like your friends, big guy," Addison said once we put some distance between the team captain and us. "I think we'll all get along just fine."

I rested my hand on her lower back and walked her into the suite. "Ted Duffy, the goalie and a big fan of your friend Nick." She gave me a puzzled look, and I added, "I'll explain later. Cory Black, Rory Dupont, Jeremy Butler, the best players in the league. This is Addison. Hands off, guys. She's with me."

My date shook her head, amused, and held her hand out to shake my friends'.

They exchanged greetings and jokes as if they'd known each other for years and hadn't just met. Another layer of calm blanketed me. Yes, the team captain was right. Addison Wilde was a keeper. Too bad I wasn't looking to get settled down.

Hours passed, and I saw exhaustion taking over her features. Her lips didn't stretch as wide when she smiled, and her eyes didn't shine as bright. Addison had been drinking only water and soda all night, yet she looked like she was about to pass out.

"You okay?" I asked, taking my place beside her on the couch when Cory Black moved to answer his phone and cut their discussion short. "You look tired."

"I'm exhausted. Sleep isn't too generous with me these days."

"Come on. Let's go home." She wrinkled her face. *Home? Why did I say that?* "Huh…I mean, to our room. Luckily, we're a couple of floors downstairs."

"Thank God. I'm not sure I would have survived a car ride."

We exchanged goodbyes with the guys, and Addison accepted the bag Ted handed her. "Hope we'll see you again. Now you'll never forget us, and maybe you'll become our biggest supporter," he said, pointing to the package I guessed was filled with merch and other Busters' memorabilia. "Don't forget to send me that custom shirt you promised. Tucker knows where I live. He'll give you my address." I had no idea what they were talking about, but by the enthusiasm pouring out from her, I had no doubt it was a big deal for her.

Rory Dupont neared us. "Addi, if things don't work out

with Tuck, gimme a call." He winked. Fucker. He was aware it'd rub me the wrong way.

I rewarded him with a murderous stare. And he smirked.

Most of the team knew about my no-dating rules, and tonight they enjoyed my presence outside my own comfort zone.

"Forget it, Dupont. She's too good for you. You can handle a puck in the big league, but you're still a novice with women."

He laughed it off. "She's too good for you," he whispered, hugging me. "She can handle your sorry ass like a champ, though. Too bad you're not in the market for a relationship. Let me know when she's a free agent."

"Never," I replied with a tight jaw.

"Oh, I see trouble in your future."

He exchanged goodbyes with Addison and walked us out before returning to his teammates.

The door clicked behind us, and I squatted down. "Hop on."

"Tuck…what? Are you offering me a piggyback ride?"

"Come on, woman."

She giggled as she placed her feet into my palms while her arms curled around my neck. "Thanks for tonight. I had a blast."

"The guys loved you. Now they'll ask about you every time we meet. You made quite an impression on them."

"Your friends are nice. They made an impression on me too."

Wearing one of my T-shirts at my demand and after she removed every trace of makeup from her face, Addison and I slid under the covers, our bodies molding together. I kept her close with my arm around her as she shifted into position.

After a moment, she twisted her neck to look at me over her shoulder. "Night, Tuck."

"Night, Wilde." I inhaled her scent. "Am I still grounded?"

I heard the smile in her voice. "No, you redeemed yourself tonight. I'm not sure I possess what it takes to stay mad at you, anyway. Tomorrow, we'll tour the city since we were too busy the last time you came here."

"I love it. You playing tour guide. Can we ride scooters again?"

"Ha, I knew you liked it the last time."

"I enjoyed spending time with you, and scooters make you happy. After all, you're the President of the club."

"Yes, I almost forgot I was at the top of the hierarchy. It's a date then. You better fight my insomnia away, though."

"Always, sweetheart. Lean on me. I have your back."

I kissed her nape, and together, we drifted to sleep. In my dreams, I prayed we could be more. So much more.

It'd been four days since I returned from Nashville, and I was in a hurry to get home to talk to Addison. I had sent her a special package, and according to the app on my phone, it had been delivered three hours ago. Before I mailed it, I had taken the time to paste a "Don't open without me" warning label on the box. My meeting had dragged on forever, and because our daily call was set for seven, I was afraid I'd be running late.

The moment I crossed the threshold of my apartment, I loosened the tie around my neck and ditched my jacket. Summer was a week away, but the city was already sizzling under the suffocating heat. Looking at the time, I realized I had six minutes to spare, so I decided to take a quick shower and change into more comfortable clothes.

My phone rang as I pulled a shirt over my head and scraped the remaining water droplets from my hair with my hand.

"Hey you," I said, excitement building in me at the thought Addison had no idea what that box contained.

"Miss me already?" Most of the time, she used this as a line of greeting. Little did she know that I did. More than I ever expected to. And more than I would let her know.

"Depends. Did you miss me, sweetheart?"

"Don't sidetrack, Tuck. The delivery guy dropped something earlier. Based on the return address label, I can tell it was sent from your city. Anything to do with you?"

"It might. You'll have to switch to video chat to be sure."

Seconds later, a notification pinged on my phone screen, and I accepted the call.

Addison, dressed down in yoga pants and a tank top, filled my screen, to my greatest enjoyment.

Her smile widened when our eyes connected.

"Fine, I missed you," she said without missing a beat.

"Good. Are you ready for your surprise?"

"Should I be?" She clutched the box and shook it. "It feels like Christmas morning. I worked from home this afternoon, and I've been tiptoeing around it for hours."

"Patience, Wilde. You'll be rewarded soon."

"Can I?"

"Have you been a naughty or a good girl?" I teased, my words expressing much more than what they said.

"A good girl." Her gaze was glued to mine, and my heart skipped a beat at the fervor of our exchange. "Always. Being naughty isn't an option. At least, for another week."

My throat worked. She followed the movement, her smile stretching bigger. Yeah, she got me there.

"Wanna play a game, Tuck?"

I shook my head with an equally wide smile. "Not before you open the box, sweetheart." Even through a screen, the sexual tension bounced between us. "Go ahead, dig in."

I sat on my couch, watching through the screen as she uncovered what I had sent.

Sitting on her bed, cross-legged, Addison unwrapped the first item. "A lavender bath bomb," she said, rolling the ball between her fingers before bringing it to her nose to take a whiff. "I love it."

"Something to appeal to your senses," I said. "It's supposed to help you sleep better if you use it before going to bed."

"Wow, thoughtful and sweet. Can I continue?"

"Yes."

I studied her while she unwrapped a pair of bright pink fluffy socks.

"Something to keep you warm. And because your feet are always cold at night."

Her eyes lifted toward mine, and I read the realization in them. "Observing and caring," she whispered. "I love your attention to detail."

Next, she pulled a scented candle out of the box.

"Something to set the mood," I said.

My pulse jackhammered while I studied her.

The corners of her lips tilted up. "Charming and seductive. So far, you've gotten a perfect score."

I high-fived myself mentally.

From her expression, I was confident in my choices.

Ripping the silk paper, she unwrapped a soft blanket next.

"Something to curl into when I'm not around to cuddle."

She stared at me, speechless. "Tuck…" She murmured my name, looking visibly touched. "Considerate and warm. You couldn't be more on point. How can you know me so well?"

"You're a fascinating subject to study, Wilde. Keep going. You haven't gotten to the best part yet."

Like a kid, she rummaged through the box and unwrapped the tissue paper around a paperback novel.

"Something to escape into," I said. "I asked around at work, and the women told me it's perfect for a romantic heart like yours."

She flipped the pages, caressed the cover, and rested it against her chest. "Generous and devoted. You asked around to get me a book?"

Was that moisture shining in her eyes?

I nodded. "I'd do it again just to see the elated expression on your face. It makes my day."

"Wow. Thank you."

She picked up a USB stick next. "What is it?"

"Something to soothe your soul. A playlist full of love songs. We won't fight over this one."

Addison blinked and cupped her chest, right over her heart. "Kind-hearted and romantic. It's… I'm impressed, big guy. You're doing amazing so far."

Seconds later, she unfolded a red lace slip, rubbing the delicate fabric between her fingers. "Tuck, this is exquisite. And provocative. You chose it yourself?"

I bowed my head. "Something to feel beautiful in," I replied, already picturing her wearing it.

She padded the skin under her eyes with her fingertips, wiping away her emotions. Yeah, those were tears I'd spotted minutes ago.

"Wilde, I can't chase away your insomnia when we're far apart. I hope this will help you unwind."

She moistened her lips with her tongue, the small gesture enough to send me over the edge, if I pumped my dick one too many times.

"There's one last thing." My voice sounded rougher now.

She opened the small black and gold box and was presented with a vibrating device.

"Something to help you relax," I said. "Orgasms are the best therapy for insomnia. Better than any massage, in my opinion."

Addison said nothing. Her chest rose and fell in a quick tempo.

"All for me?" she finally said. "You handpicked every one of these yourself? For me?"

I bobbed my head. "Yeah. I called it the 'Take It Easy Wilde Box.' I'd really love for you to get a few good nights of sleep. Dahlia needs you sharp and ready for the wedding next weekend."

"Thank you. It's the most thoughtful, naughty, and sweetest gift anyone has ever given me. I love everything. It's perfect. And I have no idea how to thank you the right way. You're too far away for a hug…or a kiss."

"One week, Wilde, and you'll be able to thank me in any way that pleases you. Now, go. By the way, I already charged it. So, you're good to go whenever you're ready."

Addison's warm laughter did strange things to me—and my body. "You thought of everything."

"I tried."

"Is it waterproof?" she asked with a quirked brow and that devious grin I'd come to love so much.

"Yep. You can lose yourself in that book, bathed in candlelight and warm lavender-scented water, after you give yourself the second-best orgasm while listening to a custom selection of romantic songs. Only to dress into something sexy while keeping your feet warm, and dreaming my arms are around you afterward. How does it sound?"

"Like we need to hang up because I'm already aroused by the description. Unless you wanna join this little party?"

I swallowed hard, my throat thick with desire. "Not this time. For once, be selfish and think only about yourself." My dick hated me for being too rational—again. He wasn't used to this altered reality. Neither was I. But I was starting to get attached to this new version of me.

"Okay, I will. This is really nice of you. Can we continue this conversation tomorrow as planned?"

"Absolutely. Go. Exhaust yourself, Wilde. Let me know tomorrow how it went."

"I will," she said, her voice already lustful. "Hey, Tuck? If this is the second-best orgasm I can get, what's number one?"

"One only Tucker Philips can provide."

"I should've guessed. I'll let you know tomorrow if you're good enough to keep the top spot."

"Yeah, you do that. I'm telling you, I'm not even scared for my title. Night, Wilde."

When I finally drifted off to sleep later, I could see her in my dreams as she moaned my name and abandoned herself to the pleasure only I could provide from a distance.

Sparks of excitement filled me. Sparks I could easily get addicted to.

Chapter 16

Addison

A week later, I swept my bottom lip with my tongue as I smoothed the skirt of my maid-of-honor pale-yellow chiffon dress. I twirled around, admiring my reflection in the mirror of what used to be Dahlia's bedroom in her old house. The gown was beautiful. Strapless, with a short train, it made me feel like a princess the first time I put it on. Having a best friend owning a bridal and evening gowns shop had many advantages. Never again would I be wearing a dress that didn't fit me like a second skin. I had picked this gown a few months back and hadn't tried it again since. Savoring its elegance, I fell in love with it all over again. Squirming, I adjusted the fabric over my breasts, annoyed about my upcoming periods making my boobs sensitive and swollen. Poor timing.

With a hand, I rubbed my stomach. My hormones had always been a crazy ride, and this time would be no exception. The wedding would be a crying fest if I didn't get myself under control. I had a tendency to be a hormonal crier. And booze would now not only feed my insomnia, but also my tears. I sighed. Getting drunk and making a fool of myself this weekend wasn't an option. Perhaps this was a good thing, though. My upcoming situation would also prevent me from jumping Tucker like a needy girlfriend the moment we met again.

The universe had decided to send me a message—a very clear message. For once, maybe I should just listen.

Or I could push the thought away and categorize it as nonsense.

Tomorrow was my best friend's wedding, and a glass—or two—of champagne wouldn't kill me. I deserved some fun of my own. Two glasses. Yes, I'd draw the line there.

With my phone in hand, I checked the time, an excuse to see if Tucker had sent me a text message. Nothing. His flight was scheduled to land sometime in the middle of the afternoon. I offered to pick him up from the airport since I got here in the morning, but he had a rental and was meeting Nick for some last-minute tuxedo adjustments.

I loved the friendship thing we got going on. Physical, sexual, emotional, intellectual. Over the past six weeks, we'd grown really close. Inserting himself into my daily life, Tucker had taken over a huge part of my time. We clicked. No better word described us. I cherished every second we spent talking and goofing around and confiding in each other.

We'd graduated from superficial conversations full of sexual promises and innuendos. Everything about Tucker Philips made sense to me now. His fears. His doubts. His insecurities. The only thing I still hadn't figured out was the shadow I sometimes perceived in his gaze. My gut told me it was quite recent, nothing related to his childhood.

When he thought no one was paying him attention, it languished there, in the darkness of his chocolate-brown irises. I'd noticed it. More than once.

Someday, I'd ask him about it. If our friendship survived this weekend because we were supposed to have sex again—as a part of our agreement. My body tingled just at the thought of it. The memories of that day, when we singed the sheets of my hotel room, still made me hot, even over a month later.

His lips on my skin. His hands everywhere. The way he transformed me into an inferno, burning hotter for him the more we pleasured each other. And the promises of a repeat performance this weekend before going our separate ways.

How could I not be obsessed with him? Still, I had no idea how we both kept things PG-13 both weekends we spent together considering the sizzling chemistry and undeniable attraction we shared.

The thought of never lying in his arms again after this weekend twisted my stomach with foreign sensations. It'd be the end of many chapters we were writing together, and the end of that physical connection I'd never experienced with anyone else before him. Despite myself, I loved us together. Even when sex wasn't a part of the equation.

My heart rate accelerated at the thought. Something coiled my insides.

A million questions swirled in my head, and a wave of uneasiness slowly crept through me. I had no answers, but deep down, I feared that getting intimate again might put our blooming friendship at risk and break the fragile equilibrium between us. I loved the chase. Our relationship. The restraint and the magnetism pulling us toward each other. All of it. Tucker and I were both sexual people. We loved sex—a lot. Somehow, we had both resisted our number-one temptation while growing closer and getting to know each other. Pride danced in me at the thought. I also relished how we completed each other and could rely on the other when we lacked strength. Still, every time we spent time together, we risked being burned by the fire threatening to consume us, and it became harder to resist.

I inhaled, wishing it would calm the bouncing balls of nerves pounding against the walls of my chest.

The way Tucker held me in his arms—when I visited him in Chicago, and again two weekends ago in Nashville —as if I mattered to him, as if I were his whole world, played havoc with my emotions. Now I feared I'd become too attached to him—more than I should, more than I was allowed, more than I had promised. With someone else, a relationship, love, could be possible, but not with a man allergic to commitment. I would only set myself up for disappointment in the end…and another broken heart. My heart had enough scars already. It wouldn't survive another blow.

Yeah, I'd ridden that rollercoaster before. We shared great sex. I fell in love. Then the guy decided I wasn't worth whatever attachment issues he struggled with. Result? Another Addison Wilde's failed love story. Instructions? Start over and repeat. Until the parts of my heart, held only by a flimsy thread, healed while I vowed to live a celibate life. No, thank you. I yearned for love spelled in giant glittery letters. The one you could never overcome because it rattled your core just thinking about losing it. The thing movies and novels were made of.

Since last night after we hung up, my heart and head had been debating if Tucker and I should go forward with our plan or forfeit it and continue to nurture our friendship instead. In a platonic way. One option kept my heart safe, the other put it at risk. Our relationship meant a lot to me.

It defied logic. Even my own. But I wouldn't want to live without it for another day. God, how much more complicated could it get? My thoughts were spinning at a dizzying speed, none agreeing with the others.

With my gaze locked on my figure, I twirled one last time, loving the cascade of the fabric as the dress fell back into place. I lowered the zipper, watching the gown billow to the floor at my feet before picking it up and hanging it behind the door. I ran my fingers over the bodice, caressing the delicate fabric, my mind drifting to Tucker. Again. A stupid smile curled my lips. My heart sang in my chest. Seeing him tonight meant making a decision, and my head and heart hadn't settled yet. I required more time. Whatever my heart desired, the guy didn't do relationships. He'd been adamant about it—multiple times. Yeah, I had to follow my head. Our off-the-charts sexual compatibility shouldn't be explored any further. Okay, I would talk to him. Yes, I could do that. Explain how I felt. Make him understand the situation from my perspective. He would agree because it made sense.

I nodded, confident in my position.

Our insane chemistry should be put to better use.

Doubts crippled me. How could I stay friends with a guy my heart ached for without risking everything in the process?

A dreadful feeling washed over me, and I buried my face in my hands with a growl.

Why did it trouble every cell in my body to think we might never be intimate again?

Despite what I told myself, I couldn't imagine a life without Tucker Philips in it. One in which he called me every day, held me at night, chasing away the bad guys in my dreams or fighting my insomnia. Just picturing him in pressed suits, or catching his enticing smirks directed at me with barely contained lust, made me giddy, but also shot me with unexpected doses of calm. Even when I tried to lock my heart away from the hurt, I realized the man with dark skin and sparkling eyes had already stolen a huge chunk of it.

No. *No, no, no.* I refused to acknowledge what I already knew. I would fight this. With everything I possessed.

Closing my eyes, I counted to three, and leaving my new resolves behind, I grabbed my phone again, re-reading our last text exchange.

Yeah, I was that weak.

TUCKER

Counting the days till I see you again.

I lied.

ME

Why? When?

TUCKER

It's more like hours, to be honest. Sweetheart, we've been patient enough. I want you. Under me. Over me. Sitting on my face. On all-fours. And in a dozen other different ways.

ME

Oh, Tuck. I want you too. I want it all. That tongue of yours... Just thinking about it makes me wet.

The smile stretching my lips probably mirrored the one I had at the same exact moment we exchanged this. The anticipation tumbling in my lower belly had only grown stronger over the hours. Even if I wanted to, I couldn't lie and pretend otherwise.

ME

Tuck...

TUCKER

What's wrong, Wilde?

ME

I'm happy. How did we get here?

TUCKER

What do you mean?

ME

Us. How did we grow so comfortable around each other? So close? Our friendship. It matters to me.

TUCKER

No idea. But I regret nothing. You've become the most important person in my life. With you, I don't feel like I'm stuck. I feel like I'm living.

Stuck? I hadn't noticed the word the first time. Could it explain the shadow lingering in his eyes? One day, I'd get to the bottom of it—soon—because I hated the idea that something was bothering him and he didn't feel safe enough to open up about it.

TUCKER

Oh fuck. Can we talk later? I'll be late if I don't leave in like ten minutes.

ME

Sure.

TUCKER

I'll see you soon, sweetheart. Don't miss me too much *winking emoji* And don't miss your bus or I'll come get you myself.

ME

You wouldn't.

TUCKER

Try me. I already did. Twice.

ME

I know. Wanted to hear you say it.

See you later.

I laughed because I loved the idea of him coming to get me, all caveman-style, handsome and sexy, scooping me over his shoulder to carry me wherever I was supposed to be.

With a shake of my head, I erased my stupid grin. My heart banged a little faster. That man... Gosh, I really missed him. A warm shiver zipped through me. And now I was lying to myself. *Ohmyfuckinggod.*

I sighed, cursing at myself, and rummaged through my suitcase to find something to wear tonight, trying to keep the images of him away to avoid transforming into a puddle of arousal. And locking the desire center of my brain to make sure it would not interfere with my new dedication to keep our relationship platonic.

In an attempt to focus on something else, I turned my laptop on and lost myself in my newest designs. Much later, when I noticed the time, I fumbled to save the open file. "Oh no. And now I'll be late."

Dahlia and Nick had invited us to a pre-wedding dinner in an hour, so I should hurry. At least, for the length of an afternoon, I had left my naughty thoughts where they belonged—far away from here.

See? I could do this. Be strong. And resist Tucker's charms.

I showered and applied my makeup, doing a great job

at thinking about anything but the man I had no right to think about.

My mind drifted to the wedding the next day instead.

A new set of jitters swam in my belly. Flowers. Music. Food. Love. I placed a flat palm over my chest, calming my thudding organ, and gave a pep talk to my reflection through the full-length mirror on the bedroom wall. "Things will work out when the timing is right."

I firmed my back. Confidence slithered through the cracks of my vulnerability, growing roots.

I'd questioned it earlier, but now I was convinced I had to keep the man at arm's length, aware that my heart would probably let him slither in if I wasn't careful. Weakness was not an option. I had to grow a backbone.

With a little insight, Nick and Dahlia's warning was fitting. Maybe they knew me better than I knew myself. Would they agree to be the protectors of my heart from now on if I asked? Because I had failed at the task once again… big time.

Great, I was rambling in my own head and thinking about asking my best friend and her future husband to micro-manage my love life. This was bad.

I bet they sensed Tucker and I would hit it off, and they knew us well enough to guess it could be disastrous if we ended up in bed together. *Me*, the romantic. *He*, the guarded womanizer…or ex-womanizer. Yeah, a love story doomed from the start.

"See, Tuck? That's what spending too much time with you does to me," I said out loud. It fucked with my mind… and my body. Not fucked. No. Confused. Confused my mind and my body. "See? It happened again. Why do you have to be so irresistible all the time? And smell so great? And be nice and caring. And freaking hot."

Dressed in a denim skirt and an off-shoulder white top,

I climbed behind the wheel of Dahlia's car. The one she lent me for the next few days since I had traveled here on bus. I checked my reflection one last time in the rearview mirror and fixed my lipstick before driving to my friend's place.

Carter and Jack were kicking a soccer ball on the front lawn when I pulled into the driveway.

"Hey guys," I said as the toddler ran into my wide-open arms when I squatted before him.

"*Addidi*," he screamed when I lifted him and spun him around.

"Ohmygod, you're so tall. Did you grow a foot in the last month?" He bobbed his head as I lowered him back to his feet after hugging him. This kid owned a big slice of my heart. Jack Hills topped the list of my favorite human beings in this world. Right next to his mama.

"Hey you," Carter greeted me as we kissed each other's cheeks. "Dahlia said to meet her inside as soon as possible. Some maid of honor emergency…huh, I think." He shrugged and picked up Jack to position him on his shoulders while maneuvering the ball with his feet. They always looked so happy together. As if they belonged to a world nobody else had access to. Like he and Dahlia did when they were kids.

He kicked the ball in my direction, and I blocked it. From his perch, Jack applauded.

"Guess I should go. See you later, you two," I said as I made my way inside, adjusting my skirt. "Hey, girlfriend. I'm here. What's the problem?" I asked as my feet met the plank floor. I scanned the main level. It looked nothing as it did the last time I was here. "Wow, you guys did an amazing job. I'm speechless. This is so beautiful. No doubt why you're getting married. You make a terrific team."

The farmhouse had been turned into a more modern

version while maintaining its old charm. The wooden floors and ceilings were the same but refreshed, and everything else had been changed. The kitchen now stood where the living room used to be, and vice versa. The walls that used to be a silvery shade of gray were now white, giving a fresh vibe to the place. The old staircase had been sanded and re-stained the same color as the floors. Here and there were black and purple accessories. It looked country-chic, modern, and vintage all at the same time.

One day, I'd like to own a house. Just like this one. Some place warm and cozy. Some place to call home.

Dahlia met me in the kitchen and pushed a wine glass into my hand. I discarded it on the countertop, my stomach churning at the thought of an early drink.

"What's going on? Carter was being cryptic outside."

She took a seat beside me at the island. "The lady who was supposed to come over to do our makeup tomorrow bailed on us. She had to leave town. An emergency. I was thinking, with your mama owning a beauty salon which means being a makeup wizard runs in your veins and your genes, if perhaps you'd agree to replace her. I know I'm asking a lot, and you have plenty of maid of honor and organizer's duties to deal with, but if you could find some time to do my mama's, mine, and Mrs. Peterson's makeup, you'd save my life."

I pulled Dahlia into a hug as tears filled my eyes. "Nothing would make me happier and prouder, girlfriend. You've always been my favorite model. Remember prom? And that night at the music awards? I'm very flattered you asked." I leaned back to wipe my teary eyes.

"Ohmygod, you're crying. Everything okay?"

I sniffled. "Wedding jitters. Your getting married is making me emotional. I'm so happy for you. And Nick. But mostly for you."

Dahlia brushed my hair back with her hand. We stayed in each other's embrace for a minute.

My tears dried, and I straightened my back. "Anyway, I'm sure we can delegate most of my tasks to Tucker. No way will he be sitting around on his ass all afternoon drinking whiskey while we get everything ready. Consider it done. I'll deal with him."

Dahlia pulled back. "Oh, Addi is back. You look good, girlfriend. I'm sorry I haven't been available lately. This craziness is almost over, and things will go back to normal." She hugged me a little tighter. "I've been yearning to ask… How is it going between you two?"

"Tucker and me?"

"Yes. You seemed to get along just fine in Nashville. Did you guys keep in touch? Did you convince him to take part in that secret project of yours?"

I swallowed before speaking. "Yeah, we're fine. We messaged a few times. Mostly wedding stuff." And one half-naked selfie. Two late-night raunchy video chats. One date. A weekend sleepover. A weekend getaway. Hundreds of hours over the phone. Too many text messages. But hey, mostly wedding stuff, right?

"Good. I feared you guys would either hit it off or wouldn't be able to stand each other. Both of you are much more alike than you think." A long pause. "How is it going with the *I'm done with men* thing? Changed your mind already? Who is your mysterious plus-one?"

I let out a heartfelt laugh, my mini meltdown forgotten, and my best friend joined in. "Fine. You knew I'd never go through with it, even if I think it'd make my life easier and my heart much safer. I had lunch with Felicia, my college experiment, as you called her." I sighed. "It kinda sealed the deal. I'm not made for this. I love men too much."

Dahlia snickered. "Promise me you won't date the first

one you meet, okay? You deserve someone great. Someone who will love you and put you first."

The door yanked open, and laughter reached us, cutting short our conversation. The one with a deep baritone sent my heart into a frenzy, and all my hair stood on end. This was bad. Very bad. I wasn't ready to see him just yet. And, for some reason, in the last half-hour, I'd convinced myself he would skip being here tonight…or that his flight had been delayed. Just the idea of Tucker standing feet away from me turned me into a horny time bomb. Having him too close, while I was still debating the right course of action, was dangerous—all the more so with our friends surrounding us. His presence destroyed my resolve and toyed with my stupid hormones. *Get a grip on yourself, Addi.*

"Hey, Tuck," Dahlia greeted, rising to her feet to meet him. "How was your flight?"

"Great."

"Remember my best friend, Addi, your *bride* and the woman you sang to?" she asked with a half-smile.

"Hey you," he said, staring at me for far too long. The column of his throat worked. His pupils dilated. His lips parted.

My skin tingled, and my face heated up under his heavy gaze.

Warmth shot through me, and desire welled up between my thighs.

I shouldn't want him. Not if I wanted to stay true to the promise I had made to myself to find the right person for me. No more one-night stands. I thought I could do rebound sex, but I was bad at it. With him, my heart sometimes forgot about the no-strings-attached rules because Tucker Philips was the one my entire body longed for. My weakness. The man who should share my bed and rock my nights.

He inched closer to me, stealing every remnant molecule of oxygen meant for my lungs.

When his lips connected with my cheek, I caught fire. His presence invaded my senses. I fisted his shirt, a reflex I hadn't grown out of, to keep my balance. Goose bumps blossomed on my arms. My breathing picked up, and my heart galloped in my chest.

Oh gosh, disaster was looming. A collision of desires we had leashed in for far too long.

I took a whiff of him, closing my eyes as I savored the clean and manly scent he wore so perfectly. Ocean breeze. And him.

"Miss me, sweetheart?" he asked in a husky voice with an edge that only I could hear.

I nodded. Barely. But enough to see the dangerous twinkle in his eyes. A devilish smile broadened his lips.

Every cell in me throbbed at his proximity.

Nick touched his friend's shoulder, breaking the spell. "Whiskey or beer?"

I resumed my breathing. If we weren't careful enough, we'd get caught. Now wasn't the time to stress our friends with our antics.

Tucker cleared his throat, finding his composure back and stepping away from me. "Beer. For now. Anything for you, Addison?" he asked holding my eyes, articulating each syllable of my name in a way that made my legs weak.

Was my face all flushed? And my armpits drenched? I hooked a finger into the collar of my shirt and motioned it back and forth, bringing much-needed air to my combusting self.

"Water's fine. Thanks."

Tucker walked past me and whispered, so once again

only I could hear him, "Am I making you all hot and bothered, sweetheart?"

I met his eyes for a split second and looked away. "No," I murmured through clenched teeth. The game was on. I could already imagine how we'd implode together. And yet, I was unable to stop the imminent clash.

He let out a low chuckle. "We'll see." He winked, then followed Nick. There. I almost lost the fight in me at that instant. Our connection had intensified since the playoff game two weeks ago. The stakes had gotten higher. And Tucker had transformed into an addiction whose sole mission was to ravage me. Mind, body, and soul.

Hours later, the five of us sat around the table, now that Jack was in bed.

"To family," Dahlia said, her wine glass in hand. "You, my friends, are our family. We love each of you so much. Thanks for being here with us tonight. It means more than you'll ever know."

The cook they had hired for tonight brought us some fancy salad after we clinked our glasses. I was about to bring my fork to my mouth when warm fingers slithered their way to my pulsing center, sliding my panties to the side and gliding into the depths of me. I yelped and shut my eyes for a second, trying to act casual.

The sparks spiraling through me were foreign. And intoxicating. As if I was being touched this way for the very first time.

A truckload of sensations, each more pleasurable than the others, washed through me. It took all I had not to roll my hips, chasing the friction between my thighs.

"Are you okay?" my best friend asked, worry swimming in her hypnotic moss-green eyes.

"Yeah," I said, my voice stuck in my throat. I downed my water, trying to cool myself off.

Beside me, Tucker pinched his lips, acting as if his fingers weren't buried inside me, playing me like a love song. The heel of his hand brushed my clit, and my blood turned to lava. Shudders infiltrated my entire body as it came alive under his expert caresses. Yeah, I had no self-control when he was involved. I chewed on a piece of lettuce longer than needed, unable to focus on the conversation going on around the table.

"Addi, you gotta settle this debate. What do you think?" Nick asked, his fork suspended mid-air, waiting for me to answer a question I had no clue about. I blinked.

Under the table, Tucker applied more pressure to my throbbing bundle of nerves. I clenched my thighs, trying hard not to squirm on the chair and moan at the top of my lungs.

"I think you're right."

Nick's fork fell to his plate, and he went "Ha, ha. Told you, guys."

I had no idea what I had just agreed to. Who cared? My body tensed. No way would I come undone right here at the table surrounded by my closest friends.

Tucker spread my wetness over my folds, teasing me, my body too sensitive to be fiddled with.

Pleasure blinded me while it pulsed through me, and I punched the table. All eyes drifted in my direction.

"You sure you okay?" Dahlia asked. "Your face is all red."

I nodded. "Yeah. Something's stuck in here," I said, massaging my throat.

She rose to her feet. "Let me get you more water."

A throaty "Thanks" bubbled out.

The cook came to the table and asked Nick something, who stood to follow him.

As if pulled by a magnet, my head turned toward

Tucker. His eyes gleamed. A victory smirk hung from his lips, the one I was dying to feed on. I rubbed my cheek against his sleeve. How did I transform into a pathetic aching puppy? Heavy lids and teeth biting into my tongue, I hid my face in the crook of his arm, angling my body to increase the friction between us.

"You guys are so bad," Carter stated, finishing his plate, acting as if nothing was happening three feet away from him. "You could at least be subtle about it. It's written all over your faces you're sleeping together. Just a question, though. Where are your fingers, Tuck?"

I clenched my jaw as a first wave of pleasure hit me, strangling Tucker's hand between my thighs. A deep-throated groan whistled out of me.

Tucker kissed the tip of my nose.

I swallowed and blinked. "Please, Cart. Don't say a word. They don't have to know." I gasped, my eyelids fluttering, wondering how long I could last without detonating.

My voice sounded so unlike mine.

Dahlia entered the room, and Tucker and I broke apart.

My chest heaved. I kept my gaze down, trying to even my shallow breathing.

She put a glass of water before me on the table, and Carter stood up before she could sit back.

"Dah, can I talk to you for a minute?" She nodded. "In private. I think Nick should come too."

She turned her head to face us. "Sorry, guys. It won't be long. Meet me in the den, Cart. I'll go get him."

Carter eyed us for a long second and whispered, leaning forward, "You have three minutes to finish what you're doing."

Now boiling with need, I pivoted in my chair until I

faced Tucker again. He curled a hand around my nape and kissed me as if it would be the last time, his fingers diving in and out of me at a dizzying pace. The orgasm built inside me, and in no time, I liquified around his digits. He removed his hand, and with his thumb coated in my arousal, he skimmed the length of my lower lip. The taste of me on his fingers turned me on in a way no words could express. With the tip of my tongue, I licked his fingers clean while he watched me.

"Good girl. God, you're hot. I've missed you, sweetheart."

We fixated on each other for a long moment. Tension coiled around us, ribbons of pleasure tying us together.

After a beat, I found my voice. "Tuck, we're not supposed to. We said after the wedding, remember? Friendship and sex are blurring the lines."

"Fuck the wait. You want it as much as I do. I paid penance. I can't wait to have a taste of you later. It's all I've been thinking about. Taking you on this table. On the island in the kitchen. By the front door." He brought my hand over his erection, his dick twitching under my touch while I massaged it. "See? I'm not waiting another night."

"What about your words?" I asked, breathless, falling under his charm. "Our deal?"

The more he stared at me like this, with hunger and lust, the more I drifted toward him, unable to resist the pull.

"Let's talk about it later," he said as footsteps neared us, and we moved apart as if nothing had happened. I kept my head low, knowing my face was flushed, and excused myself from the table the moment everyone sat, needing a minute—or many—to regain my composure and get my hormones back under control. And to cool off.

My body still pulsated, desperate for more.

In the bathroom, I splashed cold water over my face, doing my best not to ruin my makeup. I shook my hands, trying to infuse myself with words of wisdom.

Control yourself, Addi. You can do it. Just for a few hours. Remember what you decided earlier? Resist. Be strong. You can do this. He'll understand.

The door opened when my hand wrapped around the knob, and Tucker slid his tall self into the opening.

I startled back. "What are you doing here?" I asked in a whisper, my heart rate picking up at his closeness, and my fragile composure slipping.

"Dahlia is wondering if you're all right." He shrugged. "I offered to come get you." He flipped me around and nestled his hard length between my ass cheeks, grinding his hips against my backside.

I whimpered, clutching the counter with both hands to prevent my knees from buckling. His palms ventured underneath my shirt and dragged upward until he cupped both breasts, my nipples stiff enough they could drill holes through his flesh. He traced the length of my neck with his lips. Okay, I was melting right here. On my best friend's bathroom floor.

"Fuck, Wilde. I've missed you."

I shook my head, unable to open my eyes, the sensations rushing through me and threatening my balance.

"No, Tuck. You can't miss me. The only thing you're allowed to miss is our friendship. Not my body."

I inhaled through my mouth, calming myself, and spun around between his arms now caging me. I tilted my head back to lock eyes with him, his warm breath sweeping across my cheek. With one hand sprayed on his broad chest, I kept him at a safe distance.

"Wilde, this weekend will be torture if I'm not granted permission to touch you. To fuck you with my tongue. My cock. My fingers. Told you already. You're all I think about. All. The. Time. Help a guy out. We deserve our playtime. We've been reasonable long enough."

I shook my head. "Listen, we gotta stop now. We'll get caught. For the rest of tonight and the weekend, we better stay away from each other."

He blinked. "Is that what you want?" he asked, a perplexed frown wrinkling the contours of his eyes.

My throat closed. *No. Yes. For my heart's safety.*

I hung my head low and looked away. "It's for the best. Being selfish and jeopardizing the wedding isn't smart."

He tried to meet my fleeting gaze. "Wait? You serious? This makes no sense. I've missed you. I thought we agreed to spend this weekend together. When did you change your mind? Why didn't you tell me last night when we talked?"

Because it's all new. I realized I could easily fall for you, and it scares me because I know you won't reciprocate my feelings if it happens and I'm being honest about how I feel. Our friendship is sacred to me, and I won't spoil it. I've had too many failed relationships in the past.

I wiped my watery eyes with my fingers. Why was I crying all the time? Dahlia's wedding was happening at the worst time.

Tucker's voice softened as he held my upper arms, leveling his eyes with mine.

"Hey, why are you sad? What's going on?" He pushed my hair away from my face, and I stared at a spot behind him. "Addison, talk to me. Last time we discussed it, you said you couldn't wait for the weekend to arrive and have me all to you. You even made dirty promises."

Worry billowed in his eyes. Why did he have to be so damn handsome? And so caring? It wasn't fair. My dream man was a Mustang. One who could never be tamed.

I shrugged. "Nothing. Wedding jitters. This thing is

making me all emotional. I love weddings. Always have. True love. Soul mates. They mean something to me. Something I aspire to. Someday." He brushed my cheek with his knuckles, but I jerked away from his touch. "Don't worry. I'm fine. Imminent period. Girls' stuff." I sniffled. "I'm okay. Now let's go back before our friends start wondering what we're doing."

He dropped his head and blew out a breath. "Fine. You win. We'll do as you say. You'd tell me if something was bothering you, right?" he asked, shoving his hands into the pockets of his dark trousers.

"Yup. Everything's great. Better than great. Our best friends are about to get hitched. Yay," I said, pumping my fist.

Tucker studied me for a long, fat minute, trying to read me. Or that was what it seemed like. I fixed a smile onto my face, straightened my back, and exited the bathroom without another glance in his direction.

———

"How long are you in town, Tuck?" Carter asked when we were all sitting in the den, the guys—except him—now sipping on whiskey, and Dahlia and I drinking tea instead.

"Two weeks maybe. Not sure yet."

My heart pounded at Tucker's words, and I couldn't even explain the reason.

"You never told me you accepted my offer," Nick chimed in with a frown.

"It will be fun to have you around for a little while. Where are you staying?" Dahlia asked next.

"For all I know, your old house. Nick offered it to me when he came to visit a few weeks ago."

Dahlia winced.

"Is there something wrong?" he asked.

My best friend's gaze ping-ponged between us.

"Well, Addi has moved in for the weekend." She turned to face her almost-husband. "Babe, you didn't tell me you had promised it to Tucker."

Tucker's eyes moved to me for half a second before drawing back to Nick.

"You can stay here while Addi is in town. It's only for a few nights, anyway. Then you decide if you wanna move there instead. The offer to stay in town for a couple of weeks still stands. Your choice." Nick shrugged as if it was no big deal, when in fact it was a very big deal.

"Nah, I can't stay here. You guys need your space. You're getting married tomorrow. So, a hotel it is. No worries. I'll find a decent place in town."

"You could stay at Cart's," Dahlia suggested. With her mug nestled in her hands, copper hair cascading freely over her shoulders, and legs tucked under her, she looked relaxed about her upcoming nuptials. The opposite of how I felt.

Carter shrugged. "Sure. There are plenty of rooms if you're looking for a place to crash. I don't offer room service, but other than that, it's rent-free."

Tucker shook his head. "No way. Jack is going home with you, and you're all entitled to your privacy. I'm just an outsider here. The hotel's fine. I'll decide what to do after a few nights."

"Or you could stay with me," I offered, not bothering to look at him, busy nipping at my fingernails. "There's enough room for both of us. And like Nick said, I'm just in town for three days, anyway. Soon, you'll have the entire place to yourself."

Nick's voice broke the awkward silence, and he

scratched his temple. "Guys, I'm sorry we both offered you the house without talking about it first."

"Then it's settled. We're shacking up together, big guy."

"You sure?" His glance said far more than his words.

"Yep." I looked away, but his stare burned the side of my head.

Carter snickered behind his hand and fake-coughed when my laser-beam eyes landed on him, ready to turn him into a roasted chicken.

My heavy stare pinned him to the spot, and he reeled his laughter in.

On my feet, I hugged my best friend. "I love you. I should go. Tomorrow is the big day. You should get some rest."

Tucker joined me. "Sweetheart, let me walk you to your car. It's my unofficial job as the best man to make sure the maid of honor is always safe and sound and accounted for."

I rolled my eyes, pretending to be annoyed, when little fireworks exploded inside me instead. Tucker had a way of making me feel special. No wonder women fell at his feet all the time. He and I never got into details about his past *sexcapades*. I didn't want to know all the specifics, anyway. *No, thanks, hard pass.* Still, I could recognize his power of seduction.

My eyes took him in, and I enjoyed the sight. The attraction searing between us didn't only come from Tucker's model-face or football-star physique. Nor from his panty-melting grin or the way he undressed me with his eyes. It was a mix of everything combined with his huge heart and sense of humor. Plus the caring and sweet side of him that he hid from most people. Altogether, it was a deadly combination.

If he were after my heart, I'd offer him the entire organ without second-guessing myself. Because that was how I was wired. Love and love hard. Trust and trust harder.

No, Addi, a voice in my head warned me. *Stop doing that. Take your time. Don't fall in love so quickly. Make sure that whoever you entrust your heart to is truly the right person. Please, no more broken hearts.*

"Come on, Wilde. Let me do this." His words carried more meaning than anyone else could understand.

I sighed and shut my eyes for a second. "Fine. But I'm pretty sure walking to my car isn't a hazard. Even if it's late."

Dahlia and Nick hugged us, teasing about how if we spent too much time together, we'd drive each other nuts, as Carter joined us, a sleepy Jack tucked in his arms.

"I'm ready, big guy. Show me the way," I said, pulling Tucker's hand. The warmth of his palm against mine propelled shivers down to my knees, then to my toes. My body woke up. Tingles moved along my vertebrae.

Next to my car, he leaned in until his forehead rested against mine.

"Wilde, I can keep you company tonight. Just hold you. We're getting good at this cuddling thing. Or help you relax with whichever part of my body pleases you. All you have to do is say yes. I've missed you so damn much. Two weeks without seeing you was boring as hell. My bed is empty without you in it."

My heart flipped around in my chest at the sound of his breathing and closeness. He spoke the words I was dying to hear, but in another context.

With courage in my hands, I shook my head *no*, hoping he'd understand. Regardless of the lust screaming inside me, begging him to take care of all my needs. "We better not. I shouldn't have let you touch me earlier. It was a mistake. I fucked up all the signals."

"Which signals? I want you. You want me. Let's not complicate things."

I lifted a hand between us and rested it over his heart, relishing the strong rhythm underneath my palm. I toyed with the fabric of his dress shirt with my fingers as I avoided looking at him. "This thing between us is getting out of hand. We gotta stop before it's too late. Hooking up will affect our friendship. How could it not? I'm not risking it. Being your friend is all I can give you, or everything we are will shatter. You know I speak the truth… Over the last few of weeks, I've got very attached to you... More than I should… And very attracted to you. I miss you like crazy when we're apart. You've starred in all my dreams too. Refusing you, *us*, is super hard right now."

And all I want is to protect my heart. Same as you do. Because knowing we would be together this weekend made me feel something I never thought I'd feel again—but bigger and rawer. It's precious to me. Being your friend is getting harder than I thought because you're not supposed to be obsessed with your friends and wish you could see them every day of the week. Or share every insignificant detail of your life with them. Even the things that don't matter because their smiles are enough to make everything better and bring you to a place where you're at peace.

"I'm that bad looking, huh?" Tucker teased, breaking the trance I was falling into.

I shook my head, a small smile peeking out. "I wish." A lone tear escaped, and he used the pad of his finger to wipe it off. His lips, soft and delicate, erased the last trace of moisture, and right there, I almost forgot all about my stupid decision to stay away and nearly kissed him. My voice trembled as I spoke, "I'm so sorry. I-I know we had a plan… And…huh…I was really looking forward to it, but

I'm afraid I won't be able to keep the 'no strings attached' promise from my end. You're not looking for a relationship, and I am. Well, not now, but eventually. I'm done…I'm done settling for less than I deserve. It's best if we keep our distance so my heart can get tougher. It must harden up. Together, we're explosive, and if we're not careful, it'll all blow up in our faces."

He cleared his throat. "You have no idea what I want, sweetheart. You never asked."

"I don't have to. You've said your piece from the start. It's all on me. I'm the one unable to follow the rules now. I thought I could, but I was fooling myself. It's over. Let's not make this weekend weirder than it has to be."

As if I'd poked him, Tucker jumped back, hurt flashing in his dark irises. "Fine. Message received. See you tomorrow, Wilde. I'll book a room at the hotel after all. Call me if you need help with the wedding plans." Without another word or glance in my direction, he stepped back, with his shoulders rolled forward and his hands stuffed deep into his pockets.

I swallowed the rock-hard lump sitting in my throat, slid behind the wheel, and drove away, feeling as if I'd broken something that didn't even exist.

Chapter 17
Tucker

Was she joking? Was this a prank? I blinked. And blinked again. Just to make sure I'd heard her right and this wasn't some nightmare I had agreed to partake in.

Addison left me high and dry in our friends' driveway without another glance in my direction. She. Fucking. Left.

Stunned, with mixed emotions brewing inside me, I watched until she made a right turn, her taillights fading from view. With heavy steps, I trudged toward my rental car, parked at the curb, kicking clouds of dust around me.

With a hand clutching the door frame, I glanced back in the direction she disappeared. Just in case she realized she'd spoken nonsense and decided to come back and explain herself.

I waited. One. Two. Ten minutes.

Nothing.

Twenty-four hours ago, we were both eager at the idea

of finally being together again. And now, out of nowhere, she rambled about getting attached, panicked, and drove away.

I had my fingers inside her pussy mere hours ago, and back then, she didn't seem to be against the idea of an *us*.

I plugged my dead phone into the charger. A single text message pinged, cutting through the silence of the night.

ADDISON

I'm sorry.

With my palm, I hit the steering wheel. The worst was that I wasn't even mad at her. Not really. I was angry at the circumstances.

We spent countless hours on the phone over the course of the last few weeks, and each time we met in person, we refrained from having sex when we shared a bed. Even though we were both ripping at the seams in such close proximity, we cuddled all night, because that was the only closeness we allowed ourselves to indulge in.

Memories of our time together flooded my mind, followed by flashbacks of the day we locked ourselves in her hotel room six weeks ago. Right now, it seemed like so long ago. Her face took center stage in my thoughts. I could see her, feel her, smell her. As if she were sitting right next to me. My dick sprang to wood in my pants, and I pushed it down. "Not tonight, buddy."

Yeah, Addison Wilde was the girl we both craved.

The yearning wasn't only physical—it was visceral. I wanted all of her. Every single inch of her body, mind, and soul.

Driving to the outskirts of town, I booked a room in the only hotel around. Padding to the sixth floor using the stairs—I really needed to expel my frustration—I fumbled with the key card, my nerves getting the best of me. How much would I pay for a gym right now to exhaust my body and mind? Waiting for some miracle—a call, a message, anything—I didn't shower and lay on my back on the bed, still dressed.

With my eyes closed, I replayed the last month and a half in my head. Where did I go wrong? Had I missed a hint?

Nothing. I couldn't come up with anything that explained why she backed out on us. *Us.* Why did I keep using this word? We were friends with benefits with *no* benefits. Not a couple. Not a thing. Just people enjoying each other inside and outside the bedroom. But without sex.

Yet, something felt like a mistake. My skin tingled. My stomach roiled. All signs I was missing something right in front of me. Why was I too blind to see?

With my phone in hand, I re-read her last message again.

ADDISON

I'm sorry.

Emotions layered my throat, making it tight. I swallowed around the lump that was suffocating me.

"Me too, sweetheart."

I imagined a life without her…or with her only being partially in it. Living in different states and barely having time to meet anymore. Not being each other's last call of the day.

Once again, I saw her, as clearly as if she were in the room with me right now, holding hands with another guy. Kissing him. Fucking him.

Cold chills skittered along my nape.

Hell rose inside me.

A mass clogged my airways.

Sweat beaded on my temples.

I held my breath, thinking the sting would go away. That the hand tightening around my heart would release its grip. But it didn't. Instead, it squeezed harder. As if someone had cut off my air supply. My only source of oxygen.

Then it hit me. Like a tidal wave, it crashed over me, stealing my breath. Emotions I had pushed down most of my life resurfaced. The sound of an internal alarm rang in my head.

I put my hands over my ears, trying to quiet all the evidence that I was losing my mind. Big time.

My lips parted, straining to voice the words I feared, but they would not cross the threshold of my mouth.

Could this be real?

Could I be that guy?

No. I shook my head. It was all a nightmare. I had to be dreaming. None of this was real. Panic dug its claws into my heart. A cry tore from my throat. Darkness swallowed me.

Why couldn't I wake up?

I searched for an exit, an out. Nothing.

Springing upright, I ran a hand over my face, my lungs collapsing as I drew in a jagged breath. The burn lingered.

Was I asleep?

Or trapped in some alternate reality?

I scanned the room, and it took a moment to remember where I was.

Grabbing my phone, I looked at the time. Only minutes had passed, and yet it felt like a lifetime since I'd been on this bed.

What was going on with me?

I exhaled. My body shook as the truth sank in. I could

no longer hide from my emotions. Or from this new reality.

ADDISON

I'm sorry.

Her words took my eyes hostage, flashing as if they were neon signs.

Sweeping through the pictures I took in the last six weeks, I stopped to stare at every one of them where we were together. And the ones I snapped of her when she wasn't looking.

"Wilde, I'm in love with you."

The words left my mouth by themselves, and this time, they didn't hurt. Instead, they sent a spark straight to my heart.

"I love you," I told a picture of her at the game, wearing her Honky-Tonks purple jersey, eyes locked on the action unfolding on the ice.

Jumping to my feet, I grabbed the car keys I'd tossed aside when I arrived, only to sink back onto my bed again, my elbows propped on my knees and my face buried in my hands.

I couldn't go to her and reveal my consuming feelings. No. Not without a strategy, some carefully thought-out plan. She was clearly emotional tonight, and I couldn't just spill the words to her without making sure she was in the right frame of mind to receive them.

Fear crippled me. How would Addison ever believe I spoke the truth? She'd been played by losers too many times to count. And like a fool, I'd been declaring my non-commitment to her from the very moment we met.

I peeled off my clothes, my body igniting as my thoughts spun wildly inside my head. This was a clusterfuck. Nothing made sense anymore. Everything I'd ever believed—or lived by—was being challenged.

Under a stream of cold water, I showered, hoping it would calm the jitters in my stomach and put some order into my thoughts. I was Tucker Philips. I didn't do love. I didn't even have an idea what a committed relationship would ask of me…or what it would look like.

I repeated the words, loving how they sounded, getting used to them. "I love you, Addison Wilde." Blood flowed to my dick because he enjoyed her as much as I did.

I curled a fist around the girth, working it until I couldn't stop, and shooting my release became my only way out of the tornado I found myself spinning in.

Tremors shook my body.

I pumped myself faster.

My head snapped back, cold water cascading down my face, the muscles of my jaw taut.

A tingle of electricity raced down my spine, and my balls ached.

I increased the pace of my hand around my shaft.

My forehead banged against the wall, my lungs struggling to inhale any fresh air.

With one last flick of my wrist, I let go.

My load sprayed the floor, and some of my apprehension left me.

Oxygen made its way back to my brain.

My shoulders dipped forward.

Jesus, I was in love.

Bare-assed, I went back to bed, tossed and turned for hours before I surrendered myself to sleep. In my dreams, I wished I could test run the idea of an *us*. Followed by a heartfelt conversation with the woman who had inserted herself into my heart and stolen a chunk—rather the whole organ—without warning me.

Chapter 18

Addison

The next morning, I woke up with a stiff neck. I'd flailed all night, unable to find a soothing position. My insomnia had returned in full force over the past week. After the weekend at Tucker's place in Chicago, and the confidences we'd shared, it had eased. But now it was back, relentless, and I spent my nights awake, barely able to keep my eyes closed for more than two hours at a stretch. The realization I was falling for the best man didn't help. He occupied too many of my thoughts and dreams.

Today was Dahlia and Nick's wedding day.

My nerves bounced around in my chest. I tried to control my breathing. It didn't work. In addition to making sure everything ran as planned and being the maid of honor, I had agreed to be the makeup artist.

A fresh batch of jitters hit me, and I leaped to my feet,

rushing to the bathroom. I didn't remember the last time I'd been so nervous.

It's just for today, I reminded myself. *Everything will be fine. Dahlia hired that wedding planner to deal with the last-minute details so I would have time to enjoy the night I'd helped to organize. And Tucker will have my back.*

I prayed he would put his hurt over being rejected on the back burner for a day. I could act as if everything between us were fine for a day, and wish he could do the same.

Skipping breakfast for obvious reasons, my stomach still unsteady, I showered and got ready, humming the wedding march song as I did. Yeah, I was a sucker for happily-ever-afters.

Around ten, I arrived at Dahlia's, just in time for the hairdresser to tame the wild mane I'd kind of neglected since I woke up.

Around noon, a server passed *amuse-bouches* around as I finished applying makeup on Mrs. Ellis, Dahlia's mother.

"Addison, you're still very skilled. Your mama taught you well."

I air-kissed her cheek, my eyes filling with moisture. My mother owned a beauty salon back in our hometown of White Crest, Tennessee. Dahlia and I spent countless hours getting pampered there as teens. I started working at the salon on the weekends at fourteen and had absorbed everything beauty-related. Back in the day, I would practice my skills on my best friend, from hair to nails to the latest makeup trends.

"Thank you, Mrs. Ellis," I said, cupping my heart with both hands. My eyes drifted to Dahlia as her future mother-in-law helped to zip her gown up. The river down my cheeks intensified. I brought my gaze back to my best friend's mother. Tears shone in her eyes too. "Please don't cry, Mrs. Ellis, you'll ruin your makeup," I said in a teasing tone. She watched her daughter with so much pride as I continued, "She's gonna be okay. Dahlia is strong. She went through awful things and is still standing tall. Nick is perfect for her. He will pick up the stars for her if she asks him."

She nodded as she grabbed one of my hands, cradling it between hers. "She's been through a lot. I'm glad the storm has passed. Witnessing her hit rock bottom had been one of the hardest things I've ever gone through in my life. My heart broke when she pushed us away. I'm glad Carter stayed at her side during that time. Deep down, I've always known she would come back to us… On her own terms… When she was ready. Look at her now. Radiant. And thriving. It's all I've been asking for. Everything I ever prayed for each night before going to bed—for the longest time— was that my baby would find her way back toward the light. Because her heart is in the right place. Always has been. Even when she had to make tough choices." She paused, using a tissue to dry her teary eyes. We both watched my best friend twirl in front of the mirror, admiring her dress, a beatific smile tugging at her lips. "Nick is good for her, I agree. They make a great pair."

I nodded, sniffling.

"Are you okay, Addison? You're all pale? Do you need to sit? Some water?"

I shook my head. "I'm just tired. And…and emotional. Nothing to worry about. Today is precious. I want everything to run smoothly. To be perfect. She deserves the best." I turned to face Dahlia again. "Hey, girlfriend. Now that you're dressed, come here. I'll finish the work of art on your face." I winked at her, and she lifted one finger as if to say, 'Just a minute,' while listening to something Nick's mother was saying.

Her mama reached for my wrist. "Honey, you would tell me if something was wrong, right? We've known each other forever. I'm here in case you need to talk about it. Just remember that."

She fixed her eyes on mine and arched one brow, saying so much to my soul without her speaking a word out loud.

It? What did she mean by it?

My thoughts evaporated as Dahlia joined us.

"I'm ready," she said, sitting next to her mother.

I placed a hand over my mouth. My tears resumed. "Ohmygod, you look so beautiful. Nick is going to go crazy. He's a lucky man."

She got up and pulled me into her arms. "One day, it'll be you, Addi. I promise. And I'll be *your* maid of honor."

I pushed my emotional overload away and focused on my task: helping my best friend be the most beautiful bride.

The ceremony passed in a blur. It took place on their property, just next to the barn Nick had built behind their house.

The entire time I was up at the altar beside Dahlia, I avoided looking at Tucker. I felt his heavy stare on me— every second of the ceremony. We linked arms after the bride and groom exchanged vows and kissed. All the while, I kept my gaze fixed straight ahead.

My eyes drifted to the wooden garden chairs, the giant white bows linking them together to line up the aisle, the carpet of white petals. Long reclaimed barn wood tables were set up further on our right, decorated with golden plates, white candles, and more ivory white petals. I watched Jack squirming in Carter's arms, and the sight of them calmed my mind.

Carter and Dahlia's ex-bandmate, a great guy named

Stud, was playing the guitar and singing a melody I couldn't hear, the beating of my heart deafening.

A makeshift dance floor was on our left, garden lights hanging from the tree branches above.

The set-up was magical. Perfect. Mesmerizing. And just as Dahlia had imagined it in her head. Months ago, I had submitted to the wedding planning team the sketches I'd drawn, and under my watch, they did an incredible job of bringing her vision to life.

My grip around the bouquet of white lilies in my hand tightened.

All day, I'd dodged Tucker, piling tasks on his to-do list. Playing makeup artist earlier had ended up being the perfect excuse to avoid engaging with him.

"Later, can we talk about what you said last night?" he asked, his mouth close to my ear.

Tremors shook my body at the intimacy we shared. His scent invaded my senses, and I shut my eyes to force some control over myself.

"Are you sad? I thought you were looking forward to this day. I'm used to you being full of life when there're people around. Mingling, chatting, and entertaining the crowd. Almost annoying with your *everything is a celebration* attitude. So far today, you haven't come up with any wild plans, insane ideas, or silly challenges." He adjusted the tie around his neck. "You're avoiding me. All day, you've barely said a word to me, and you tasked me with supervising other people's work. You're fighting back emotions. Those tears can't be only wedding jitters."

I sniffled, refusing to look at him, patting under my eyes with a tissue I'd stacked in my bra, making sure my mascara didn't leave stains.

We walked away from the altar and stood to the side as

we watched our best friends come our way, the small crowd cheering them on, their eyes locked on each other. I swept my lower lip with my tongue and plastered a bright smile on my face, clapping and ignoring the man whose eyes were trained on me.

"Tuck, I'm fine. Stop worrying about me for a sec," I whisper-yelled through pinched lips. "Why is everyone on my case today? A girl is allowed to cry when her best friend is getting hitched for the second time after her first husband died and she thought she would never fall in love again."

Dahlia and Nick followed the photographer, Carter in tow with Jack in his arms, his face a mask of contained pain.

I supposed we all felt different about this day.

People spread out on the lawn, mingling and sipping champagne. I pushed away from Tucker, desperate for a breath of fresh air. Away from him.

A few strides and he was on my heels, his hand on the small of my back. "Wilde, we gotta talk. At some point, we'll have to discuss *us*."

"Tuck, no. Gimme time. And there's no *us*, remember?" I rubbed my temples, my lids sealed as I tried to block every stimulus from reaching me. "Just this once, let me be. If you wanna talk, we'll do it later. Now isn't a good time."

He said nothing for a while, then stepped back

The more distance he created from me, the easier I breathed.

The constant pull zigzagging between us always jeopardized my dedication to stay away. Anytime he stood too close, my entire self started reacting to his presence, and I lost all sense of self-control.

He returned to my side. "Wilde, I'm not buying it. Let's talk." His voice sounded more like a plea than a demand when he whirled around to face me.

One stride forward and panic swirled inside me. Before he could catch up with me, I lifted the hem of my gown with one hand and ran toward the barn. I covered my mouth with my free hand, trying to confine my despair. My head and heart pulled me in opposite directions, and right now, I had no clue which one to trust. Once I slowed down, I glanced at him over my shoulder through the curtain of tears clouding my vision. His arms hung at his sides, and he looked defeated—and baffled by my rejection and refusal to engage with him.

A storm, agonizing and devastating, raged inside me as I rested my body against the wall on the other side of the barn.

I felt lightheaded and sad. Hopeful and anxious. Such a confusing combination.

My emotions were all over the place.

With a deep sigh, I tried to regain my joyous state. In vain.

Mrs. Ellis joined me. She enveloped me in her arms when uncontrolled sobs poured out of me. Everything today appeared to be a bigger deal than it really was. And yet, I couldn't evade the overwhelming frenzy flowing in me.

My best friend's mom wiped my eyes with a tissue and held me until I calmed a little. Gripping my upper arms with her hands, she leaned back, her eyes full of compassion. "Honey, have you told him yet?"

Her words passed through my foggy mind, and my brows creased, having no clue what she was talking about.

"I can tell he's a nice guy. Last month, in Nashville, he

couldn't take his eyes off you. Nor today at the altar. The chemistry you two share is almost palpable. How long have you two been together?"

"He…huh…what? How? Who?" I dragged a hand over my face and shook my head, trying to make sense of what she was saying because none of her words today did —not to me at least. Was she privy to a secret nobody had shared with me?

"Tucker. Addison, the guy is really fond of you. That much is evident. He looks miserable out there by himself."

I cocked my head to watch him. Hurt painted his face. Raw sadness carved his features.

"Did you tell him? If he messes with you, I'll kick his shin myself. We Southern women must stick together. Did he say something to upset you? I hope he'll take care of you. You deserve to be happy, honey. And loved. Especially in this condition." She rubbed my back with her hand as if to infuse me with the courage I lacked. And some much-needed affection.

I stood there, my body tensed, and my brain not processing anything she'd just said.

She must have sensed it because a soft smile curled her lips. She pushed strands of my hair away from my face with her fingertips. "Oh, you didn't tell him. Am I right?"

I scratched the side of my head, my insides now tied in a series of knots. What was I missing?

A shiver ran through me, and I fanned myself with one hand. I was right. There was a secret. The truth hovered just out of reach, yet no matter how hard I tried, I couldn't grasp it. Fear grew inside me, crawling along my spine. What was I supposed to know and didn't? How bad was it?

So far, this day had been nothing like I expected. It felt as if nothing could surprise me anymore.

Mrs. Ellis dried the last trace of tears from my cheek with her thumb, her eyes brimming with softness.

"I-I have no idea what you're…what you're talking about," I murmured, my voice weak, and my body trembling.

"Addison, I think you're pregnant. I thought you knew."

I stood there, frozen, unable to move or speak.

My heels dug into the perfectly manicured lawn.

My throat closed. Not even a breath could come in or out.

No. Mrs. Ellis was mistaken. She had to be wrong. She knew nothing about me. Or Tucker. Or our relationship.

"You're wrong. I'm not…I can't be." I took a deep breath. "You're mistaken. Mrs. Ellis. I'm not pregnant… You're mistaken."

She offered me a stern glance as her green irises focused on me, reminding me of Dahlia's eyes when filled with empathy. "Are you sure? All the signs are there. You barely ate all day. You scrunched up your nose every time there was food around. You're tearing up for nothing. I'm sorry to tell you that, but we've known each other for a long time. Honey, your breasts are fuller. That's an unmistakable sign. And I know for a fact my daughter wouldn't have outfitted you in a gown strangling your chest. You really had no idea?"

I shook my head, but it felt as if someone else did. Like I was in another dimension and this wasn't my body—nor my life—playing in front of me.

I tried to swallow but failed.

Balls of angst pinballed inside me.

She was wrong. Dahlia's mama was wrong.

"Addison, it will all be okay. I think you should tell him. By the look of it," she angled her head to watch Tucker, and I followed her gaze, "I'm pretty sure he'll do right by you."

My eyes lingered on the best man for a bit longer. He stood by himself, an empty flute of champagne in one hand, kicking the ground with his expensive shoe, his other hand stuffed in his trouser pocket, looking lost.

His usual cockiness was missing. Somber face, loosened tie, dejected expression. He reminded me of the version of himself I encountered the night we spent on the rooftop. That was when I saw him at his most vulnerable.

"He worries about you. He wanted to run after you, but I told him you and I had to talk first."

I nodded. What else could I do? Open and close my mouth like a stupid fish? No way. So I clamped it shut.

In that instant, I didn't feel like crying anymore.

The fear brewing in me multiplied, coiling my stomach in steeled bands.

I still believed Mrs. Ellis had no idea what she was talking about. My period was due any day now. It explained every sign she interpreted as a pregnancy.

"It's that time of the month. It makes me bloated. And turns me into an emotional wreck. Nothing unusual here. And yes, I'm tired. I've been working long hours for months."

Mrs. Ellis caressed my bare arm. "I'll leave you to it. You know where to find me. If you need my help, for whatever reason, just say the word." She turned on her heel but halted mid-step. "And for what it's worth, I'm pretty certain you love him too." She offered me a tight-lipped smile. "The same way I've always known Carter was in love with my daughter and that she had feelings for him, but not as strong as the ones she bore for Jeff. You're not as unreadable as you think you are, Addison. Your eyes speak the truth. They never lie."

She walked away.

No matter what I did, oxygen refused to reach my brain.

My legs wobbled. Back dots blurred my vision. I shut my eyes, unable to stand upright.

Chapter 19
Tucker

S he rejected me. For hours, I'd been following the instructions she laid down in her wedding-planning notebook. Dahlia and Nick had hired people to take care of this, but still, Addison had requested I made sure nobody undermined her work. And since I couldn't refuse her anything, I'd been playing along all day.

Flower arrangements at the altar: *check*

Table centerpieces: *check*

Fairy lights over the makeshift dance floor: *check*

Rose petals spread down the aisle: *check*

Band setup: *check*

These last-minute tasks had helped me keep my mind off everything—except for the conclusion I came to last night. That I had fallen in love despite myself, with my best friend, a woman who was both my equal and my biggest challenge. My other half and my wildest dream. She fooled herself if she thought that by now I wasn't attuned to her.

The sparks in her eyes were missing today. She looked paler and thinner than usual. As if life had given her a hard time lately other than her recurring insomnia. I wasn't aware of anything else eating her up. Last week, she couldn't stop gushing about the wedding, and now she appeared as if she wanted to be anywhere but here. Anywhere but next to me too.

We locked eyes from a distance after she rushed away. Something wasn't right. The space that separated us last night had grown to a full-size canyon today.

Riley Burns, Dahlia's ex-manager whom I'd met at the bachelor party, approached me. "How is it going? Tucker, right?"

I accepted the flute of champagne he handed me.

"Good."

We chatted for a moment, and the entire time, my gaze did not drift away from the clearly upset maid of honor. Minutes later, Stud, the guy playing the guitar during the ceremony, stole Riley away after we agreed to continue our discussion later.

Whatever haunted the woman my body and soul recognized as mine, it affected me too. I longed to be by her side, transforming her rain into a rainbow and her frown into a smile.

"If you'd listen to me for one sec, I'd tell you how much you mean to me," I said, chugging the rest of the bubbly alcohol.

I was in love.

The concept didn't compute with me, but it didn't scare me either. Even if I had no idea what it meant to be in a committed relationship, or whether my feelings were reciprocated, even though I suspected they were—at least, to a certain extent. Unless we had that talk, I had no way of being completely sure.

Addison broke into sobs, and the sight devastated me. My feet strode forward, always going in her direction. No matter how hard I fought it, my body had a mind of its own.

Mrs. Ellis comforted her, and my chest deflated. Now I was jealous of a middle-aged lady hugging my woman. Yep, over the last month and a half, Addison Wilde had become mine. To love and to care for.

The thought sent my heart cartwheeling behind my ribs.

Their exchange had heated up, and Addison was now gesticulating, new flames I'd never seen before dancing in her eyes. The sight cut me deep inside. Could we be so connected that her pain became mine? That her struggles hurt me too?

I chased the displeasure taking over my face with a hand.

Yeah, I had no clue how to be in a relationship or to do love, but with her, I was willing to try.

Mrs. Ellis left her, and I was about to look the other way to give Addison the space she'd pleaded for when I noticed her knees bending and her balance shifting.

"Wilde," I yelled, rushing to her side before her limp body hit the ground.

To be continued in **Brittle Scars**...
(book two in the *Breathless* duet)

emmanuellesnow.com/products/brittle-scars

★★★★★ "This is not a romance, it is a story about first love, first heartbreak and growing up."

A compelling tale of love, friendship, and self-discovery that will tug at your heartstrings.

Start Dahlia's story now

———

Cruel Destiny

★★★★★ "Wow. Just wow. If that could be my review, that is all I would write."

★★★★★ "Emmanuelle has done it yet again. She found a way to slip into my mind and heart with her words and the creation of characters you can't help but fall in love with."

★★★★★ "This book broke my heart in the first twenty five percent and sewed it back together."

A story of healing, second chances, and the risks of opening your heart to someone new. Can they trust each other with their hearts, or will their pasts keep them apart?

Read Nick and Dahlia's love story now

———

Wild Encounter

★★★★★ "This is by far one of the most well-written

book I've read this month. It is dynamic, intriguing, interesting, unafraid to go there and most of all touching."

★★★★★ "I personally wouldn't call this book JUST a romance novel because it's so much more. I 100% recommend it no doubt in mind."

A tale of passion and perseverance that will leave your heart racing and your spirit soaring.

Read Tucker and Addison's love story now

———

Last Hope

★★★★★ "This book was not only about the darkness but it was about pure love, hope, spice, family, and friendships on point with just the right amount without overpowering the storyline at all."

★★★★★ "Devon and Riley's story is a beautiful one with a lot of emotions. The subject matter is intense but it is handled very gently."

A tale of resilience and second chances in a world where love and danger intertwine.

Read Riley and Devon's love story now

———

Midnight Sparks

★★★★★ "The characters, the love, the humor, the steaminess, the emotions… it's everything I hoped and more."

★★★★★ "I think that is one Emmanuelle Snow's sexiest novels yet."

Welcome to the island where Holiday magic meets unexpected romance and a chance at a fresh start.

Read Gavin and Aisha's love story now

————

Fallen Legend

★★★★★ ""The love that grows, not only through tough angst but through unconditional moments had my heart. This is a spicy and riveting book"

★★★★★ "Emmanuelle Snow doesn't just tell a story, she creates an entire world."

A poignant and uplifting journey of hope, love, and the power of second chances.

Read Sam and Madison's love story now

————

Snowbound

★★★★★ "5 big stars from me for this amazing story. Absolutely loved it!"

★★★★★ "Emmanuelle Snow's stories are always full of angst, and Snowbound is no exception."

The intertwined lives of two strangers bound by fate in the midst of a snowstorm.

Read Anderson and Abigail's love story now

———

All available at emmanuellesnow.com

ABOUT THE AUTHOR

Soulfully Beautiful Love Stories

USA Today Bestselling Author Emmanuelle Snow is an author of contemporary YA and women's fiction love stories, who gives life to strong characters who'll fight with all they have to reach their life goals and find their own happiness. She loves her characters to be relatable and realistic.

Emmanuelle is in love with love. Especially complicated, deep, and passionate feelings that make a relationship extraordinary and complex all at the same time.

In her spare time, when she's not writing or reading, she likes to go on road trips—with her four kids and her own soulmate—watch movies, paint, or do some DIY, always with a cup of green tea in her hand and listening to country music.

She splits her time between beautiful Canada and the small US towns she adores.

Find all of Emmanuelle's books here:
emmanuellesnow.com

———

ALSO BY THE AUTHOR

CARTER HILLS BAND UNIVERSE

(suggested reading order)

Carter Hills Band series

False Promises

HEART SONG DUET

Blindsided

Forevermore

Whiskey Melody series

Sweet Agony

SECOND TEAR DUET

Cruel Destiny

Beautiful Salvation

BREATHLESS DUET

Wild Encounter

Brittle Scars

Upon A Star Series

Last Hope

Midnight Sparks

Love Song For Two Series

SAVE THE DATE
LOVE
L O V E
& NICK
Green Mountain, Tennessee
WEDDING
NASHVILLE
HOCKEY
HOCKEY
PLAYO